BEHIND A LIFE OF OPULENCE
LAY THE DARK PAST—
THE TERRIBLE PRICE
STILL TO BE PAID

Trent Kiferson—The brilliant betrothal she had engineered would make her the queen of New Orleans society, but the reckless path she chose would lead to danger, adventure—and love. . . .

Kyle Kiferson, Trent's father—A shipping magnate, he had forged a new identity in America. But in spite of vast wealth and exalted social position his life was a dangerous masquerade. . . .

Hall Fargo—Handsome, seductive, a charming shipowner who was equally at home in the plush brothels of the French Quarter and the gilded mansions of the aristocracy. But buried in his past was a legacy of hatred—and a murderous debt to be paid. . . .

Count Flaubert—A vicious slaver, he had plotted for years to destroy his arch-enemy. Now he was ready to spring his deadly trap—with beautiful young Trent as bait!

BARBARY BOUNTY

Melissa Masters

A DELL/BRYANS BOOK

Published by
Dell Publishing Co., Inc.
1 Dag Hammarskjold Plaza
New York, New York 10017

Dell ® TM 681510, Dell Publishing Co., Inc.

ISBN: 0-440-10461-0

Printed in the United States of America

First printing—May 1980

To Jo Irwin, Jim Bryans, and Richard Gallen, who weathered the storm; Frank Lauria, who kept a sure hand on the helm; and Magi Prins, who poured oil over troubled waters . . .

CHAPTER ONE

New Orleans was enjoying a magnificent season.

Its abundant wealth, regal splendor, and lusty pleasures made it the most fashionable port in the New World. Adventurers, artists, whores, prophets, kings, scholars, saints, outlaws, and dreamers of every persuasion were drawn to its allure—like moths swarming over a jeweled lantern.

Great ships crammed the harbor, their sails filling the sky with a rich tapestry of color. Each day the docks were glutted with fresh cargo: spices and fabric from the Orient, weapons and tools from Europe, and, most valuable of all, African slaves.

Melba Sanjin vividly recalled her own voyage to America though she'd been barely ten. Her mother's death aboard the sunless, filth-sotted slave ship was among the horrors etched in her memory.

But the nightmare ended when she reached New Orleans. Fate delivered her to the benign care of the Kiferson family. She was reared with their daughter Trent, and treated more like a companion than a servant.

For this reason Melba was the only one who understood why her mistress rebelled at any form of authority. Lady Trent was too honest for pretense and strong enough to stand alone. Unfortunately she was also too proud to admit her mistakes.

That fiery pride illuminated Lady Trent's beauty as the carriage edged along the bustling harbor. Few men failed to note her passing and most paused to admire her progress. Indeed it was a dazzling sight.

Trent Kiferson floated above the crowd like a flame-crowned angel on a white carriage drawn by two white stallions. Her long red hair shimmered beneath the white parasol shading her ivory skin from the afternoon sun, and she wore a white shantung suit that enhanced her slim, supple body and flawlessly sculpted profile.

Her driver also wore white as did the maidservant who sat facing her. The wench's sensual features and proud bearing complemented Lady Trent's aristocratic charms. But for her dusky skin, it would have been difficult to distinguish slave from mistress.

Trent was well aware of the stir caused by her leisurely drive through the streets. Although she ignored the gawking pedestrians, she reveled in their adulation.

It wasn't merely vanity. She had no need for petty gratification, knowing that beautiful females abounded in the flesh markets. Instead Trent accepted it as confirmation of a deeply sensed compact with destiny—one she intended to honor, despite her family's disapproval and her own misgivings.

Because Lucille Fontaine believed that price was the truest measure of excellence, she over-charged her customers outrageously.

There were many expensive salons on the Place D'Armes, but none as popular, or as prosperous. This was more a tribute to her tenacity, than to her taste in fashion. Madame Fontaine took great pains to satisfy her clients' slightest whims. She entertained them, acted as social arbiter, and served as personal confidante. The choice gossip she gathered did much to nurture her natural flair for public relations.

Time, and a weakness for pastry, had thickened Madame Fontaine's hourglass figure, but she still had a sharp eye for profit. Despite her poor view of the street, she was the first to spy Lady Trent's carriage.

She rushed from her office, waving at her employees, like a buxom duck herding her brood toward water.

"Muriel . . . see to the refreshments. Edna . . . stop daydreaming and fetch the seamstress. Ambrose . . . never mind the new shipment . . . we have a very special visitor."

Ambrose dropped his hammer immediately, recognizing the urgent note in her voice. Hastily donning his tailcoat, the elderly black man hurried out of the storeroom to open the door.

"Good afternoon, mistress," he droned, clicking his heels with a military flourish as Lady Trent swept past, followed by her maid.

"*Chérie,* you're simply incorrigible," Madame Fontaine clucked. "You're days late for your fitting. How will we ever have you ready by tomorrow?"

Trent snapped her parasol shut. "Please don't scold, Lucille. I've had a beastly day."

"Not a lover's spat with dear Gavin?"

"What an amusing idea," the girl answered with a faint smile. "Wouldn't Julie Devon just love it? Not to mention my dear family."

"Have they been at you to postpone your betrothal again?"

"It's hardly worth discussing. Let's get on with the fitting. A new gown always brightens my mood."

Madame Fontaine curtailed her curiosity knowing that Trent resented any intrusion in her personal affairs.

"Of course, darling," she cooed, taking Trent's arm. "Let's retire to my sanctum. We can sip some champagne and I'll tell you what Julie Devon has been saying about you this week."

"I'll accept the wine gratefully. But spare me that cow's sour milk."

Trent was delightfully candid concerning her rival for Gavin Radcliffe's affections. But as usual she deftly avoided comment on her family's objections to the union.

She was a true Kiferson, despite her rebellious streak, Madame Fontaine reflected dourly. Although Trent's father controlled the richest shipping fleet in the Americas, he remained aloof from social contact, rarely extending or accepting invitations. Over the years this preference for isolation provoked much speculation about the mysterious Lord Kiferson, and his wife, Lady Trevor.

Their daughter retained the same infuriating air of self-sufficiency. Unlike most of the local debutantes, Trent had been educated in England. She'd been home less than a year and had already managed to impress—or insult—everyone worth knowing in New Orleans.

Needless to say, the plantation-bred belles despised her.

At first they tried to freeze her out, but the intense enthusiasm Lady Trent sparked in male circles soon melted the barricades. Today, not even Julie Devon would dare omit Trent from an invitation list. And Miss Julie had good reason to hate her.

However, Madame Fontaine had always admired Trent and was pleased that age hadn't dulled her instincts. A few weeks earlier she had had serious doubts.

While some were disturbed by Trent's outspoken manner, most found her fascinating. Her beauty, wealth, and disarming wit discouraged her detractors, until one of her escapades erupted into a major scandal.

It happened during a large, and very boring, dinner at the Radcliffe mansion. Trent mentioned that roulette was the latest rage in Paris, and suggested an excursion to a gaming house.

Julie Devon reminded her that a lady of breeding would never enter a public gambling hall.

"A lady of breeding is above bourgeois conventions," Trent retorted, and to prove her point insisted that Gavin escort her to the notorious Creole Queen Casino.

The incident loosed a rash of vicious rumors—all vigorously circulated by Julie Devon's coterie—that threatened to destroy Trent's reputation.

Trent squelched the threat with a single, brilliant stroke. She decided to accept Gavin Radcliffe's proposal of marriage.

The news stunned New Orleans aristocracy. Gavin was heir to an empire that extended from the Carib Isles to Africa. Many believed his father, Moss Radcliffe, would someday be governor. Public reaction was swift and emphatic.

Within the week a group of highborn matrons risked censure by organizing a roulette party at the Creole Queen. The well-attended gala confirmed

Trent's elevation from fallen woman to Caesar's wife.

One thing was certain, Madame Fontaine mused as she watched Trent being fitted, the bride spent money like Cleopatra. Her gown cost more than most men earned in a year.

"This bodice is a disaster," Trent announced, waving the seamstress away. "Lucille, come look at this. I specifically asked you to lower the neckline. It's practically around my throat."

"But *ma chérie,* you exaggerate," Madame Fontaine murmured, "the neckline is perfect." She slowly circled Trent, squinting through her pince-nez with owlish concentration.

The garment was a masterpiece.

Made of rose-tinted moiré, it flared from the hips in a shimmer of long pleats, emphasizing Trent's slender waist. Each pleat was seamed with hundreds of tiny seed pearls that had been carefully hand-pierced before being sewn into place. Twenty-one of these pearly seams lined the tight midriff like a finely-ribbed corset. The illusion called attention to Trent's high, rounded breasts, and also served to commemorate her twenty-first birthday.

The offending neckline was simple, but quite dramatic, being a curved edge with black lace that peeled away from her shoulders to expose the barest hint of cleavage.

"It's perfect," Madame Fontaine repeated. "You look absolutely divine. The empress Josephine herself would weep with envy. Take my word, darling, it's devastating."

She glanced at the mirror to pat a stray curl into place. Then she saw Trent's unsmiling face and realized her word wasn't enough.

"I pray you remember our last discussion on this

matter," Trent said in a cool, cutting tone. "We agreed the neckline would start here." She tugged the bodice down, revealing the creamy fullness of her breasts.

"But, *ma petite*, it's too blatant for someone of your position. This is your betrothal, not a Mardi Gras."

Trent's gray eyes glinted like crystal darts.

"Do you presume to educate me, Madame?"

Her query punctured Madame Fontaine's composure and a stream of doubts filled the silence. She couldn't afford to offend one of her most influential clients—nor could she afford to overlook the sizeable sum invested in the gown. On the other hand, what Lady Trent demanded was impossible.

"My dear, please don't misunderstand my intentions," Madame Fontaine twittered anxiously. "My sole concern is your happiness on this important occasion. The neckline can be altered to your wish . . . but it will take much work . . ."

"Naturally I'll pay for the added labor."

Madame Fontaine's hands fluttered in protest. "Oh, no, *chérie*. Money is not at issue here. It's a matter of time."

"Surely twenty-four hours is ample to snip a few inches of silk." The girl scoffed, turning back to the mirror.

"It will take at least forty-eight hours even if we work around the clock."

Trent whirled. "That's out of the question. This gown must be ready tomorrow."

Madame Fontaine's plump features folded into an imploring pout. "To open the seams we must unstitch every tiny pearl. Then after the bodice is reshaped they must be sewn back. This is not a common garden frock, dear lady. Please try to understand my position."

"You understand this, Madame. If my gown is not ready by tomorrow eve, I shall be sorely disappointed." The icy authority glazing her delicate porcelain features made it clear that disappointment meant instant excommunication.

Madame Fontaine began to perspire and she signaled for more champagne.

The cold wine did little for her parched throat or her desolate spirits. She'd eventually recoup the money invested in the garment, but not the loss of her professional reputation. Most frustrating of all, it was due to nothing more than a childish tantrum. At some lighter moment the young heiress would have adored the exquisite creation. Numbly she watched Lady Trent start to remove the gown.

The maidservant moved to help, then paused and murmured something to her mistress.

A positive chord in Trent's response alerted Madame Fontaine and she inched closer.

"See there, missy?" the black girl was explaining. "It's just this ruffle that needs trimming."

"Are you sure?" Trent moved to the mirror. "It does look nice."

"Looks better than that," the maid assured.

"It is superbly detailed . . . but the bodice . . ."

The black girl smiled. "Your beaus won't be disappointed. Their imagination can lower that bodice quicker than any seamstress."

Their whispers dissolved into muted giggles. Trent's lighthearted mood encouraged Madame Fontaine to risk an intrusion.

"Now, now, there'll be no naughty tales in this

salon," she warbled, as she approached the pair. "Unless, of course, I'm privy as well."

Trent shrugged. "It's hardly naughty, but you might find our tale to your liking. Melba has devised a compromise."

"The art of compromise can be highly rewarding," Madame Fontaine chirped, beaming at the black girl. "What do you suggest?"

Melba ran her finger along the thick ruffle of black lace edging the bodice. "If you trim it here in front and tuck it back"—she pinched the fabric to illustrate—"it opens the neckline without tearing out any seams. Of course, it changes the effect."

"But it's absolutely charming, my dear. A stroke of genius," Madame Fontaine crowed. She clapped her hands and set the seamstress to work before Lady Trent's humor turned.

While Trent was occupied, Madame Fontaine took Melba aside. "You're a very bright girl," she whispered, pressing a coin into her palm.

Melba stared at the gold piece, then looked up.

She was tall and willowy, with the elongated neck and angular features of an Egyptian statue and her amber eyes reflected an ageless calm that belied her tender years.

"What is this, mistress?" she asked softly.

"It's a gift for you. Because I like smart girls. Take it, child. Buy whatever you want."

To Madame Fontaine's utter astonishment, the girl gravely returned the gold coin. "Begging your pardon, mistress," she said, lowering her gaze, "but I have everything I want."

When Lady Trent took her leave, Madame Fontaine's airy farewells were underscored by a profound sense of relief. Even the Kiferson slaves were a strange breed, she noted, watching the pair stroll to their carriage.

She lowered the shade and locked the door. The brief skirmish with Lady Trent had left her too exhausted for further dealings that day. Retreating to the office, she poured a generous measure of brandy and gulped it down.

God help Mister Gavin Radcliffe, she reflected grimly, refilling her glass. Or any other poor devil who fancied the fire-haired hellion.

Eubert had a way with horses.

The Arabian stallions responded like farm mares to his sure touch as they cut through the tangled streets. His master often said he rode ahead of his steeds rather than behind them, and Eubert valued the compliment highly. He considered Lord Kiferson to be the wisest gentleman on earth.

Of course Eubert knew that the highly strung thoroughbreds were better suited to a racing saddle than carriage harness, but Lady Trent decided to wear white on her outing. And he wasn't fool enough to argue. Not even Lord Kiferson could budge his daughter once she fixed her mind on something. As it happened, her decision gave Eubert a long-desired opportunity to show off his prized charges. The pair of matched white stallions were more than equal to the challenge. They sailed grandly through the crowded boulevards, manes billowing above their sun-rippled flesh.

As the carriage coasted serenely in their wake, Eubert kept his head high, scanning the flow of traffic ahead. Occasionally his concentration would be distracted by stray comments, and while he maintained a militant indifference to the flattery, his chest swelled with pride. Minutes later the bubble burst.

A mule-drawn lorry loaded with hay lumbered across their path, forcing Eubert to pull up.

The mules balked, stalling wagons on both sides as the driver exhorted the animals with a volley of lashes and loud curses. A circle of spectators shouted advice from the sidelines until finally someone suggested using a torch to drive the stubborn mules from the intersection. But after lighting the torch the driver made the mistake of approaching the animals from behind. One of the mules suddenly kicked and sent the man sprawling. The torch flew out of his hand, spraying sparks like a pinwheel and within seconds the hay wagon was a raging pyre.

The stallions, already made jittery by the noisy crowd, panicked when the blaze erupted. They reared up, hooves flailing at the bright yellow flames, before they bolted for the sidewalk.

Eubert managed to yank them aside from a group of pedestrians, but as the horses swerved, the carriage tipped over on two wheels, catapulting him to the ground. Trent grasped the door handle with one hand, and Melba's arm with the other, preventing the girl from tumbling out of the careening vehicle. Both women were hurled to the floor when the wheels slammed down, but Trent scrambled to her knees, and crawled over the cushions, frantically trying to reach the driver's seat. Then she saw her efforts were useless. The team was stampeding toward a narrow gap between a stack of crates and a large freight wagon. The horses had a slight chance of breaking through unscathed, but the carriage would be shattered like an egg. With horrified fascination she watched the barrier rush closer. As she braced herself for the crash, a dark figure swooped beside the wildly galloping stallions. With a fluid motion he leaped astride the nearest animal, grabbed the reins, and brought the carriage to a shuddering halt, a scant three yards short of the looming crates.

Trent gaped at the rider in stunned silence. Although his back was turned, she sensed something familiar about the black-clad figure.

"Missy . . ."

The cry pierced her numbed thoughts and she turned to help Melba.

"Are you hurt, Mellie?" she murmured, bending over the prostrate girl.

Melba pushed herself to a sitting position, and gingerly fingered the back of her head. "I'm all right, just a bump." She smiled weakly. "How did you manage to stop them?"

"I had no part in it," Trent assured her.

"Anyone hurt?"

For a moment Trent was unable to answer.

She stared at the man leaning casually against the door, as if trying to recall a forgotten name.

The man wore a black silk suit and satin waistcoat over a ruffled jabot that set off his finely-chiseled face.

It was a face composed of contrasts.

The magnetic intensity of his ebony eyes was muted by dark lashes and gently arched brows, while a sensitive mouth softened his sharply cleft chin. One might have taken him for a sensitive young scholar except for the steely cynicism edging his lean features.

Truly he was the most attractive man Trent had ever encountered. Even more exciting was the flare of recognition he ignited within her.

Gathering her composure she coolly met his gaze. "We're both uninjured. Thanks to your intercession."

"Thanks to a swift horse," he corrected, inclining his head toward the glistening black steed tethered nearby. "It was just my good luck to be riding her."

As Trent stepped out of the carriage he proferred his hand. His touch sent a quick shock across her skin and a flicker of tension tightened his fingers, before he reluctantly released her hand.

"Hall Fargo at your service," he announced with a courtly bow.

His vibrant tone made it seem more a promise than an introduction. Trent's pale smile was equally promising.

"I'm indebted to you, sir."

Fargo's dark eyes burned into hers. "Your beauty absolves you from all debt, milady. Save one."

"What has greater value?" she mused playfully. "Profit or power?"

"You forget pleasure, milady."

"And what is your pleasure, sir?" Trent inquired with a guarded smile.

"Nothing can afford me more gratification than to hear your name," Fargo said softly.

She responded with a graceful curtsy.

"Lady Trent Kiferson, at your service."

Her lighthearted announcement faded into frozen silence. Sensing a sudden shift in Fargo's mood she looked at him questioningly.

His eyes were hooded and his expression had the detached glaze of a bored guest determined to be polite. His comment was also less than inspired.

"Yes, a lovely name. Is it English?"

"My mother is English," she answered crisply, stung by his abrupt manner.

Hall Fargo didn't seem to hear, intent on the crowd milling at the corner.

"I suggest you tend to your driver," he said, glancing at Trent. "I'll take care of the horses."

"You're quite right," she snapped, turning on her heel. As she strode away, a smoldering anger smothered her concern for Eubert. She felt humiliated by the callous dismissal and somewhat disappointed. Very few men failed to appreciate her attentions. Of course this was an awkward moment she noted, quickening her pace. She'd settle accounts at a more opportune time.

Fortunately Eubert was merely shaken up by the fall. When Trent reached him, he was on his feet, carefully testing his bruised limbs.

"Are you all right?" she asked briskly.

"Yes'm. Be worse tomorrow." Eubert squinted at the carriage to avoid her icy stare. "Sure hope Miss Melba and the horses weren't hurt."

"I can vouch for Miss Melba's health. However, the horses are your responsibility," Trent reminded, turning to resume her conversation with Fargo. She focused full attention on charming her inscrutable rescuer, as she walked back to the carriage, a few paces ahead of Eubert's limping gait. While Hall Fargo spoke with a gentleman's tone, his elegant manner had a rough edge, Trent reflected. He could be an actor or an entrepreneur, judging from his rather dramatic mode of dress. Whatever his profession, his arrogance hinted at success, she decided. And she meant to tame his unbridled behavior.

Trent veiled her thoughts behind a ravishing smile when she neared the carriage. A moment later her expression sagged. Melba stood at the rail where the horses were tethered, but Fargo had departed.

"The gentleman left his regrets," Melba explained.

"He was called to a previous obligation. He asked me to convey his apologies."

The message was both cavalier and challenging. Trent fumed. It was also insufferable. She refused to allow a swaggering lout to demean her so casually.

"Where did he go?" Trent demanded, peering at the large warehouse blocking the end of the street.

"I'm not certain, missy," Melba said carefully.

Trent glanced at her. "Don't you dare lie to your mistress."

"Just trying to remember," the girl replied with a reproachful pout. "I think he went into that fancy place with the big sign."

"Very well. Come with me," Trent ordered, moving toward a building across the street, adorned by a large gilded slipper.

"Missy, wait," Melba implored, looking at Eubert for support.

The driver tended to his horses, unwilling to tempt Lady Trent's wrath a second time.

"We can't go in that place," Melba implored, hurrying after her mistress. "It's not proper."

Trent stopped a few feet from the entrance. "I'll decide what's proper. Now open that door."

Melba shook her head. "I can't do it, missy."

"Are you defying me?"

The sharp question glanced off Melba's stubborn frown. "If I opened that door for you I'd be defying your parents," she said firmly. "It's unseemly and you know it."

"We'll discuss this later," Trent promised. Lips pressed in a bloodless scowl, she strode to the frosted glass door and pushed it open. To her relief the place was empty.

Chairs were stacked atop the tables, and only one

of the chandeliers was lit, sending long shadows across the cavernous room. A lone employee, wearing a red striped shirt and black tie stood behind the carved mahogany bar methodically polishing glassware. He held each to the light before depositing it on the shelf behind him. The man paused as Trent approached.

"Would you be good enough to inform Mr. Fargo that Lady Trent wishes to see him?"

The man gaped at her, hand still uplifted. "Lady Trent is here to see Mr. Fargo," she repeated impatiently.

"Maybe I can help, milady."

Trent turned and saw a plump, black-haired woman with heavily shaded eyes and greasy red lips emerge from behind a pile of chairs. She reeked of sweat and cheap wine and her slack, servile grin had a sour twist.

"I can take you to Mr. Fargo," she declared.

Suppressing an urge to retreat, Trent took a step toward her. "I'd be much obliged for the assistance."

"How much obliged is that?" the woman asked slyly.

Trent opened her purse and fished out a five-dollar gold piece.

"This much," she said, voice barbed with contempt.

The woman snatched the coin from her fingers and bade her follow. Weaving slightly she led Trent across the darkened room toward a stream of illumination trickling through the folds of a thick velvet curtain.

"Mr. Fargo is inside," the woman hissed, motioning her closer.

As Trent neared she was alerted by the woman's malicious smirk, but before she could react the woman flung open the curtain, drenching them both with light.

Some fifteen men were gathered around a large table beneath a glittering chandelier. Seven were seated in high-backed chairs playing cards, while the rest stood watching through a haze of cigar smoke and silence. Most of them were well dressed, and they all looked up in surprise when the woman stepped inside the room.

"Lady Trent to see Mr. Fargo," she announced with mock formality.

Trent shrank back into the shadows, berating the impulsive decision that left her vulnerable to compromise by a common trollop.

"There you are, dearie," the woman snorted, shuffling back to the bar.

Her taunt went unheeded. Trent's attention was completely taken by the dark figure approaching the doorway.

Hall Fargo's face reflected neither amusement nor displeasure at her intrusion. "What occasions this call, milady?" he inquired, ebony eyes as distant as his tone.

Trent smiled. "I'm here to proffer proper thanks for my well-being."

"As I stated earlier, you're released from any obligation."

"Somehow it seemed better stated the first time," she observed.

The wry comment softened Fargo's reserve and his smile was almost apologetic.

"My manners suffer the urgency of the business at hand, but my admiration endures."

"I shan't tax you further then," Trent said lightly.

"Just long enough to extend an invitation to my birthday ball tomorrow eve."

Fargo's expression clenched like an iron fist. "My deepest pardons, milady," he murmured with a curt bow. "Unfortunately I'm previously engaged. Now if you'll excuse me . . ."

"Excused!" Trent spat vehemently, storming toward the exit. Despite the unfamiliar surroundings, her seething rage propelled her unerringly through the darkened maze. When she neared the hazy arc of sunlight circling the frosted glass doors, a grinning, bovine face appeared from the gloom.

Seated directly in Trent's path, her chair tipped back and frayed red shoes propped on a table, was the black-haired slattern.

The woman brandished her glass like a sword, cutting off Trent's progress. Her gesture bristled with menace and a threatening whine edged her voice.

"Not leavin' so soon, your Ladyship?" she demanded. "You must do me the honor of havin' a drink first."

Without pausing a step, Trent brushed her hand aside. As she marched past, some combative reflex hooked the handle of her parasol to the woman's chair.

But the frantic bellow signaling the trollop's violent clash with the floor failed to appease Trent. The white-hot fury roaring through her brain consumed all sense of triumph.

Nothing would ever satisfy her rampant hatred of Hall Fargo—save his damnation. . . .

The gentlemen seated around the table became engrossed with their cards when Fargo returned. Having received Lady Trent's visit without comment, they also avoided any mention of Fargo's absence from the poker game. Their tact marked them as men of breeding.

Unfortunately Captain Woodrow Hayes had lost too much money to afford the luxury of discretion. As the master of a slave ship he had little use for fine manners, and over the past two days he'd watched Hall Fargo rake in the profit from a six-month voyage.

Be it for a pound or a penny, Captain Hayes didn't like to lose. He studied Fargo carefully as the cards were dealt, searching for a sign of agitation. The dark features were as impassive as carved wood. Still, Captain Hayes knew from experience that the sturdiest wit could be shaken by a wench. And poker was, after all, a game of wits.

"Five hundred to you, Captain."

Hayes tossed in his chips automatically. He continued watching Fargo from the corner of his eye, like some bald, bearded gorilla stalking a bird.

With a bit of spunk he might recoup his losses, Hayes decided.

Lady Luck seemed to smile on the thought. He won the hand with three queens, giving him confidence.

He paused to light a cigar as Fargo began dealing a new hand. The game was five-card stud, first card down and the other four open.

After giving each of the seven players a down card, Fargo deftly flipped the others face up.

The high card fell to Hayes.

"Ace bets," Fargo announced.

"Wasn't that Lord Kiferson's daughter?" Hayes inquired as he dropped two white chips into the pile.

Fargo's gaze moved past him. "Two hundred to

you, Doctor Mason," he intoned briskly. Mason called, as did the next man, but Fargo raised the bet two hundred.

It wasn't a wise move, Hayes gloated. Obviously his baiting had been effective. He decided to push harder.

"They say Kiferson has the richest shipping franchise in New Orleans," he commented, when Fargo started dealing the third card.

"A real gentleman, Lord Kiferson," one of the other players said with meaningful emphasis.

Hayes ignored the warning. He was more interested in the second ace Fargo dealt him. With the one underneath, he had three.

"Maybe so," he drawled, counting out five hundred-dollar chips. "But his daughter sure gets around."

"Lady Trent is a fine girl," Doctor Mason remarked pointedly, as he folded his cards.

As Hayes expected, Fargo raised the bet to a thousand dollars.

Hayes surveyed the open cards on the table, and raised another thousand. He could see that the best Fargo could have was three kings. The fool was betting with his emotions, not his head, Hayes reflected smugly.

The heavy betting on the next card drove out everyone except Judge Paxton, Hall Fargo, and Captain Hayes. When the last card was dealt, Hayes knew that he'd won.

It was the fourth ace.

Hayes bet two thousand and Judge Paxton displayed his wisdom by dropping out. Fargo promptly raised it to ten thousand dollars.

Having only a thousand in chips, Hayes called.

"You're nine thousand shy," Fargo observed.

"I'm known to these gentlemen," Hayes said crisply. "However, if you wish my personal receipt I'll be glad to oblige."

"Your receipt is unacceptable."

The cool, measured statement silenced the room.

Frozen between anger and anticipation, Hayes glared across the table. "Are you questioning my word?"

"I question nothing," Fargo snapped. "I'm saying your word is as worthless as your honor."

"Gentlemen, gentlemen . . ." Judge Paxton murmured. But it was too late for mediation.

"I'm going to kill you for that," Captain Hayes said hoarsely. "How do you want it?"

Fargo's dark eyes burned through the smoky haze. "I want nothing from you. The time, place, and weapons are at your convenience."

The spectators retreated hastily as Hayes pushed away from the table and got to his feet.

"Right here and now, then," he rumbled, clenching his huge fists.

"And the weapon?" Fargo inquired.

Hayes stared at the dark, slender figure seated at the table. He was stronger than Fargo but a bullet made all men heavier and equal. No doubt the fop was skilled with both dueling pistol and a sword as were most gentlemen in New Orleans. But there was one weapon that gave Hayes an advantage, being accustomed to the more savage modes of combat aboard ship.

His hand slipped inside his coat and pulled a seven-inch blade from its sheath. "Let it be knives, damn you."

"Gentlemen please . . ." Judge Paxton interjected. "This is hardly proper procedure."

"Knives it is," Fargo said, still watching Hayes intently. "Perhaps the judge will be good enough to act as referee."

"Since you both insist on this foolish contest, I suppose I have no other choice than to see that it's conducted in accordance with the code in such matters," Paxton sighed.

He stood up and motioned to the spectators. "All disinterested parties please stand at the door. Doctor Mason will act as witness, seconds aren't necessary in this case. And, oh yes . . . can someone provide Mr. Fargo with a suitable weapon?"

"That won't be necessary," Fargo announced, producing a bone-handled knife that was concealed in his boot.

Hayes was more curious than worried. He'd seen a similar blade somewhere, but couldn't quite recall the place. No matter, he thought, preparing himself for the duel, the knife would make a handsome souvenir of the occasion. For Hayes had no doubt about the outcome. His superior height, strength, and experience put all the odds in his favor.

Nonetheless he wrapped his coat carefully around his left forearm as a shield and examined the fighting area for hidden obstacles. Years of armed combat had taught him that readiness was the key to survival, even against amateurs.

The rules were simple.

The field of honor was an open area at the end of the room. Both men stood ten feet apart, with Judge Paxton between them. After calling time, he would withdraw to the sidelines. The man who drew the first blood would be declared the winner.

While Hayes waited for Paxton's signal, he studied his opponent.

Hall Fargo's dark face was impassive and his tall, slender body had an almost casual slouch. He also held his weapon too loosely, Hayes noted.

"Time, gentlemen. You may begin."

As Judge Paxton retreated, Hayes slowly advanced, body crouched and blade held low.

The first thing that impressed him was Fargo's quickness. The slender man nimbly ducked under Hayes's sweeping thrust and leaped away from a second. *Easy now,* the Captain told himself, *it's just a matter of time.* Instead of rushing forward, Hayes circled his opponent, cutting off his possibility of movement.

His massive arms and huge girth devoured the space between them until Fargo was boxed off, with nothing behind him but the wall. Hayes advanced slowly, made wary by Fargo's surprising agility. Suddenly the dark figure feinted, slipping out of striking range like an elusive shadow. Hayes blocked his escape, however, and closed in, knife cocked like a sharp, shiny finger as he selected the most vulnerable part of Fargo's body.

Fargo made it easy when he extended his arm in a futile gesture of surrender.

"Here's mercy, you damned fool," Hayes roared, ramming his blade at Fargo's heart.

Then he saw Fargo's arm lash out and realized the gesture hadn't meant surrender at all. An instant later his lungs exploded with pain. As Hayes slowly collapsed, he gaped at the blood-soiled blade jutting from his belly. He remembered where he'd seen it before. The distinctive carvings on its bone handle marked it as a Barbar throwing knife. His bulging eyes remained fixed on the weapon long after he died.

Fargo removed the blade and wiped it clean with a lace handkerchief as Doctor Mason, Paxton, and the others crowded around the body.

"Get the undertaker," Mason intoned.

"He threw that knife faster than most men can shoot," someone said in a hushed voice.

"It was a fair fight, conducted according to code," Judge Paxton declared, returning to the table.

The others murmured agreement as they drifted back to their places. Their voices faded into silence when Paxton casually turned over Hayes' hole card. It was the ace of spades.

"Four aces," he croaked, regretting his foolish impulse.

Everyone stared at the three kings lined up before Fargo. Even with a fourth hidden underneath, he was a clear loser. Fargo slowly folded his cards and tossed them aside. "Since nobody called, looks like kings take the pot. Unless there's some objection."

Paxton hastily assured him there were none, having seen what happened to people who offended the dark, soft-spoken gambler.

Fargo raked in the large pot, then carefully placed a stack of hundred-dollar chips on the ace of spades.

"That should cover any inconvenience," he said calmly, as if apologizing for a spilled drink. "Now let's have some fresh cards for the dealer. These have gone cold."

CHAPTER TWO

For the first time, Melba understood what it meant to be a slave.

Of course she knew that Lord Kiferson was an exceptionally generous master. Despite her cloistered existence she'd heard how blacks were treated on the neighboring plantations. Until now she'd offered fervent thanks to the gods who guided her to the Kiferson estate.

Like the other servants and field hands who maintained the lush sanctuary, Melba was paid for her work. She was also given comfortable quarters, pretty clothes, and Sundays off to pursue her studies. Although it was against the law, Lord Kiferson insisted that all of his slaves learn to read, write, and count. His greatest boon however, was hope. After ten years of service, he allowed them to buy back their freedom.

But as Melba watched the lavishly costumed guests streaming into the mansion, she realized the long cherished promise was a cruel lie. Lord Kiferson couldn't restore her freedom. No more than he could return her mother to life. Her freedom died the day she left Africa.

Whether she returned to her tribe or remained in America, she'd always be an outcast. A legal paper couldn't redeem her birthright, or change the color of her skin. Black girls didn't have elegant balls on their birthdays, nor were they betrothed to fine gentlemen. She would never be courted, pampered, or spoiled—merely groomed for use as a beast of burden.

Half-concealed behind a marble column, Melba peered through the slits of her scarlet mask, like some exotic fawn at the edge of a glittering waterfall. Waves of bright color covered the floor while sweet music washed over the high-pitched babble pouring into the domed ballroom. But despite the swirling confusion, she never lost sight of her mistress.

A luminous aura highlighted Lady Trent's shimmering beauty. She drifted through the crowd like a masked sea nymph and her radiance seemed to enthrall every man in the room except one.

Lord Kiferson stood alone beside the arched entrance, his grim smile edged with contempt as he watched his daughter flirt brazenly with her flocking admirers. As if sensing he was being observed, he abruptly glanced in Melba's direction.

Though Lord Kiferson wore no mask, his striking, gold-flecked eyes and long blond hair gave his face a lionlike cast. The impression was heightened when he moved toward her.

He slipped past the revelers with the unhurried ease of a stalking cat, eyes narrowed in a pensive frown.

Melba wanted to lose herself in the crowd, but she didn't dare. Few people had the courage to defy the powerful, sun-bronzed figure. And save for his daughter, none had succeeded. All she could do was bury her resentments beneath a respectful smile and wait.

"Are you hiding from us?"

The gentle question scratched at her composure.

Unwilling to answer and unable to lie, Melba shook her head.

Lord Kiferson regarded her thoughtfully. "I've been meaning to speak to you about something."

"Yes, milord. What is your wish?" she murmured.

"It's your wish we must discuss," he said carefully.

"Yes, milord, thank you," she said, trying to avoid his probing gaze.

"On the eve of your mistress's betrothal it's fitting that you too receive a bounty. Therefore I've decided to grant your freedom."

His gold-tipped eyes seemed to peel away her mask, uncovering the naked fear. "Of course this will always be your home," he assured.

"Thank you, milord. I'd like to stay," she mumbled, voice hardly audible over the swelling confusion.

He smiled. "Now that our business is settled, I'd like to request the honor of this dance."

Melba shrank back in panic. "Oh, no, milord, it's not allowed."

"Slaves aren't allowed to dance with their masters. But you're a free woman now," he reminded.

She pulled away. "Please, milord, I can't . . . I don't know how . . ."

He reached out and gently took her hand. "You'll never learn until you try. It's quite simple really," he added, guiding her toward the crowded floor. "You'll be fine after a few turns. Everything takes practice at first—even freedom."

His last few words were still echoing in Melba's memory when the music faded.

For years Millicent Devon had been longing to be invited to the Kiferson estate.

Like everyone else in New Orleans she was fascinated by the mysterious shipping magnate, but Lord and Lady Kiferson had consistently rejected all overtures. Indeed, very few had ever set foot inside the mansion. And now that she'd finally gained admittance Millicent wasn't disappointed.

The palatial splendor of its mosaic halls and gilded ceilings was enriched by a profusion of treasures. The Chinese vases, Persian rugs, Indian tapestries, Egyptian scrolls, Italian paintings, French furniture, and English porcelain adorning the rooms were intermixed with a vast array of weaponry that spanned everything from war clubs to dueling pistols. There were also tall glass cases housing tiny jeweled boxes, golden figurines, and a large collection of exquisite timepieces, all precisely timed to chime the hour of Lady Trent's birth.

But Millicent was most impressed by Lord Kiferson himself. She could almost feel the magnetic power he generated as he moved through the crowded ballroom. His body seemed charged with seething animal energy that made her skin tingle whenever he came near.

Quite a few others shared Millicent's admiration for the golden-maned figure, judging from the comments she overheard in the dressing room.

"He looks like that Greek god . . . Apollo," one young matron gushed breathlessly.

"Honey, if he's Greek I'm going to immigrate," her companion declared.

The matron heaved a mournful sigh. "Too bad about his wife."

Millicent knew exactly what she meant.

Lady Trevor Kiferson had that rare combination of beauty, self-assurance, and wit most men prized in a woman. She was alluring without being vain, and maintained a sensible outlook without sacrificing her charm. In short, the sort of female Millicent despised.

However, she knew that even perfection had its limits when it came to sensual pleasure. She'd learned from experience that the most effective aphrodisiac was variety.

After primping her jet-black curls and adding a spot of rouge to her pale, vaguely oriental features, she tugged at her bodice to expose a bit more of her plump, powdered breasts. The only one who'd be shocked was her husband, Millicent calculated smugly. And he didn't matter.

Nothing mattered except the raw need guiding her toward the ballroom like a heat-crazed bitch drawn by the irresistible scent of excitement.

It took all of Lady Trevor's patience to respond politely to the blatant arrogance exhibited by her guests. Most were merely bores, but some, like Millicent Devon, had a vicious streak.

She was also shameless, Trevor noted. *If the woman's bodice were an inch lower it would reach her waist.* As it was, she looked more like Lady Godiva than Marie Antoinette, despite the diamond-starred tiara adorning her elaborate wig.

"Dear Lady Trevor," she gushed with exaggerated sweetness. "Why, I declare, you could be Trent's sister."

The compliment was well deserved.

Although modestly garbed compared to the lavish finery displayed by her guests, Lady Trevor's gown focused attention on her flawless beauty.

Its severe cut emphasized her lushly curved form,

while the rich, black velvet dramatized the milky smoothness of her skin.

A single ruby dangled from her black pearl necklace like a drop of blood. Its warm, red gleam highlighted her hair's fiery sheen and her clear, crystal eyes. She had the same long-limbed grace, chiseled features, and youthful vibrance that favored her daughter Trent. Indeed the two were often mistaken for sisters.

"You must tell me your secret," Millicent pleaded. "How do you keep so well with three children to raise?"

Trevor shrugged. "I suppose it's the reward of temperance."

"Now you're really too modest, darling. I'm sure Lord Kiferson contributes a goodly measure toward preserving that rosy bloom," Millicent confided with a sly smile.

I'm sure you'd love to sample the cure yourself, Trevor thought. However, she managed to maintain her humor. "That's something my husband can answer better than I."

"Where is the dear man?" Millicent whined, "I haven't seen him for hours."

"Take heart. The evening is still young."

But Millicent wasn't listening. "There he is!" She cooed, craning her neck. Then her mouth fell open.

"But who is he dancing with?"

Trevor glanced across the room and saw her husband waltzing with a slim black girl. "I believe that's our Melba," she said casually.

"You mean she's one of your slaves?" Millicent demanded.

"Not really. She's been given her freedom."

"But my dear, she is a servant after all," Millicent

reminded indignantly. "I mean . . . her with Lord Kiferson . . . it's hardly proper."

Trevor's smile faded. "Actually we consider Melba part of the family. Now, if you'll excuse me . . ."

"Of course, darling," Millicent purred, gazing intently at Lord Kiferson. "Don't worry, surely I'll find something to amuse me."

"No doubt you're easily amused," Trevor muttered as she hurried outside for a breath of air.

She slipped through a side door and heaved a grateful sigh when she found the veranda was empty. Though the ball had only just begun she was exhausted.

She also felt a profound sense of futility. Somehow her daughter had become a complete stranger. Trevor vividly recalled her own youth and admitted to having been a thoroughly spoiled, ill-mannered brat. Unfortunately Trent had inherited her mother's temperament as well as her looks.

However, Trevor had always maintained the dignity befitting her station. Her reputation was beyond question.

The question had no meaning to her daughter. Trent wasn't merely headstrong or high-spirited. Since her return from school she'd comported herself like a common slut.

While Trevor accepted full responsibility for failing to win her daughter's trust, she placed most of the blame on her husband. It was his fault for many reasons, some of which were beyond his control.

The matter of his tainted bloodline couldn't be ignored as a significant factor. The secret hovered over their lives like a predatory bird.

To be sure Lord Kyle Kiferson was of noble birth and exemplified the finest qualities of an Eton gentleman. His high moral standards gained as much public repute as his wealth. It was commonly known that Lord Kiferson refused to haul slaves on his ships despite the enormous profits in human cargo. But if his ethics drew a great deal of interest, they earned very little sympathy. Even close associates considered him an eccentric. They underestimated him.

Lord Kyle Kiferson was actually a thief, reiver, kidnapper, and killer—as well as an impostor. He was better known to the fierce sea-raiders of North Africa as Kahlil el-Kifer—undisputed king of the Barbar coast. His noble birthright had been sealed in the fires of a hundred battles as chieftain of the Barbar pirates who plundered the waters separating Europe from the New World.

Neither Trent, nor her younger brother Kevin, had ever been told of their savage legacy.

But blood will tell, Trevor reflected grimly.

Little was known of the Barbar tribe. Some claimed they were descendants of the people of lost Atlantis; others believed them to be the lost tribe cited in the Old Testament. But one thing was certain. They were a heathen race.

Barbar law accorded women equal privilege, including sexual freedom. Indeed Trevor had often berated her husband's laxity in dealing with Trent's indiscretions.

It was useless. The fact that he adored his daughter exacerbated his natural tolerance. As a result, Trent had no regard for parental authority, social convention, or Christian decency. Only a savage or a prostitute would auction her troth to the highest bidder. Certainly Trevor couldn't believe her daughter wanted Gavin Radcliffe for anything more than his money.

As she peered through the window she caught sight of Trent's intended spouse. Gavin Radcliffe's red mask and satin brocade tailcoat failed to disguise—or flatter—his flaccid paunch and receding chin. He stood at a discreet distance as his fiancée entertained a trio of admirers, lurking in Trent's shadow like a sleek, overfed rodent.

Damn her Barbar blood, Trevor raged helplessly. The curse froze on her lips when she spotted Shan.

The black-haired girl stood alone at the edge of the floor, and even at a distance Trevor could see her disapproving expression.

Shan's face was unmasked, but an icy contempt glazed her turquoise eyes and dark, sensual features. Since Shan was her foster daughter, Trevor immediately recognized the disdain behind the girl's polite smile. In many ways she felt closer to Shan than to her natural child.

Trevor also recognized her own tragic error. Her stepdaughter's dignity, devotion, and honor bore proud witness to her Barbar heritage. If Trent's vices were evidence of bad blood, Shan's virtues proved the real sin lay with her mother. It was a damning indictment of Lady Trevor's guilt, and the decadence of Christian civilization.

Judging from the licentious behavior exhibited by her guests, Trent was merely following the example set by society. Vanity, avarice, gluttony, and lust seemed to be common practice among her aristocratic friends.

As was adultery, Trevor thought dourly, when she spotted Millicent Devon dancing with Lord Kiferson. Like most of the highborn ladies in New Orleans, Millicent had the morals of a cobra.

Her skin crawled as she watched the half-naked fe-

male coiling lasciviously around Kyle. Though fully
confident of her husband's ability to resist Millicent's
wanton embrace, Lady Trevor despaired for her
daughter. Somehow she knew that the jaded whore
with the jeweled mask heralded Trent's unholy destiny.

During his extraordinary career, Lord Kiferson had
crossed swords with every breed of criminal from
Marseilles to Mecca.

But none so corrupt as a Southern belle, Kiferson
reflected as he held Millicent Devon at bay.

He was more embarrassed than excited by the
woman's attentions. Undaunted she pressed closer,
rubbing her breasts seductively against him in full
view of her husband and daughter.

And they call my people savages, Kiferson mused.
*Yet Barbars didn't betray their friends or dishonor
their family. Nor did they barter human slaves. Such
traits better distinguished civilized gentry.*

Indeed, he'd been forced to keep slaves on his estate. A wealthy landowner without servants would
surely arouse suspicion. If anyone exposed his Barbar
roots, his wife and children would be branded as outcasts. For their sake he endured the demands of
convention.

However, Madame Devon was sorely testing his en-
durance. Firmly, if not too gently, he pried her off his
chest, and waltzed toward the refreshment table. His
dancing partner deftly countered the move.

"I feel faint," she murmured, sagging limply in his
arms. "Pray assist me outside for a breath of fresh
air."

Although the main terrace was cool, quiet, and
comfortably appointed with lounge chairs, Millicent
found it overcrowded.

"Perhaps a walk through the gardens would clear my head," she suggested. "I'm still a bit dazed. Can you bear my company a while longer, milord?"

Kiferson doubted he could, but he had no choice.

"Certainly madame," he muttered.

Millicent leaned heavily on his arm as he escorted her through the scented groves that bordered the mansion. To his relief he saw a few other couples strolling nearby, their costumes illuminated by the necklace of colored lights encircling the darkness. Their presence had little effect on Millicent.

She stopped abruptly and drew him into the shadow of a large tree. "I'm burning with fever," she whispered breathlessly. "Just feel my skin." She pulled his hand to her breast and held it there.

The feral passion steaming from her liquidy flesh flooded Kiferson's senses. Reflexively, his fingers stroked the stiff, throbbing nipples thrusting from her bodice.

A catlike smile drifted across Millicent's lips. With deliberate slowness she stepped back and unfastened the pearl buttons at her waist. As her gown fell open she removed her mask and tossed it aside.

She had the high cheekbones, dark, almond eyes, and sensuous mouth of a Russian ballerina, but her ripe, swollen breasts and voluptuous thighs suggested earthier pleasures. The animal lust danced across her smile as she slowly sank to her knees.

Desire boiled through Kiferson's brain, searing away his civilized veneer. Stripped of restraint and charged with anticipation he crouched like a golden-eyed lion as Millicent clawed at his trousers, mewling hungrily.

A sudden trill of female laughter floated through

the darkness. The muffled sound smothered Kiferson's excitement and he drew back.

"Don't leave me," Millicent hissed, clutching his boot.

"Only for a moment," he assured, easing out of her grasp. "I want to make certain we're undisturbed."

Actually he intended to be away much longer.

When he left the grove he strode briskly toward the house and didn't slacken his pace until he was inside.

Left parched and perspired by his bout with temptation, Kiferson headed directly for the punch bowl.

As soon as he entered the ballroom he was met by Millicent's husband and daughter.

Eustace Devon had unwisely chosen a matador costume for the occasion. The snug-fitting tights exaggerated his wide buttocks and spindly legs, making him resemble nothing more than a glittering sausage. His bulging, pink eyes and the blue veins mottling his bulbous nose attested to his advanced state of intoxication.

"Just the man I've been looking for," Devon brayed. "Allow me to present my little girl, Julie."

Kiferson bowed mechanically. "I'm honored, mademoiselle."

"Now that your daughter's gettin' hitched it's high time your son took a wife. And he could do a lot worse than my little Julie."

"That's something he'll have to decide for himself." Kiferson smiled. "If you'll excuse me, I must speak to my wife."

Devon clapped him on the shoulder. "Tell her to save me a dance. I'm really taken by that woman of yours."

"It's your wife that requires attention," Kiferson snapped coldly. "She's waiting in the garden."

Devon blinked. Though confused by his host's message, there was no mistaking the steely menace in his tone.

"The garden . . ." he echoed inanely, wilting under the relentless glare of Kiferson's sun-flecked eyes. ". . . I'll attend to it immediately." He mumbled, retreating toward the door.

The solace afforded by his hasty departure was short-lived.

"It seems I've been deserted." A feminine voice observed coyly.

Kiferson turned and saw Julie Devon smiling at him. Unlike Millicent she was tall and fair, with long flaxen hair that fell to her waist. Except for those differences however, Julie clearly favored her mother. The family resemblance was marked by the insolent thrust of her hips and well-exposed cleavage, as well as her seductive manner.

"I've been yearning for a handsome dance partner, but I fear I need instruction," she confided, taking his arm.

"Then my duty is clear, mademoiselle."

"I'm in your hands," Julie purred. "What do you suggest?"

Kiferson managed a weary smile. "I suggest we find my son."

It had been a long, frustrating evening for Kevin.

Not that he'd been ignored by the ladies at the ball. He'd been flattered, fussed-over, and besieged with proposals of every type. The local belles accorded him singular attention, aware that Trent's betrothal afforded them a rare opportunity. They knew Kevin didn't share his sister's enthusiasm for social gatherings. Away at school most of the year, he spent his brief sojourns with his family in seclusion. Like his father he was something of a recluse.

Unfortunately the comparison magnified Kevin's deficiencies. His blond hair and golden eyes marked him as Lord Kiferson's heir, but his sensitive features and tall, slender frame lacked his father's raw-boned power.

Kevin was awkward as well, with a tendency to blush that belied his father's magnetic aura of authority.

While some young ladies were disappointed, none were discouraged. They knew Kevin had yet to reach full maturity, being barely eighteen and without worldly experience. Only time could measure his manly virtues.

They also knew it didn't matter. Even if Kevin fell short of his father, time would endow him with Lord Kiferson's empire. Indeed, a few of Kevin's admirers considered his youth a distinct advantage and attempted to dazzle him with their feminine wiles.

When he failed to respond they were undeterred, certain that sooner or later he'd succumb to the lure of nature.

Their assumptions were accurate, if belated. Since childhood Kevin had been hopelessly in love with his foster-sister, Shan. And for years she'd rewarded his devotion with scornful indifference. He'd always believed that when he came of age Shan would consider him an eligible suitor, but she continued to treat him like a bothersome infant.

Though only five years his senior Shan possessed the serene self-assurance of a matriarch. Trent and her fashionable friends were childlike imitations of womanhood compared to his foster-sister.

The sole reason Kevin endured their transparent

advances was to pique Shan's jealousy. That too, proved to be a false hope, however. His foster-sister remained oblivious to his presence all evening.

She can't deny me one dance, Kevin fumed, impatiently scanning the throng.

A quick jolt of anger wrenched his awareness when he saw her across the room, talking with Trent's fiancé. Gavin Radcliffe's very proximity to Shan seemed profane—like Judas paying court to the Holy Madonna.

Kevin tried to calm his emotions as he threaded through the crowd.

It's just brute jealousy, he told himself. *Radcliffe didn't matter.*

His anger subsided immediately. He knew it was true. Trent's intended had nothing in common with Shan. Anyone who spoke to her aroused his resentment. That much he'd learned from experience.

His thoughts crumbled when Shan looked up.

The moment she saw him approaching she turned and said something to her companion.

Kevin came to an abrupt halt as Radcliffe took Shan's hand and led her onto the dance floor. He wanted to rush away but his limbs refused to respond.

He stood there helplessly, gaping in stunned disbelief—his will shattered by Shan's deliberate rebuff.

Gavin Radcliffe proved to be clumsy as well as dull.

The oaf also has bad breath, Shan noted, forcibly pushing her dancing partner back a few inches. *Still he was the lesser of two evils.*

She didn't want to hurt her brother, but to encourage him would be far more cruel. For both of them.

"Now it's your turn to find a husband," Radcliffe remarked tactlessly. "After all, you're the oldest."

"Wine tastes sweetest when it's ripe." She replied with a polite smile.

If Radcliffe heard, it wasn't apparent by his response. "Oh, there's Sybil Reynolds," he piped, waving at a fat woman dressed as Cleopatra.

It was just as well. Shan had no intention of discussing her marital status. Lately, however, the question nagged at her thoughts with increasing persistence. As did her long-suffering beaus.

Unfortunately Shan knew the answer. She would never marry.

Despite her proper English education, she was a Barbar maiden. She wouldn't wed without love, and very few of the men she'd encountered were worthy of respect. Compared to a Barbar seawolf they were timid lap dogs. But though painful to admit, Shan understood she was unfit to be a Barbar wife after so many years among foreigners. Of course, El-Kifer was hardly a foreigner. Shan considered herself privileged by his bounty. Lord Kiferson had always granted her the same devoted care given to his natural offspring. *Now she had to pay the price,* Shan reflected somberly.

Perhaps it was cheap at that, she decided, glancing at Radcliffe.

Neither wealth nor her loyalty to El-Kifer—her beloved father and king—could induce her to take such a simpering mouse as her husband.

And yet, if Trent's choice was appalling, the union did solve a serious problem. Her stepsister would never learn of her savage heritage.

That alone was a priceless blessing, in light of her erratic conduct. Trent couldn't be entrusted with her father's secret. Her self-indulgent temperament would endanger them all.

In time, when El-Kifer deemed him ready, Kevin would be told of his birthright as a Barbar prince. If he proved worthy he might even inherit his father's crown. If he proved worthy . . .

A pang of remorse cut through Shan's speculations. She loved Kevin—but only as a brother. While his puppylike adoration was touching, it embarrassed her. Shan yearned for a man who would tame her wild passions, not a moonstruck schoolboy.

More than that, Kevin belonged to another world.

He needed a woman of his own caste. Someone bred to share his future, rather than his past.

Shan could only pray that it wasn't someone like his sister.

Lady Trent felt marvelous.

Her exhilaration was amplified by the heady awareness of victory, as she accepted the tributes of her fawning audience. She was also aware that it was money, not love, that powered her triumph. Trent had suffered too long to forget. For years she'd endured the bitter sting of humiliation. Ever since childhood, she'd been considered an outcast by the social arbiters of New Orleans—and by her own family.

As a young girl her classmates made fun of her father's unconventional reputation. When she went to England to finish her education, she was ostracized for being an American. Her aristocratic peers made it clear that titles, like vintage wines, didn't travel well.

Trent cared little for their petty opinions. She adored her father and admired his staunch independence. But in time, she became embittered by his indifference.

Away at sea for long months, her father spent the brief interludes between voyages doting on his son. Kevin had always been the family favorite, while Shan could do no wrong. Indeed her mother often cited Shan as an example of maidenly decorum, during their disagreements. However, Trent learned early in life to assert her own values. She considered pride a precious luxury, and by exploiting her exceptional beauty she'd earned her vindication.

Her marriage would give her wealth, position—and freedom from her parents' domination. That it was merely a union of convenience didn't matter. She had long realized the futility of love.

Certainly Gavin's aesthetic shortcomings hadn't dissuaded her rivals, Trent observed with cynical amusement.

"My sincerest wishes for your future happiness, mademoiselle. And my deepest regrets."

Trent looked up and saw a tall gentleman, attired as a French musketeer. Although he was masked, she recognized him immediately. As well she should; Jason Dean was a part of her future, being a full partner in the firm of Dean and Radcliffe.

"Why your regrets, sir?" she inquired demurely.

"I only regret my own loss," he quipped. "Time put you beyond my reach."

"There's still ample time for a dance."

"You've rejuvenated my hopes," Dean replied, taking her hand.

She accepted his flirtatious remark as a polite compliment. Most Southern gentlemen were prone to excessive flattery. For the same reason she accepted his invitation to join him on the veranda.

"The quiet is so refreshing," Trent sighed gratefully, leaning against the rail. "I needed this brief respite from the festivities."

Dean moved closer, and removed his mask. "At my age, one appreciates the pleasures of solitude."

"Shall I leave you then?" Trent teased.

"Not so soon, mademoiselle."

His sharp tone alerted Trent, and she gave him an appraising smile. "I do have my guests to consider."

"I believe I fall into that category," he reminded. "You may also count me as one of your admirers."

"I'm flattered," Trent said lightly. In truth she found his interest rather intriguing. Jason Dean was quite handsome for an older man, with rugged, sea-weathered features and deep-set blue eyes that boldly challenged her.

"We'll get to know each other better, when you're Gavin's wife," he confided. "No doubt you'll welcome the distraction. A woman like you needs more than tea parties."

Trent bristled at his implication.

"And just what kind of woman is that, sir?"

Dean roughly pulled her closer. "This kind . . ." he whispered hoarsely, pressing his lips on hers.

She recoiled from his whiskey-fevered kiss, and twisted free.

"I demand an apology," she hissed.

"You needn't play the virginal bride for my benefit," he assured, voice slurred by sarcasm. "We're too much alike to pretend."

As he reached for her, Trent lashed out, vehemently.

Her slap drove Dean back, but failed to dislodge his knowing smirk.

"You will apologize, sir," she repeated, "or I'll inform my fiancé immediately."

Dean snorted derisively. "Your precious fiancé is hardly a threat."

Stung by the truth of his words, she turned and hurried inside. Her rage was further spurred by panic. For despite her scandalous reputation, she was indeed a virgin.

If Trent had sold her troth, it was an honest bargain. And she intended to defend her honor.

She was oddly comforted when she saw Gavin dancing with her stepsister. *At least Shan can be depended upon for support,* Trent reflected, as she beckoned to her fiancé.

Gavin stopped dancing and trotted over like a well-trained terrier, dragging Shan with him.

"Where've you been, sugar angel?"

The familiar endearment stoked Trent's outrage.

"If you're truly interested, I've just been molested and insulted by your friend, Mr. Jason Dean."

Gavin pulled the mask off his face.

"Jason . . . ?"

"You doubt my word?" Trent asked, voice edged with fury.

"Oh no, dearest," he assured hastily. "It's simply that I'm shocked beyond belief . . . ah, that is . . . I'm absolutely stunned."

Shan gently touched her sister's shoulder. "Did he harm you?"

"The cowardly swine left his mark," Trent declared, lifting her arm.

Gavin stared at the bruises smudging her white skin in slack-jawed amazement. "Jason did that?"

"He did indeed, sir. Now what do you intend to do about it?"

He continued to peer at the marks, as if expecting them to provide the answer.

"Don't worry, dearest, I'll settle this matter," he assured, avoiding her fiery gaze. "I'll ask him to leave immediately."

"It's not enough. I demand full satisfaction for this dishonor."

Shiny beads of sweat bloomed on Gavin's pudgy face. According to the code, he was obliged to challenge Jason to a duel. And he already knew the result. Jason Dean was a master swordsman, who'd survived numerous challenges, while Gavin hadn't lifted anything heavier than a wine goblet for the past decade.

"There he is," Trent exclaimed. "If you don't confront him, I will."

The threat roused Gavin from his stupor. Blinking like an alarmed rooster, he reluctantly shuffled toward Dean.

Few people noticed the trio in the crowd of revelers. Jason Dean was one. Another was Kevin Kiferson. He spied Shan and his sister following Radcliffe to the veranda, and hurried after them.

Kevin knew that Shan couldn't refuse him in front of Trent and her betrothed. He also understood he was playing the fool, but couldn't rein his emotions.

Spurring his haste was the fear that Shan would take another dance partner before he reached her. His fear turned to hostility when he saw Radcliffe approach Jason Dean. Dean's arrogant manner confirmed his impression. The man's blustering tone could be heard above the noise.

Although Kevin's thoughts centered on Shan, an odd sense of menace slowed his pace. Then he saw Radcliffe's expression and realized something was wrong.

Gavin was gaping at Jason Dean like a landed fish,

eyes bulging from his gray, sweat-drenched face.

"Mister Dean, we demand an apology," he wheezed. "In all respect to the long friendship between our families."

"Apologize, you say? To whom must I apologize and for what?"

"Why . . . to Lady Trent, of course."

Dean shrugged. "I don't see why I should."

"Then look at this, you contemptible coward!" Trent snapped, displaying her bruised arm. "If I were a man I'd take a whip to you."

"We find your actions highly insulting," Gavin added lamely.

"Take care," Dean warned, ignoring Trent. "A rash tongue could prove fatal. Your false accusations try my patience."

Gavin blinked and stepped back. "False, you say? Then you deny making advances toward my fiancée?"

Dean's frown became a righteous sneer.

"My advances were encouraged. What else would a man expect when a woman consents to join him alone on the terrace? A woman dressed in such provocative fashion."

His retort gave Gavin the opportunity he'd been searching for, and he seized it frantically. "Well . . . now, sugar . . . you didn't mention this . . . this er . . . tryst," he stammered, glancing at Trent.

Before she could reply, Kevin elbowed Gavin aside and struck Jason Dean in the face. The open-handed blow caught Dean by surprise and he reeled back, more confused than hurt.

"Your slurs are intolerable," Kevin said, voice trembling with anger. "I'm at your disposal."

"Don't be foolish," Shan exclaimed, sure his act

was a reckless bid to prove himself an adult.

Jason Dean took a harsher view of the matter. "No man strikes me and lives," he snarled, reaching for his sword.

"What's the trouble here?" The question stayed Dean's hand, and he glared at the intruder. His scowl softened when he recognized Judge Paxton.

"The fool is eager to test his mettle," Dean muttered indignantly. "He attacked me without warning."

Kevin's gaze didn't waver. "I repeat sir, I'm at your disposal."

Judge Paxton stepped between them. "Gentlemen, this can be discussed calmly. We must respect the sanctity of the occasion."

"Some things can't be discussed," Dean rasped.

"I urge you to reconsider, Mr. Dean. He's just a high-spirited young buck."

Shan caught sight of Lord Kiferson and discreetly waved him closer. She was relieved by his alert response.

"Let him suffer the consequences," Dean insisted, gripping the hilt of his sword.

"Can I be of assistance?"

"Daddy, you're just in time," Trent cried, rushing to Lord Kiferson's side. "This scum vilified my honor. Kevin merely tried to defend me." She lifted her arm with a flourish. "This should be evidence enough."

Kiferson barely glanced at her bruises. "What happened, Kevin?"

"He slandered Trent," the boy replied, eyes still on Dean. "Any man would have been offended by his swinish conduct."

Gavin understood the remark was a partial rebuke but remained silent, thankful he'd been spared from certain death.

"Surely, Lord Kiferson, you'll forbid this ill-advised challenge," Paxton drawled. "In light of your son's age . . ."

Dean snorted impatiently. "If he's old enough to bear insult he's old enough to apologize."

There was really no other choice, Kiferson reflected. *If he forced Kevin to withdraw, the boy's pride would be crushed. And apology was out of the question. Better he die in combat, like a true Barbar.*

"My son is a man," he said quietly. "I cannot interfere. I can only suggest that this affair be settled quickly, with a minimum of inconvenience to my guests."

"The sooner the better," Dean sputtered, somewhat bewildered. He'd fully expected Lord Kiferson to negotiate for his son's life.

Shan, too, was startled, certain El-Kifer would personally avenge his daughter's dishonor.

But Kevin accepted the decision as the highest form of praise. His father's statement meant more to him than a blessing.

Lord Kiferson continued to question his own judgment as he waited for the duel to begin.

A small corral behind the stables had been selected as the field of honor, and the area was illuminated by torches. There were a handful of spectators huddled at the rail; Gavin stood beside his father, Moss Radcliffe, while Trent exchanged whispered comments with Millicent Devon.

Though disturbed by Millicent's presence, there was nothing Kiferson could do. Her husband had agreed to serve as Jason Dean's second. At the moment, Kiferson was more concerned by the menacing whistle of Dean's sword.

The man's too strong for Kevin, he speculated.

Jason Dean moved with practiced ease, as he executed some preliminary maneuvers to acquaint himself with the battle area.

Kevin stood in a corner, intently going through a number of limbering exercises, using the fence rail to stretch his legs. He seemed awkward compared to Dean, like a gangly-kneed gazelle preparing to battle a tiger.

Stop fretting like an old woman, Kiferson chided silently.

As Kevin's second, his task was to aid and advise the boy, not discourage him. And in truth he'd underrated his son's abilities. Kevin had earned distinction as Eton's best fencer during the school term, and was no stranger to violent combat, having been bloodied on his first sea-voyage.

And yet, Kiferson knew it wasn't enough.

Galley fights and fencing contests meant nothing against a veteran killer.

"Time, gentlemen," Judge Paxton droned.

The announcement cut off Kiferson's broodings and he concentrated on the task at hand.

"Don't rush him," he warned, moving to Kevin's side. "Your best course is a sturdy defense. Is that clear?"

Kevin looked up. "Parry, boy, parry," he recited with a slight smile.

The familiar admonition reassured Kiferson. He'd repeated it constantly while teaching his son the rudiments of armed combat.

He was further comforted by Judge Paxton's decree.

"As official arbiter of this dispute, I hereby bind all litigants to specific rules of conduct," he said sternly, making sure Dean understood. "In light of the obvious inexperience of the challenging party, *first blood* shall be deemed full satisfaction—and will decide the winner. Any questions, gentlemen?"

Dean's scowl revealed his frustration but he knew better than to object. The referee had final say according to the code, and Paxton exerted considerable legal influence. His word could change an affair of honor to a criminal offense.

"Seconds will now withdraw," Paxton called. "Parry boy . . ." Kiferson murmured before stepping back.

While relieved by Paxton's ruling, he was still anxious for his son's safety. If he'd learned anything from his warrior years it was to take nothing as certain. And everything about this skirmish seemed bizarre. Except for Kevin and himself, all the participants were in costume, and one of the spectators, Moss Radcliffe, wore a mask.

Jason Dean was dressed in the full regalia of a musketeer, including a plumed hat, which he didn't deign to remove, either as a demonstration of his scorn, or to conceal his receding hairline.

The sight of Judge Paxton in the center of the corral attired as a revolutionary general would have been comic but for his function. He stood between the two combatants holding a handkerchief aloft. When the tips of their swords were poised on each side of the white lace, he gave the signal.

"*En garde*, gentlemen," he intoned, letting the handkerchief fall.

As it fluttered to the ground, Dean lunged.

His vicious thrust drew a gasp from the spectators, but Kevin alertly deflected the blade and assumed a defensive stance. At the first clash of steel, Kiferson's senses quickened with primitive emotion. This was his heir's baptism as a Barbar warrior.

Although the duel would be settled by a single wound, that injury could well be mortal.

And Dean seems to be trying his damnedest for a kill, Lord Kiferson observed grimly.

Dean advanced relentlessly, his sword humming like a deadly hornet as he darted from side to side, seeking an opening. Many times he could have ended the duel with an arm or shoulder sting but he preferred to wait for a more telling stroke.

Fortunately, Kevin was prudent as well as agile. Wisely following his father's counsel, he maintained a flawless defense.

His style was an unusual blend of classic Italian and little-known Barbar techniques, which kept the more experienced swordsman at bay. But the most important factor was Kevin's natural ability. No longer awkward, he dodged, circled, feinted, and parried with the nimble ease of a dancer.

After a few minutes, however, Dean began to penetrate with great frequency.

He constantly probed Kevin's guard with swift, accurate thrusts that threatened to pierce heart or lung. Only the boy's extraordinary reflexes saved him from harm.

With each passing moment, Kevin's advantage increased. By neutralizing Dean's furious attack he was wearing him down. Though a masterful swordsman, Dean's age was beginning to weigh against him. His weapon seemed heavier and his footwork slower.

Lord Kiferson knew it was the most dangerous part of the battle.

The boy's overconfident, he noted anxiously, as Kevin feinted Dean back.

Jason Dean saw the same thing. He took off his plumed hat and threw it aside, as if readying himself for an all-out assault.

Kiferson couldn't warn his son without violating the code. Helplessly, he watched Kevin enter the trap.

As Dean retreated, he dropped his blade an inch and Kevin couldn't resist. Expecting to surprise his opponent, he lunged.

In one smooth motion Dean parried, and swung his sword at Kevin's exposed neck. Instinctively the boy fell back, blade flashing in the torchlight. His wild chop caught the hilt of Dean's sabre, and the weapon flew from his hand.

Dean looked up, body frozen in place.

"Arm yourself," Kevin said curtly.

As Dean bent to retrieve his sabre he suddenly grabbed a fistful of gravel and hurled it in the boy's face.

Kevin's momentary confusion enabled Dean to scoop up his sword and strike. The hurried thrust gashed the boy's forearm, jolting his weapon loose.

"Apologize," Dean demanded, pressing his blade against Kevin's throat.

"Hold!" Judge Paxton shouted.

Dean didn't hear. "Apologize or eat steel," he rasped.

The boy remained motionless, as the sword tip punctured his skin.

"Hold!" Paxton repeated, moving hastily toward them.

Before he'd taken two paces, Lord Kiferson hurdled the fence and sprinted across the corral, to Kevin's side.

When Dean saw him loom into view he lifted his sabre.

"Hold, man!" Paxton insisted.

Dean stepped back but kept watching Kiferson intently, as if expecting him to spring.

"I declare this contest a draw," Paxton said hoarsely. "Mr. Dean's untoward action violates the code of combat."

"Just as he violates my house with his presence."

Kiferson's voice cut through the quiet like a gust of snow. There was no mistaking the threat in his soft tone and although he was unarmed, Dean declined to challenge the powerful, golden-haired figure.

He shrugged and lowered his sword.

"We'll settle our accounts without prejudice the next time."

"At your convenience," Kiferson replied, as he turned to examine his son's wound. Kevin's arm was sliced from wristbone to elbow, and his sleeve was sodden with blood. Luckily the slash proved to be much longer than it was deep. "Probably won't even leave a scar," Kiferson announced.

Kevin seemed disappointed. He was on the verge of speaking, then glanced away, jaw clenched stubbornly.

"Should be washed as soon as possible," Kiferson went on. "I'll ask Shan to bandage it . . ."

"That won't be necessary," Kevin blurted. "It's just a scratch . . ." he added lamely, avoiding his father's puzzled gaze.

"As you wish," Kiferson said, stroking his chin. "But don't delay. Infection can be deadlier than a coward's sword."

Kevin looked up, eyes flaring.

"I hope I didn't embarrass you."

As Kiferson met his stare he slowly understood.

The boy thinks he lost, he realized with mild astonishment.

"I'll be as clear as possible," he said finally. "I'm proud of you. As of now you're a full-time associate in my firm. And when you sail to Africa with me this June, you'll be my second mate. Is that proof enough?"

It took Kevin a moment to comprehend. Then a wide, foolish, grin dissolved his anger.

Before he could reply, Lady Trevor and Shan rushed to his side, followed by the other spectators.

"You're hurt," Trevor cried.

"Don't worry, Mother. He barely nicked me."

"He's all right," Kiferson assured.

Lady Trevor glanced at her husband.

"Shall we call a doctor?"

"It's not necessary."

The affirmation quelled her fears.

"Then I suppose we'd better return to our guests," she said, trying not to look at Kevin's blood-soaked arm.

Moss Radcliffe removed his mask and stepped forward.

"I pray this unfortunate incident won't mar our friendship," he droned anxiously. "Or weaken our family bond."

While repelled by the thought of kinship with the pompous hypocrite, Kiferson forced a smile.

"Rest easy, Mister Radcliffe. I seek no quarrel with my daughter's future happiness. Nor do I blame you for another man's actions. In fact I've arranged a special gift for the couple."

"How marvelous," Gavin blared. "I can't wait to find out. Can you, sugar angel?"

A flicker of suspicion crossed Trent's smile.

"I'm burning with curiosity. What have you arranged, Father, dear?"

Lord Kiferson took her hand. "Paris, London, Barcelona, Rome, Venice, and Athens. That's my surprise for you both. I've arranged receptions in each city; you'll be formally introduced to the most distinguished families in the old world. And on your return you'll be wed right here, in the home where you were born."

"You mean a sea voyage?" Gavin sputtered.

"It's more of a Grand Tour. You'll travel in splendid comfort I assure you."

"Oh but I can't . . . I mean . . . my business commitments . . ." Gavin stammered, mopping his brow with a satin handkerchief. "It could take months."

"Six months exactly," Kiferson told him. "You'll be sailing on my fastest clippers."

Moss Radcliffe pushed his son aside. "It's impossible. Gavin's needed here. You understand, I'm sure."

"Maybe for our honeymoon, sugar angel," Gavin whined, glancing at Trent.

"I can cancel the receptions," Kiferson said curtly.

"Do I have a voice in this?" Trent inquired.

Gavin flinched. "Of course, angel. What do you suggest?"

"I for one am deeply moved by my father's generous gift and fail to see why I should suffer because of your dreary business affairs."

"You're absolutely right, darling. This requires careful deliberation. But it's almost time to announce our troth," he reminded, blinking nervously. He gingerly took her arm and nudged her toward the house. "I promise we'll reconsider. Won't we, Father?"

"Certainly . . . certainly . . ," Radcliffe croaked, waddling after them.

Lady Trevor regarded her husband sternly. "Haven't you spoiled her enough?"

"More than enough," he admitted, with a rueful sigh.

"Then why do you indulge her so?"

"My madness is not entirely without method," he confided. "Since it's obvious your daughter will never yield to our wishes, we must rely on her obstinate nature. A prolonged absence from her fiancé might change her outlook."

"Suppose he decides to join her?"

He smiled and drew her close. "It's common knowledge that Gavin Radcliffe is terrified of water. He's never been on a paddle-boat, much less a real ship."

"You've always been a brilliant tactician, milord," Trevor admitted, giving him a kiss. "Let's hope you win this campaign. I don't fancy having Gavin sire my grandchild."

As Lord and Lady Kiferson strolled away, Shan glared at Kevin. "I'm not impressed by your heroics," she said coolly.

He glanced around as if awakening from a deep sleep. Jason Dean and Eustace Devon had already departed, while the others were walking slowly toward the house.

"I did it for my own sake," he murmured, dabbing at his arm with his shirttail.

"You're lucky to escape with your life."

Ten minutes earlier, her icy scorn would have shriveled his confidence, but now it barely touched him. He was still basking in the warmth of his father's proud words. "It was worth the risk."

"I'm sure you treasure your wound like some badge of honor. But it merely proves your bone-headed stupidity."

He shrugged. "It was the only way."

"The only way to prove you're a fool," she corrected, her voice rising angrily.

"How else could I lure you close enough to claim the next dance?"

His rueful grin—and a sudden curiosity—dissolved Shan's rage. Kevin seemed different somehow, as if he'd just returned from a long voyage.

"I suppose it's my family duty," she sighed. "But not before you change your shirt."

Trent made sure that Gavin didn't forget his show of cowardice. She found it quite convenient to keep him on the defensive. If nothing else, it obscured her own culpability in the affair.

"I'm still in shock," she exclaimed, glaring at her fiancé. "How could you abide such a despicable insult?"

"It happened so fast, sugar," Gavin whined, looking at his father for support.

"Jason was a bit inebriated," Mr. Radcliffe said hastily. "I'm certain he'll offer a full apology at a more propitious moment. But right now we've got more pleasant matters to consider. Don't we, son?"

Gavin nodded enthusiastically, and took Trent's arm.

"Daddy's right, my sweet. It's almost time for our announcement."

Trent pulled away. "Perhaps we should postpone it until a more . . . *propitious moment.*"

"We're all overwrought. Why air soiled linen in public?" Mr. Radcliffe clucked.

"You put it quite aptly," Trent observed, as they neared the light-festooned mansion. "Better we save everyone further embarrassment."

At the stroke of midnight, Lord Kiferson made a brief statement. The crowd hushed immediately when the tall, golden-maned figure mounted the musician's podium.

"I bid you welcome," he said curtly. "As you know we're here to celebrate a birthday. However, my daughter Trent has a surprise for you all. Please permit me to introduce Mister Moss Radcliffe."

There was a smattering of applause as Radcliffe took the stage.

Hardly an overwhelming tribute from a proud father, Trent observed bitterly.

Although she knew it didn't matter anymore, frustration gnawed at her triumph. She wasn't comforted by Radcliffe's forced joviality.

"Time to unmask, dear friends," he sang out cheerfully. "And to reveal our special surprise."

As Trent glanced around the room a dark, hawk-featured face fluttered into view. The shock of recognition scattered her thoughts and she instinctively moved toward the black-clad figure far across the floor.

". . . with deepest pride I announce the betrothal of Lady Trent Kiferson to my son . . ."

"Where are you going, angel?" Gavin cooed anxiously. "Daddy's waiting for us."

Scarcely aware of him, or the excited murmur stirred by his father's statement, Trent edged through the throng, heartbeat racing wildly.

"Look out!"

Gavin's cry drew her attention to a burly man attired as a sea pirate pushing his way toward her. He roughly knocked her aside as he charged through the crowd.

When he neared the podium the man stopped short.

"Lord . . ." he rasped hoarsely. The man lurched forward, arms extended, and embraced Lord Kiferson. Then he went limp, legs sagging slowly as if floating in water.

"Why the old cutthroat's drunk," Judge Paxton chuckled.

Trailed by a ripple of laughter he helped Kiferson steer the man to the outer hall.

"Let's all drink and be merry," Radcliffe declared. "I offer a toast to the happy couple."

Trent barely heard, as she kept searching for the man in black. He had disappeared in the milling confusion.

If he'd ever been there at all, she reflected.

She wasn't even sure who—or what—she expected to find.

"Come, sugar . . . everyone's waiting . . ." Gavin stammered, gingerly tugging her arm.

His damp fingers froze her uncertainty. *There's nothing out there,* she decided, turning back. *I have everything I want.*

But later as she stood with Gavin, basking in the crowd's adulation, she continued to gaze around the room, like a child straining to glimpse the Christmas angel.

After forty years in politics, Judge Paxton had no illusions. When he saw the knife jutting from the man's side, his first reflex was to prevent a senseless panic. As Kiferson carried the limp figure into the hall, Paxton walked beside them, shielding the man from view.

"Give him air, please," he drawled loudly, whenever a guest strayed too near.

His calm was the residue of long experience with violence. Neither the duel, nor the wounded intruder, surprised him greatly. He knew that men like Lord Kiferson had many enemies.

For that reason, he didn't question the presence of the guard outside Kiferson's private study.

However, Paxton gaped in astonishment when he entered. A rich patchwork of carpets covered the floor and the walls were swaddled by exquisite tapestries whose gold and silver patterns glimmered in the candlelight. The only furnishings were three ivory mosaic tables and a number of silken pillows scattered about the room. In every detail it resembled the chamber of an Oriental potentate.

It was then that Paxton realized the servant at the door wasn't black, but some strange breed of Indian.

On closer inspection the wounded man had a similar appearance. His wrinkled shirt and worn pantaloons suggested that he wasn't in costume, while the coarse sounds rumbling from his slack lips were evidently some alien language.

"Baraka . . . El-Kifer . . ." the man grunted, as Kiferson eased him down to the floor.

"Saf . . . Saf . . ." Kiferson responded, in the same guttural tongue.

Though unable to understand what was being said, Paxton could hear the desperation in the man's tone. He also saw it was hopeless. A dark red stain was spreading rapidly across the man's chest and his face had the blue-white pallor of candlewax.

He was dead by the time the servant returned with a medical bag.

Kiferson heaved a weary sigh and stood up. "It's over."

"Better call out your servants to search the grounds," Paxton exclaimed.

"That's been taken care of."

"Do you know this man?"

For a moment Kiferson studied Paxton. "I owe you a debt of gratitude, my friend."

"Seems you have a serious problem. From a legal standpoint, that is." The sharp edge in Paxton's tone made his warning clear.

Kiferson nodded thoughtfully. "What do you advise?"

"I don't know the facts," Paxton reminded, glancing at the body. The servant was kneeling beside the dead man, carefully sponging off the blood.

"His name is Asmad," Kiferson said softly. "He is an officer on one of my ships."

"Did he say who killed him?"

"There wasn't time. He came to warn me of an attack on my shipping vessels."

"Pirates?"

"Perhaps. Or a competitor. Asmad didn't . . ."

They were interrupted by a light knock at the door.

Like the servant attending to the body, the man who entered was attired in a headdress and pantaloons.

He bowed and whispered something to Kiferson.

"My men are out combing the area," he explained. "They suggest using the hounds."

"Might work. Trail's still fresh."

"With hundreds of people swarming all over the

house?" Kiferson bent to pick up the knife lying beside the dead man. "No, my friend. Dogs are only useful in the forest."

"You think it possible that one of your guests killed him?"

"Most of them are strangers—and all had ample opportunity. Look at this."

Paxton stared at the knife Kiferson held out for inspection. It was about ten inches long, with a finely sharpened tip. Except for the deep grooves scored in the handle, there was nothing unusual about the murder weapon.

"Notches seem fresh-cut . . ." he ventured. ". . . but what's that to do with anybody here?"

"The notches were cut to balance the blade's weight," Kiferson said slowly. "Making it easier to throw. Anyone in the ballroom could have killed Asmad. Perhaps it was intended for me."

Paxton thoughtfully hefted the weapon in his palm. "Throwing knife, eh? Funny . . . just yesterday . . ."

Then he remembered and his voice trailed off.

"What happened yesterday?"

"Er . . . nothing much," Paxton stalled. He knew it was useless. Kiferson's gold-flecked eyes seemed to burn into his thoughts.

"Just that I happened to recall a gentleman who seemed skilled at throwing knives. As are lots of people in these parts," he added quickly. "This fellow's name was Fargo, I believe." He neglected to mention that Hall Fargo demonstrated his ability while defending Lady Trent's honor.

Fortunately Kiferson had other concerns at the moment.

"No one must know what happened here tonight," he said, watching Paxton intently.

The judge nervously fingered his white goatee. He knew an inquiry would severely damage Lord Kiferson's reputation. But concealing a murder was a hanging matter.

"You know, of course, what you're asking?"

He didn't expect an answer. As Kiferson's attorney he'd learned years ago that the wealthy shipper seldom sought a favor, and never asked twice. It wasn't his way to bargain, or plead. And yet Paxton had an obligation deeper than friendship—his duty to the rule of law.

He squinted at the dead man. "What about him?"

Kiferson sensed his unspoken question.

"Asmad will be avenged. In full accordance to the law of his people."

Despite his calm tone, the statement had the intensity of an oath. And Paxton suddenly realized he was also bound to comply.

"Let his justice prevail, then," he muttered. "I'll say nothing of this."

Kiferson gave a guttural command to the servant waiting nearby. Immediately the man moved to help his companion. The muted light and exotic tapestries emphasized the quiet as the two men began wrapping the body.

"Within the hour he'll be at sea," Kiferson murmured.

"His assassin will still be here," Paxton reminded him gruffly.

Kiferson's smile was like the flicker of a distant storm. "That's what I'm counting on, my friend."

CHAPTER THREE

It was a beautiful day for sailing.

The smooth, blue water mirrored the sky so perfectly that one might believe the white puffs of foam were clouds—and the ships a flock of kites, bobbing in the morning breeze.

On such days Malcolm Gaines wished he were putting out to sea aboard a full-masted schooner instead of plodding to his office.

Not that he was dissatisfied with his lot. As deputy clerk of the *White Star,* his future was assured. In time, he'd be made a full clerk, and after a few years he might even succeed Mr. Timwell as office manager.

An image of Timwell's bulldog scowl quickened his pace.

Malcolm knew only too well what would happen if he was late. Mr. Timwell made sure to give tardy clerks the dreariest task on hand.

The streets around the harbor were gorged with freight wagons, stevedores, sailors, and food vendors, slowing Malcolm's progress considerably. He arrived with a minute to spare and paused to adjust his tie before he entered. The fleeting moment of vanity altered the course of his life.

The shipping firm faced a large wharf where a merchant clipper was being loaded. Malcolm heard a

warning shout and glanced back. The loveliest
woman he'd ever seen was stepping out of a white
carriage, completely oblivious to the cargo net sweeping down on her like a ragged spider. Some long-dor-
mant reflex catapulted Malcolm into action. He
sprinted across the sidewalk and pushed the woman
aside.

"Look out!" he croaked, as the heavy cables lashed
the carriage.

The girl coolly disengaged herself and gave him a
dazzling smile.

"I'm eternally grateful."

Malcolm stared at her, stunned by his own unexpected surge of heroism and her awesome beauty.

When he didn't respond, her gray eyes flicked past
him impatiently.

"You may leave your card with my driver. Good
day, sir."

As Malcolm watched her walk briskly toward the
ship, he realized he didn't have a card. He hastily
printed his name and address on a piece of note paper, thrust it at the driver, and hurried back to the
shipping office.

Mr. Timwell was waiting at the door: a watch in
one hand, and a sheaf of papers in the other.

Lady Trent hardly noticed the young man who'd
pushed her out of harm's way, being more preoccupied with the state of her luggage. Trunks, suitcases,
and various other bags were piled on the dock. Melba
stood beside them, gesturing anxiously.

"Are you all right, missy?"

Trent ignored the question.

"Why is my luggage still here?"

Melba shook her head in bewilderment. "The captain won't 'low it on board. Said he needs orders."

"Then I'll issue some personally," Trent declared, striding to the gangplank.

She found the captain on the bridge, conferring with his mate. He looked up, thick gray brows knotted in annoyance.

"Good day, mademoiselle," he grunted. "Are you looking for someone?"

"Why hasn't my luggage been delivered to my cabin?" Trent demanded.

His manner softened when he realized her identity. "Captain Holbrook at your service, milady. As I explained to your maid, I can do nothing without shipping orders from your father."

"Obviously there's been some error," Trent replied crisply. "My father specified I would sail on *The Mercury* to Barcelona."

"We have no passengers scheduled on this run," Holbrook told her, trying to suppress his impatience. "If there's been a mistake, it can be corrected by our office yonder."

"I shall see to this immediately," Trent assured.

Captain Holbrook bowed. "As you wish, milady."

Clearly, he hoped there'd been no mistake.

The stevedores seemed to sense the red-haired beauty's angry mood and scurried out of her path as she descended upon the *White Star* shipping office.

Lord Kiferson wasn't as fortunate. He was completely engrossed in Timwell's report when he heard the rapid knocking at his door.

"I'll send them away," Timwell muttered. Then he recognized Lady Trent, and his tone changed abruptly.

"Beg pardon, milady, but your father is in conference."

She waved him back. "I must speak to him."

"It's all right, Mr. Timwell," Kiferson said calmly. "We'll resume our discussion later."

As Trent entered, he braced himself for the imminent battle.

"Apparently your clerk has made an error," she said by way of greeting. "Captain Holbrook doesn't have my shipping orders."

"Didn't your mother receive the dispatch I sent yesterday?"

Trent shrugged. "I've been spending the last few days here in town, with Mr. and Mrs. Radcliffe. I expected to see mother at my bon voyage party."

Having been absent from home himself for the past ten days, Kiferson couldn't reproach his daughter. "I sent a letter explaining the change in schedule. No doubt your mother awaits your return."

His smile ruffled Trent's temper.

"And just why was it changed?"

"There's been some bad weather this past week. Merely temporary. You'll sail on the next clipper."

"What about my reception in Barcelona?"

"I'm sending word of your delay with Captain Holbrook."

"Then you don't expect *The Mercury* to sink before reaching Spain?"

Kiferson realized with some dismay that his daughter had seen through his excuses. "That isn't the point."

At least that much is true, he reflected dourly. Although it pained him to lie to his daughter, he had little choice. The truth would cause wider harm, especially to his wife. And Trevor had endured enough anguish in her lifetime.

"It's *exactly* the point," Trent snapped. "I've been in rough seas before. Unless you have a sounder reason, I demand you honor the promise you made at my betrothal."

Lord Kiferson steeled his emotions. He couldn't tell her what really happened that night. Nor reveal that Asmad's warning had proved accurate, and the true reason he'd postponed the voyage was that three of his ships had been captured in the past fortnight.

"The promise will be honored," he said softly, "at a more convenient time."

"Convenient for whom, dear father? If this is some ruse to prevent my marriage to Gavin I assure you it won't work."

"And I assure you it's no ruse. Much as I'd prefer a son-in-law who's seaworthy. But Gavin's your affair, as the passenger schedule is mine."

She glared at him, pale gray eyes as hard as diamonds.

"Then prove both your statements and let me sail."

"Isn't my word proof enough?"

"Which word am I to believe? The one given at my betrothal, or the one offered today?"

His patient smile concealed the bitterness evoked by the question. Despite all attempts at reason she persisted in defying him. At one time he'd attributed their differences to his inability to fathom the ways of women. However, of late, he'd come to realize that the fault lay with his daughter. Trent was simply a spoiled bitch—and neither patience nor reason could ever reform her obstinate nature.

"Believe what you like," he said, rising from his

chair. "But right now I'm due to leave for Baton Rouge. We'll settle this on my return."

"That may be your last word, sir, but be sure it's not mine."

"Of that I'm certain," Lord Kiferson declared as he flung open the door. "Until then, milady."

When Malcolm Gaines saw the red-haired beauty enter the office he thought she came to thank him.

It took him a few moments to grasp her actual destination.

He stared at the door to Lord Kiferson's chambers, trying to compose himself, but his good intentions crumbled the moment Mr. Timwell appeared. Without regard to protocol or consequences, Malcolm blocked the office manager's path.

"Who was that girl?" he blurted.

Mr. Timwell was too startled to evade the presumptuous query. "Why that's his lordship's daughter, Lady Trent. And what concern is that to you?" he added, glowering suspiciously.

"Er . . . I wasn't sure she . . . was allowed . . ."

"You're a deputy clerk, not a deputy sheriff." Timwell reminded. "Have you completed *The Mercury*'s cargo manifest?"

Gaines nodded hastily. "Ready for signature, sir."

"Then suppose you get it signed. I'm off to see Captain Holbrook."

Although Mr. Timwell meted out the task as further punishment, Gaines was overwhelmed by his good fortune. The errand gave him another chance to meet Lady Trent. He tried to compose himself for the coming encounter, but Lord Kiferson's sudden exit took him by surprise. Finding himself unable to speak, he thrust himself at his employer, blocking his path.

"What is it, man?" Kiferson thundered.

"Manif . . . fest . . . sir . . . *The Mercury* . . ." was all Gaines could manage, being completely awed by the powerful, golden-eyed figure.

"I've no time to study the manifest. Use my seal. But beware, sir, I'll not tolerate any error."

The threat had a minimal effect on Gaines, who was more preoccupied by the pair of shoes visible behind the half-open door.

It took all his willpower to wait until Lord Kiferson left the premises before entering his private chamber.

Lady Trent was neither surprised nor pleased to see him. In fact she didn't even recognize her rescuer.

"What do you want?" she inquired tartly.

Malcolm was prepared.

"I'm Lord Kiferson's personal assistant," he announced. "He asked me to sign some papers for him."

"Have we met, sir?"

"Outside. I pushed you . . ."

"Of course. How stupid of me."

Her gracious smile dissolved his defenses. "Oh no, Lady Trent . . . I understand."

"You have the advantage, sir."

"Beg pardon, milady?"

"I don't know your name."

"Ah, yes . . . Malcolm Gaines at your service, milady."

She cocked her head as if measuring him for a new suit. "What exactly do you do here, Mr. Gaines?"

"Well er . . . I'm in charge when your father is otherwise engaged," he said quickly.

The exaggeration served its purpose admirably.

Lady Trent's face registered a flicker of interest and her smile slowly returned.

"How fascinating. It must be terribly complicated, keeping track of all those ships. I'm sure it would be beyond my ability. I can barely manage to keep my social calendar in order."

"All in a day's work," Malcolm confided modestly. "However, it does require a fair amount of mathematical skill."

"Oh, I see. You're an accountant of some sort."

Her cool tone stung his pride.

"There's more than profit to the shipping business, milady. This office is the center of a worldwide marketplace that handles everything from diplomatic communiqués to royal tours. Just last month I arranged passage for his highness Prince Egon of Austria, and his entire household," Malcolm blurted before he could stop himself.

"How utterly exciting," Trent gushed. "Would you consider it too bold if I asked another favor of you, Mr. Gaines?"

"Why . . . certainly not . . ." he said, basking in her wide-eyed admiration. "Just name it."

She shyly averted her gaze. "I'd treasure a souvenir of our meeting."

Malcolm gaped at her in disbelief.

"I guess you think I'm being silly."

"Oh, no, milady," he assured. "Not at all. I was merely uncertain of your meaning. What kind of souvenir did you have in mind?"

"I don't know. Something special. Suppose we pretend that I'm taking a world tour like Prince Egon. You could give me a ticket to some exotic port in Spain."

"We don't sell tickets, we issue shipping orders," he

corrected loftily. "But I think I can grant your wish. Now let's see . . . we must choose the proper vessel."

"What about the one outside? It looks so beautiful. Like a painting by Botticelli."

A nude Venus leaped into Malcolm's mind much faster than the image of a ship, causing his skin to redden. "Uh . . . the ship outside . . . oh, yes . . . a good choice . . . *The Mercury* is the finest clipper in our fleet . . . as a matter of fact, it's bound for Spain."

"What a marvelous coincidence," Trent exclaimed, squeezing his hand. "Will you issue me passage, good sir?"

"It is a . . . bit . . . irregular . . ." Malcolm mumbled, his words lost in the breathless explosion sparked by her touch.

Trent stiffened. "Perhaps I ask too much."

"Not at all, milady," he said hastily. "Leave it to me. In a few moments I'll send you on the voyage of your dreams."

As he drew up the document, Trent followed every step with rapt interest. He answered her questions with the infinite patience only pride can evoke and when he finished, he allowed her to certify the order.

"You don't know what this means to me," she murmured, pressing Lord Kiferson's seal into the soft red wax that oozed from the flame like fresh blood.

That much was true. It took days before Malcolm understood what she had done.

Gavin was waiting with a large entourage when Trent returned to the wharf.

"Is something wrong, sugar?" he called, waddling

toward her. "The captain wouldn't let us board. I thought we were going to have a bon voyage party."

Trent patted his cheek. "Oh, but we will, darling." As she spoke, she spied Captain Holbrook on the bridge and smiled. "It will be a most memorable celebration, I promise you."

Even at a distance, Holbrook could see he was in for a difficult crossing. He slowly descended to the boat deck and met Lady Trent at the head of the gangplank.

"Now may I board your precious ship?" she demanded, brandishing her documents.

Holbrook studied them carefully before deigning to answer. "They seem to be in order," he said finally. "Welcome aboard, milady."

"I wish to see my cabin."

The curt reply failed to ruffle his crisp manner. "Perhaps you and your guests would be more comfortable in the dining room, while your quarters are being readied," the Captain suggested, beckoning to his first mate. "We'd be pleased to serve refreshments."

When Lady Trent and her coterie of admirers were safely corralled inside the officer's mess, Holbrook called an emergency meeting.

The captain cut an imposing figure, being tall and burly with a neatly clipped beard and a high, balding dome that was pleated into a permanent scowl. His dark brows hovered like storm clouds above his fierce gaze as he proclaimed the new regulations aboard *The Mercury*.

His officers accepted the stern decree without question and readily agreed to keep their passenger's identity secret until they sailed. But their assent did little to soothe Captain Holbrook's doubts. He'd weathered enough campaigns to know that secrets traveled faster than the plague aboard ship.

His apprehensions were well founded. By the time they weighed anchor, news of Lady Trent's departure was common gossip in the cafés. And a messenger was already on the high seas with a chart of *The Mercury's* exact course.

CHAPTER FOUR

Django considered himself the luckiest man aboard ship. He'd always believed that being galley master was the best job on land or sea—but now his position afforded him an extraordinary opportunity. He alone was endowed with the privilege of serving the woman of his dreams.

Again Django thanked the gods for his culinary gifts.

As a young boy in Africa he liked to help his mother prepare meals, and the lessons she'd taught him at the cooking fire proved to be a priceless inheritance.

When he was kidnapped by slavers, his talent rescued him from a life in chains. The cook on the slave ship died during the first week at sea, and by the time they reached port, Django was the youngest galley master on the trade lanes. True, he was still a slave, but that was merely a temporary inconvenience. While aboard ship he lived like a king. His master, Captain Beck, was especially fond of fine food and rewarded Django's skill with a private cabin and mate's privileges—which included his pick of the women bound for the slave market.

Eventually Captain Beck put Django in charge of purchasing fresh stores at various ports of call. One day Django went ashore at Teneriffe in the Canaries, and never returned.

He'd planned his escape carefully and an hour after leaving the slave ship he signed on a Dutch galleon as second cook. From that moment he'd remained a free man. And for the past seven years he'd enjoyed wide repute as the finest galley artist in Lord Kiferson's fleet.

His cooking skills had earned him everything a man could want—save for one thing. Django yearned to have a family. Certainly at twenty-one he could well afford to take a wife, but he'd never met the right woman.

Until this voyage, Django reflected as he prepared breakfast for his special passengers.

Ever since Melba Sanjin came aboard The Mercury *he'd felt as soft-bellied as a chocolate mousse.*

"Hey cookie, fix us a crock of tea like a good boy."

Django turned and saw Mr. Grady, the third mate, standing at the door.

"I haven't got much time," Grady wheezed.

Normally Django would have complied with the officer's request, but his orders were clear.

"You're off-limits, Mr. Grady."

"Come boy, what harm could it do?"

Django glared at the intruder. "It's my arse if you're seen here. Galley and passengers' deck are strictly forbidden to all hands except for the first mate."

"And the cook," Grady added with a smirk. "Some duty, boy. Playin' nursemaid to Lady Trent and her servin' wench."

"Right now it's my duty to order you below."

Grady's pinched features took on a menacing cast.

"I saw Dalt and Frampton having tea in here. I suppose Cap'n Holbrook invited them up."

"Mr. Dalt is first mate," Django reminded.

"What about Frampton?"

Django clenched his huge fists and took a step toward Grady.

"Mr. Frampton doesn't call me boy," he rumbled as the third mate hurriedly left the room.

A few moments of silence restored Django's good spirits, and he returned to his stove.

He'd selected almond crepes, eggs poached in brandy, cinnamon bread, and anise coffee for the day's breakfast. That each delicacy was cooked to perfection might have satisifed an ordinary chef. But Django was an artist. He made sure the trays were tastefully arranged before placing them on the dining cart.

The sprig of herbs he added to Lady Trent's tray gave it a festive appearance. They also distinguished it from the one intended for her maid. That small mark was crucial to Django's hopes. For tucked inside Melba's napkin was a special message.

"Something should be done," Mr. Grady ranted, his thin, bleached face flushing angrily. "What kind of ship is this where a nigger can insult an officer? Holbrook's lost his rudder, I tell you."

Second-mate Yeats bore the tirade with stoic detachment. Like everyone else, he'd resigned himself to Grady's constant complaints.

He scanned the horizon as the clipper whipped across the sun-gilded waters, its great sails lashing in the wind.

"Heave ho!" Yeats grunted to the helmsman. "Keep that prow steady."

"Something should be done," Grady repeated. "The blasted crew is getting out of hand."

It pained Yeats to admit the third mate touched a valid point. The unusual restrictions Captain Holbrook had imposed to insure Lady Trent's safety had alienated the crew.

"If Holbrook doesn't come to his senses, there'll be the devil to pay," Grady warned. "Mark what I say."

Yeats looked at him. "I can't mark what I don't understand."

"It's simple enough. We've got to do something about Holbrook, before it's too late."

Yeats grasped the mate's arm and pulled him to the rail. "I've heard you whine and I've heard you bluster, Mr. Grady. But I can't abide mutiny. If you utter another seditious word, I'll put you on report. Is that clear?"

"I said nothing of mutiny. I was only trying to advise the captain . . ."

"Then suppose you advise him yourself. He's right over there."

Grady jerked free as Captain Holbrook approached the bridge. "You've always had it in for me," he rasped, edging toward the stairs. "But you'll get yours. Just like him."

Despite his many preoccupations, Captain Holbrook didn't fail to note Mr. Grady's abrupt departure.

"Where's your mate bound, mister?" he asked sharply.

"Er . . . some trouble with the crew," Yeats replied, fumbling with his sextant. "Nothing serious, sir."

"He'd damn well better keep them in line. What's our heading?"

"Thirty degrees west, steady at 12 knots, sir."

Holbrook grunted in satisfaction. That, at least, was fair consolation. "Tell me, Mr. Yeats, what's the record time for the crossing from New Orleans to Barcelona?"

"Twenty-one days, sir."

"Well if the wind—and this blasted crew—doesn't slacken, *The Mercury* will beat that by two days," Holbrook declared. "What say ye to that?"

"Would be quite a feat indeed, sir."

Holbrook glared at him. "You seem doubtful, mister."

"I've no doubt this is the fastest vessel at sea," Yeats said carefully. "But there might be problems if the crew has to stand extra shifts."

"We'll offer a bonus if we break the record. That should get them stepping lively."

"It will help surely," Yeats said with forced heartiness.

Holbrook clasped his hands behind his back and regarded the water thoughtfully. "Sometimes too much discipline is worse than too little," he observed. "A good officer is always fair to his men."

"Begging your pardon, sir," Yeats blurted, encouraged by the remark. "But the crew resents the new restrictions on this voyage. They say it's unfair. After all, they have sailed with passengers before, sir." He added weakly, as the Captain's scowl darkened.

"I'll decide what's fair aboard my ship," Holbrook thundered. "Is that clear?"

Yeats snapped to attention. "Aye sir, perfectly clear."

"Then hear this. I intend to break that record and every man jack is on double watch until we reach port."

The mate's brisk salute belied his doomful expression.

"I'll inform all hands immediately!"

"You may also tell them there's two gold eagles a man if they succeed."

The news failed to ease Yeats' troubled frown.

"Very good, sir. Is that all?"

"Still don't think the bonus will bring them 'round, do you?" Holbrook growled, peering at him intently.

Yeats squared his shoulders and took a deep breath.

"The men are in an ugly mood, sir. They've been confined to quarters after duty, forced to wear shirts on deck, and denied their ration of rum. Making them stand extra watch won't be easy, gold or no gold."

"Then this might make it easier for you," Holbrook said gruffly. "You explain to them that the sooner we reach Barcelona, the sooner we'll be rid of our blasted passengers, and these bloody restrictions."

As the mate scurried below, Holbrook unfolded his brass eyepiece. *Blasted females,* he fumed, scanning the wind-flecked waves through his glass.

A wench aboard is always trouble.

His thoughts were diverted by the sight of a long, sleek vessel bobbing on the horizon. Its black hull and dark blue sails made it almost invisible as it cut through the choppy sea. Although too small and too far away to pose a threat, Captain Holbrook was disturbed by the strange vessel. It seemed vaguely menacing, like some winged insect hovering at the edge of the sky.

Holbrook wasn't superstitious, but experience had taught him there were two things to beware of at sea: a red-haired woman, and a ship *that flew no colors.*

CHAPTER FIVE

As Melba brushed Lady Trent's tresses, she could tell that her mistress was in a vile humor. She wasn't surprised.

After years of serving Lady Trent she could sense her changes of mood long before they occurred.

The first days at sea had been pleasant enough. Trent applied her energies to dispatching a vast amount of correspondence including courtesy notes to the guests at her engagement ball, and personal letters to her many admirers.

She also enjoyed a period of relaxation from the constant rounds of parties in New Orleans. In truth, Trent was a completely different person in private. She became the thoughtful, playful, delightful companion Melba had loved since childhood. Within the week Trent was brimming with vigor. It was then Melba began to prepare herself for the coming squall.

Her intuition was based on plain common sense. Beautiful young ladies—like thoroughbred racers—became high-strung when confined too long. Trent thrived on the flattery and adulation usually accorded her. But for the past eight days the officers on *The Mercury* had studiously avoided their passengers.

"I swear you can't do anything right," Trent said

sharply, snatching the brush from Melba's hand. "My hair looks awful."

"Looks fine to me," Melba said mildly. "Shall I lay out the blue frock?"

"Don't you remember anything? I want the rose chiffon."

"No, you decided on the blue . . ."

"How dare you sass me?" Trent cried, whirling to face her. "You brazen nigger."

Melba flinched as if struck. "Beg pardon, missy. I I forgot myself."

Trent dropped the hairbrush and hurried to embrace her.

"Forgive me, dear Melba. I'm all out of sorts today."

She glanced at the mirror and sighed. "Just look. The salt air is drying my skin and my hair looks like a fish net."

Melba laughed softly. "Bet you'd feel better if some nice young shark was swimmin' around."

"On this scow?" Trent snorted. "If these officers are any indication, my father's fleet is manned by jelly fish."

She was interrupted by a knock at the door.

"Breakfast, milady."

Melba threw the bolt and Django stepped inside.

"Good mornin', milady," he said cheerfully. "Hope you're feelin' well today."

"How I feel is none of your concern," Trent replied, seating herself at the dining table.

Django glanced at Melba, who shrugged and joined her mistress.

As Django set the table he wondered if the girl's gesture signified sympathy or contempt.

"I've never been so bored," Trent confided, ignor-

ing the cook's presence. "What a sorry lot of dolts.
I've seen better specimens on a shrimp boat."

Melba didn't share her view.

There was one man aboard that she found fascinating. However, she could understand why her mistress
had overlooked him. Black men were beneath Lady
Trent's notice. But Melba had long been aware of
Django's desirable qualities.

Although powerfully built, with thick shoulders
and bulging arms, he moved with stately grace.

That same air of pride illuminated his rugged features as he silently performed his duties.

The feelings he evoked were so intense that Melba
didn't dare look at him. Then she lifted her napkin
and saw the paper folded inside.

"Thank God for small favors."

Startled, Melba gripped the napkin tight.

"Pardon, missy?"

"The food is actually quite good."

"Yes indeed," Melba murmured, breathing a sigh
of relief. Her anxiety was further assuaged by the
cook's departure.

All through the meal Melba held the napkin in her
lap, reluctant to open it in front of her mistress.

Suddenly the ship rolled to one side spilling food
and plates over Lady Trent.

"My dress is ruined!"

"No harm done. I'll get it clean," Melba assured.

Without thinking she wiped Trent's skirt with her
napkin and the folded paper fluttered to the floor.

"Now what's this?" Trent inquired, scooping it up.

Melba stared at the paper. "Where did that come
from?"

"Obviously it was inside your napkin."

"What is it?"

"We'll soon see," Trent said, unfolding the paper. She studied the contents then handed it to Melba. "Apparently this is for you."

There was a message inside, carefully printed in green ink:

Mis Milba, I admir yu. Pray com viset me at nap tim

Django—the cuk man

She read it twice before looking up.

"Just foolishness. I don't know what he's talkin' about. Can't even spell my name right."

It pained Melba to deny her true feelings but she knew Lady Trent was dangerously angry and tried to make light of the matter for her admirer's sake as well as her own. Regretfully she didn't succeed.

Trent snatched the note from her fingers and stalked to the door. "How dare this animal insult me in this manner?"

"Missy, wait . . . your dress . . ." Melba cried, hurrying after her. "You can't go out like that."

"The devil with my dress!" Trent raged. "Where's the first mate? Mr. Dalt . . . Mr. Dalt!"

Both a beer belly and a broken nose hampered Dalt's mobility and he was wheezing like a trapped pig when he reached the passenger deck. He began sweating profusely when he saw Lady Trent. Her dress was stained and for a terrible moment he thought she had been hurt. Captain Holbrook had delegated him responsible for Lady Trent's welfare. If she became so much as seasick, Dalt had to answer for it. He was relieved to see her charge toward him.

"How can you allow this?" she demanded, thrusting a scrap of paper at him.

Unable to respond, he gingerly took the note from her hand.

"What do you intend to do about it?"

Dalt peered at the note intently as if hoping to find the answer.

"When did you receive this, milady?"

"It was sent to my maid," Trent said with mounting impatience. "Can't you read?"

Melba stood in the doorway, anxiously awaiting his decision. Her hopes were buoyed by his puzzled frown.

"You say the girl received this?"

"I do say, sir. And I insist this foul insult to my honor be punished forthwith."

"But if this was intended for your maid . . . er . . . how does it, er . . . compromise your ladyship?" he stammered.

"You forget she is my property."

Dalt nervously stroked his chin. "Of course . . . I stand corrected, milady. Be assured full satisfaction will be exacted."

As Melba heard the brutal dismissal of her human dignity, a cold, bitter hatred coiled around her heart. It took but a moment for her venomous rage to destroy the loving bond she had shared with Lady Trent since childhood. And from that moment she was free.

CHAPTER SIX

"Not even a rabbit is fool enough to pursue an eagle," Mustafa grumbled, scanning the empty sea. "There'll be no profit in this voyage."

Because the ship was small, his remarks were overheard by many of the crew.

Although no one else commented, Shareef Hazar knew they were waiting for his reaction. It was his first test as captain of the motley assortment of cutthroats.

If he failed, he'd lose his life along with his command. Strength was the sole law aboard a pirate vessel—and fear the most effective weapon.

"Not even a hungry dog turns on his master," Hazar observed calmly. "Unless he has gone mad. Stop howling and keep a steady keel."

The hearty guffaws elicited by his retort pecked at Mustafa's self-control. Unfortunately nature had endowed him with more brawn than humor. Standing well over six feet tall and weighing almost three-hundred pounds, Mustafa was rarely an object of derision. His arms swelled like watermelons as he gripped the wheel and glowered at Hazar.

"You promised a rich prize. Yet the clipper we hunt is too swift for your ship."

Hazar regarded him with bemused patience, as if

instructing a child. "Before tomorrow's dawn we'll have our prize. And you'll kiss these decks in gratitude."

A low murmur rippled through the crew and they paused.

Mustafa eyed the Captain warily. Despite his reputation on the Barbar Coast, Shareef Hazar seemed more like a pimp than a pirate. Unlike the others, he wore ruffled shirts and silk breeches, which enhanced his fine features. He also disdained the traditional cutlass, preferring to arm himself with knife and derringer. Still Mustafa hesitated, made cautious by the intense aura of danger generated by the dark, laconic figure.

"No prize—and no man—will make me kneel on any ship," he muttered, fingering the hilt of his blade.

Hazar's smile didn't waver as he calculated his alternatives. Killing Mustafa would leave him a hand short and the oaf was too good a warrior to lose.

Yet he had to serve as an example.

"As I said, you'll kiss the decks in gratitude," Hazar repeated.

Without warning, Mustafa drew his sword but as he lunged, Hazar was already leaping clear of the blow. Mustafa spun and slashed again, shifting his huge limbs with surprising speed. The broad blade seemed like a twig in his hand and his fierce thrusts attested to his skill. However his opponent was no ordinary man.

Whirling like a dervish, Hazar dodged a vicious chop and jumped back. In one blurred motion he yanked the braided belt from his waist and the long leather thong lashed out like a lightning bolt, hurling Mustafa's sword to the deck.

"Yield or die!"

Mustafa froze, eyes flicking from the steel-tipped whip in Hazar's left hand, to the twin-barreled derringer in his right.

"I yield," he rasped.

"Then show your gratitude for my sparing of your miserable life."

Mustafa glanced at the sword a scant six inches from his foot. Another snap of Hazar's whip sent the blade spinning across the deck, removing the temptation. It also left Mustafa no choice.

As the giant warrior squatted to kiss the deck, he vowed that nothing less than Hazar's blood would wash away his humiliation.

The crew returned to their duties with renewed gusto, seemingly awed by the demonstration. But Hazar had no illusions about their loyalty. Should his plan go awry their respect would soon turn to resentment.

I've merely won a temporary reprieve, Hazar speculated grimly, staring at the barren horizon. *If we fail to take the clipper by dawn, I'll be dead before sunset.*

Trent examined her reflection with critical detachment, unable to decide between pearls or emeralds. While both complemented her black chiffon gown, neither suited her mood.

"They just won't do," she sighed. "Perhaps the ruby locket . . . Melba, be a dear and fetch my jewel case from the trunk."

"I'm busy, Miss Trent."

Her oddly formal tone drew Trent's attention from the mirror. "Mind what I say, now. Fetch my case."

Melba was seated at the desk, writing a letter. She

looked up and coolly met Trent's gaze. "I'm occupied right now. Maybe you'll be kind enough to wait, milady."

"Don't you dare sass me," Trent exclaimed, voice taut with shock. "I'm afraid Gavin is right. Education merely teaches a slave to be insolent. Now you march over there and fetch my case this instant or you'll be sorry."

"I've decided to leave your service Miss Trent," Melba said quietly. "And I can't say it makes me sorry."

Stunned disbelief swallowed Trent's anger. "Do you realize what you're saying?"

"Every word of it."

"Then you've been driven mad."

"No, Miss Trent. I've been driven to my senses."

"If so, explain yourself in sensible terms."

"When you were betrothed, your father set me free," Melba said, voice flat and remote. "I neglected to affirm the papers he gave me, until this day."

For a moment Trent stared at her. "What reminded you, I wonder?"

"Would you care to inspect the documents?"

"I'm quite satisfied they're genuine. It's your reason that troubles me. Why did you wait until today?"

Melba shrugged. "Hard to get used to the idea, maybe. Anyhow, the reason is downright simple. I'd rather be a free woman than a slave. I'm sure you understand."

The thought of losing her filled Trent with sadness, yet she could not deny her logic. Nor could she refute the love she felt for her childhood companion.

"Of course I understand," she said gently. "I wish you every happiness."

Melba managed a brief smile.

"Thank you, milady."

Although not much more was said, Trent kept trying to locate the source of Melba's lingering hostility. Then she recalled the incident at breakfast.

"It occurs to me that I made a mistake this morning," she reflected. "Perhaps I acted too hastily in having the steward punished for a harmless flirtation."

Melba accepted the statement in silence.

"What's your opinion?" Trent prompted.

"My opinion won't change anything."

"You're right. It's up to me. I'm going to see Captain Holbrook right now and make amends."

"Please understand your amends won't alter my decision."

"It's you who misunderstand," Trent said mildly.

Melba's angular features remained impassive, yet watchful, as if weighing the possibility.

For a moment Trent grappled with her emotions, struggling for some way to breach the wall between them.

"It wasn't my intention to bribe you back into service. Your happiness is my prime concern," she said carefully. "Though it is another sort of bribe. I hoped to ransom our friendship, dear Melba. Or at least your forgiveness."

The icy suspicion glazing Melba's expression slowly melted. A familiar glow ignited her glistening eyes as she rushed to embrace Trent.

"Course I forgive you, missy. You know I love you better than a sister."

"As do I," Trent whispered. "I pray we'll always be this close."

"Nothing will come between us again," Melba assured huskily.

Trent wiped Melba's tears with her handkerchief and smiled.

"Nothing save for a certain young rogue. I'd best gather myself for that talk with the Captain. I'm sure you'll be receiving another romantic proposal with your breakfast tea."

Curse the bitch, Captain Holbrook fumed as successive waves battered the hull. *The treacherous whore's turned again.*

In this instance he referred to the sea's abrupt shift of mood. She'd been a lively playmate all afternoon, providing the brisk winds and swift currents Holbrook needed to achieve his desire. For years he'd coveted the speed record for an Atlantic crossing. He knew *The Mercury* was the fastest clipper afloat, having covered more than 400 miles in a full day's sail. *But that was yesterday*, Holbrook noted grimly. *Tonight the bitch is jealous.*

Indeed, with sunset, the waters became restless, the breeze began gusting fitfully, and a frosty mist obscured the moon—as if conspiring to impede their progress. Since both ship and sea were female, Holbrook fathomed their natural animosity toward each other.

Like having two bloody wives in the same house, he brooded, watching the prow dip listlessly through the fog.

An ominous tremor alerted him. He looked up in time to see the jib swing loose. It smacked the staysail like a wind-driven ax, until the boom collapsed, taking the foresail with it.

"Steady, damn ye!" Holbrook roared as the ship began bucking wildly.

He pushed the first mate aside and grasped the wheel. "Get below and report, you blasted lubber. I'll take the helm."

Holbrook's hand seemed to steady the ship immediately. Aided solely by instinct he managed to control its erratic course, while the first mate hurried to inspect the damage.

However, it was the second mate who returned with the report. In the navy, dung rolled downhill.

"Jib, staysail, and foresail are all down, sir," Grady said regretfully. "Take a day to repair. Maybe more."

"Any damage to the mast?"

"Just the staysail boom."

"Who was on watch?"

"I was, sir," Grady declared proudly.

Holbrook stiffened. "Then it was your bloody duty to secure the lines!"

"They were secure, sir," the second mate said hastily. "It's like I tried to tell Mr. Yeats. . . . It's the crew sir . . . them lines was cut."

"Are you saying it was deliberate?"

"Them lines was cut," Grady repeated firmly.

The captain glowered at him. "Tell me who did it."

"Don't know, sir. But I can tell you the crew's been unhappy over them new regulations, and cook being sent to the brig . . ."

"Blast them to bloody hell and you too!" Holbrook exploded. "I want the man who sabotaged this ship. His reasons will be weighed by the hangman."

Grady swallowed and backed away. "I'll find the one responsible, sir."

"You're the one responsible," the captain thundered. "Remember that, mister."

Holbrook's private view was less militant, however.

It's her fault, he admitted, as he struggled with the wheel. *Because of her, I've instituted new regulations; and was forced to discipline the finest cook under sail. And because of her, my ship was crippled. We'll be lucky to limp into port on schedule, much less set a speed record,* Holbrook reflected dourly. *Curse the bitch.*

Django didn't blame anyone except himself.

Should know better than trust a damn house nigger, he sighed, trying to make himself comfortable. The cell was damp, musty, and void of luxury. There were only a straw pallet and a jug of water. A few wisps of light filtering through the barred porthole enabled him to mark the passage of time.

Won't be long now, he speculated, stretching out on the pallet. *Come noon the Cap'n be starved for decent grub and I be topside again.*

Warmed by the thought and lulled by the ship's steady roll, he drifted into sleep.

It was night when he awoke.

His senses bristled with alarm long before he managed to focus his thoughts. He sat up and tuned his ear to the yawning darkness.

The ship's regular motion had become wildly erratic. It lurched from side to side, stern wobbling like a drunken sailor on a greased plank.

Django could hear the masts groan above the pounding seas and realized the vessel was damaged. As he struggled to stand, he clutched the bars on the porthole for support. One of them gave slightly under the strain.

Grasping the bar with both hands, he braced his feet against the wall, and exerted all the pressure his massive frame could muster.

He underestimated his strength.

The entire wall gave way, flooding the cell with a hot, sudden light that swallowed him whole.

The Mercury was listing badly when Trent came out on deck. Although fog smothered most of the ship she heard someone shout and glimpsed some men running toward the prow.

She wasn't dissuaded however, having encountered rough seas on her maiden voyage to boarding school. *But that time her father had been captain. He had a truer sense of control than most,* she noted, as the hull tilted, forcing her to grab the rail.

Undaunted, she edged through the gloom, protected by nothing more than a scarlet cloak. Pride was her staunchest ally, however, driving her on despite the lashing, wind-sharpened rain and heaving deck.

She was determined to right her mistake. For her own sake as well as Melba's. Their friendship was one of the few things she valued more than her jewels. A thick wave tipped the hull, spraying Trent with icy foam. As she reached the top of the stairs, Captain Holbrook was at the wheel, spewing a torrent of oaths, orders, and obscenities at the luckless crewmen scurrying past him.

His mouth snapped shut when he saw Trent, and his eyes popped wide, making him resemble a hairy-faced bullfrog.

"You! Get back to your cabin."

Trent stepped closer. "I must speak to you privately, sir."

"Get off my bridge!" Holbrook bellowed, shaking his fist. "Do you hear, madame?"

"I hear a vulgar lout!"

Only one thing prevented Holbrook from destroying his unblemished record in that moment of anger.

A bolt of lightning struck the bridge.

The blast hurled Trent to the deck amid a storm of flaming debris. Something warm and sticky smacked her exposed thigh. As she tried to rise she saw the object was a human arm. An instant later she recognized Holbrook's still-clenched fist.

Senses reeling in panic she turned and saw a swarm of men drop from the boiling black sky like screaming eagles. At once a flurry of gunfire rose up from every section of the ship.

Flaring pistols and flashing steel lanced the darkness and the decks erupted with violent combat. Trent fell back, gasping in terror as a turbaned savage leaped onto the bridge, swinging a double-edged ax. Then something exploded and he stopped short, blood blooming from his chest like an oversized carnation.

Acting solely on instinct, Trent scrambled down the stairs on her hands and knees, and half-crawling, half-stumbling, made her way to the cabin.

She pushed the door open and found Melba crouched behind an armchair—a bible in one hand and a bread knife in the other. She dropped both when Trent staggered inside.

"Missy, you're hurt!"

"Never mind that," Trent said hoarsely. "Help me bar the door."

Working feverishly, the two women barricaded the entrance with trunks and furniture, but it was impossible to shut out the soul-rending shrieks of dying men.

Suddenly it was quiet except for some muffled shouts and an occasional crack of gunfire. The two women huddled together clutching their weapons. Trent wielded a champagne bottle and a silver mutton cleaver, while Melba had added a flatiron to her arsenal.

Hearts booming, they listened to the footsteps outside.

Melba gasped as someone rattled the latch. She managed to stifle her fear until they began battering down the door.

"They'll kill us . . ."

"Be brave . . ." Trent urged, watching their fortress tremble under the heavy blows. A moment later it collapsed. When the door burst open Trent hurled the bottle at the first man she saw.

His surprised yowl detonated a gun shot that blasted a crater in the ceiling. Melba screamed a warning and swung the heavy iron like a discus, flinging it wildly at the blurred forms spilling inside. Someone roared in pain and they scattered.

There were six of them. And all wore the grisly stamp of their breed.

The biggest was a bald, apelike brute with a missing ear, while the smallest was a grimy weasel with a metal hook in place of a right arm. The rest were equally vile creatures besotted in blood, sweat, and the stench of death.

They circled the females warily, weapons ready to strike.

When Trent cocked her arm, however, they ducked out of range.

Melba grasped what they were doing. The beasts

wanted to take them alive. Revulsion overcame her fear of death and she charged, knife flailing desperately.

One of her thrusts sliced the weasel's cheek and he countered with a vicious swipe of his hook. The barb missed her throat, but the brass sleeve struck her skull with stunning force.

As Trent turned to help, a massive hand clamped her wrist. She kicked and struggled against the agonizing pressure, refusing to surrender her weapon.

That brief diversion enabled Melba to regain her senses. She seized an oil lamp and hurled it to the floor. Instantly a wall of flame sprang up, shielding her from the marauders.

She saw Trent outlined against the blaze, still struggling to free herself, and rushed to her aid.

Melba stabbed at the monstrous figure with reckless disregard for her own safety.

The marauder's girth was a disadvantage, offering a broad target for Melba's relentless blade. Trying to ward off her attack with a second wildcat in his grasp and a raging fire scratching his heels proved too much for him.

He shoved Trent away and retreated, spewing curses at them both.

The two women crouched behind the mounting blaze, slashing at anyone who tried to smother the flames. Without speaking a word, the pair had made a solemn pact. Both vowed to perish by fire rather than surrender to their bestial captors.

The savages darted back and forth, howling curses at the two women, as thick black fumes rapidly veiled them from view. Just then a clear, powerful voice pierced the confusion.

Though poised at the edge of death, Trent's senses

flickered. The vibrant tone stirred dim echoes in her memory.

I must be delirious, she thought, backing away from the hellish blaze. She peered through the swirling haze, trying to locate Melba.

They both spotted each other at the same time and rushed to embrace. But before they could meet, a shadowy figure swooped between them.

He disarmed them so swiftly that Trent didn't realize what he'd done until she saw the others leap through the flames.

Screeching with fury, Trent whirled, clawing for his throat. But she was too late. The black garbed figure floated out of reach like a silken bat and faded into the smoke.

As rough hands dragged her down and bound her limbs, Trent's brain kept spinning like a wheel on ice. For, while she'd barely glimpsed the dark marauder's face, she was certain of his identity. The fine, hawklike features and piercing ebony eyes were those of Hall Fargo.

CHAPTER SEVEN

It was dark and cold inside the airless cell. Fortunately Melba had some matches in her pocket and on striking a flame, spied a candle in the corner.

Since she was bound hand and foot, she was forced to crawl over to the candle. Once lit, however, the tiny flame provided light, warmth, and the means to untie their limbs.

Trent burned away the cord binding her wrists, then began separating the knots at her ankle.

"It's useless," Melba sighed. "We got no way out of here. Better we be dead."

"Maybe there's hope," Trent said softly.

"What hope? To live in slavery with such pigs as our masters?"

Trent rubbed her chafed wrists. "Perhaps it won't come to that."

"How so?"

"They're holding us for ransom," Trent explained. "They won't hurt us. We're valuable merchandise."

"But it might take weeks. Anything could happen with men like these. They're wild animals."

"Did you notice anything about the leader?"

The unexpected query left Melba confused. "Which was the leader? I couldn't tell one from another."

"The one who disarmed us."

"Oh, that one," Melba muttered. "He's quick, I'll give him that. Fact is, he came on us so sudden, I never did see him clear. How could you tell he's the leader?"

"I couldn't really. Except that he seemed more intelligent than the others," Trent said, too weary to pursue the matter of their captor's identity. Melba had seen Hall Fargo for only a few moments. She, on the other hand, remembered him vividly—having thought of him quite often since their encounter in New Orleans.

"What if we're not ransomed?"

Trent shrugged. "We have two choices. Either we wait to find out what our captors have in mind—or we tip over this candle and let the fire destroy us now."

Melba glanced nervously at the tiny flame.

"S'pose we can wait. Probably freeze to death anyway."

For some reason Trent felt certain that Hall Fargo wouldn't let that happen. It seemed preordained by fate that they should meet again, whatever the circumstances. He hadn't saved her life only to let her perish of exposure.

Her optimism appeared to be justified. Not more than an hour later they heard the thump of approaching footsteps.

"Quick, missy. They mustn't find out we got loose," Melba hissed, scooping up the discarded cord.

Both of them hurriedly rebound their ankles and then tied each other's wrists as the footsteps neared. They barely finished before the door yawned open.

The glaring light forced Trent to avert her eyes.

She squinted at the monstrous figure holding the lantern and pressed closer to Melba.

Then another shape separated from the looming shadow and bent over them. A rancid odor assailed Trent's nostrils as the man untied her ankles and she shrank back in revulsion.

The big man said something, causing both of them to laugh derisively. The other man grasped Trent's shoulders and yanked her erect. She almost gagged at the stench, provoking more laughter.

Still chuckling, they herded their captives outside. Both women were bound to each other at the ankle, and the guards posted front and rear, making it impossible to try an escape.

There's no place to run but the sea, Trent speculated as they climbed the narrow stairs.

When they reached the deck, Trent decided that drowning might well be considered a form of escape. The flickering torches added an eerie glow to the scene of carnage.

Bodies were heaped on the blood-slick deck like gaffed tuna, their grisly presence ignored by the marauders celebrating their victory with food and wine. Their coarse shouts mingled with the moans of the wounded and the harsh cries of their captors exhorted them to labor.

Despite their injuries, the prisoners had been pressed into work gangs to repair the damaged sails. The sea was still choppy and the ship bucked ceaselessly, making their task more difficult.

As the guards led Trent toward the passenger deck, she saw a man with a bloody arm crawling on the masts above. He inched painfully across the swaying boom, urged on at sword's point by one of the raiders.

Suddenly the ship rolled. Hampered by his wounded arm, he flailed awkwardly for an instant, then fell.

He smacked the deck like a sack of eggs and began groaning loudly. His cries continued until someone stilled them with a pistol shot.

However, his moans reverberated in Trent's brain as she mounted the stairs. The sound persisted for some time after they were ushered into the empty cabin. As the ghastly echoes abated, Trent slowly perceived the familiar furnishings in the room.

Her vanity table, trunks, and personal trinkets had all been transferred to the cabin. Hastily untying her bonds, Trent checked the wardrobe trunk and was relieved to find her jewel case intact. She also noted the porcelain tub filled with hot water at the foot of her bed.

The door opened, and a dark-skinned savage with tribal scars on his face stepped inside.

"Beg pardon, milady," he intoned in perfect English. "Shareef Hazar wishes to inform Lady Trent that she is expected for dinner in forty minutes' time." Having delivered the message, he bowed and took his leave.

Trent tried to gather her frayed thoughts. Her first concern was for the jewels and she scanned the room for a likely hiding place. Then she realized the effort was wasted. *No doubt they'd checked the case thoroughly and would be aware of its absence,* she reflected, setting the jewel box on her vanity table. *The best I can do is try to salvage a few of my favorite pieces and hope they aren't missed.* She chose an emerald necklace and matching ring, and a diamond bracelet, then looked for a place to conceal them. She spied an old quilted skirt and went to work with a nail scissors. By cutting a slit in the thick hem and removing some of the padding, Trent made a crude pocket. After stuffing the jewels into the opening, she replaced the flannel padding.

All this took more than five minutes, but when Trent looked up, Melba was still standing in the center of the room, staring blankly at the rope knotted around her wrist.

Realizing the girl was in shock, Trent gently took her arm and led her to the bed. She covered Melba with a blanket, then strode to the door.

Finding it bolted, she knocked until the guard responded. He seemed startled to see her glaring at him and totally perplexed by her demands.

"Bring hot tea and brandy right away. Do you hear? Don't stand there like an ass," Trent railed, angered by his mulelike stare.

The English-speaking messenger came to his rescue.

"Tea and brandy will be served immediately, milady," he assured her, shutting the door.

Trent chose a gown while she waited. In a short time the guard entered with a tray, placed it on the floor, and darted outside as if afraid of being contaminated.

As soon as Melba gulped down the tea and strong brandy, she dozed off, and Trent returned to her toilette. She hastily bathed the grime from her body, then scented her skin, slipped into her gown, brushed her hair, and was just clasping a string of pearls around her neck when the messenger entered. "Good evening, milady. Are you ready for dinner?"

"Don't you ever think to knock?" she snapped.

"No, milady . . . since it is I who must open, and not otherwise," he replied solemnly. "Are you ready to go?"

"I certainly am not. Please be kind enough to wait outside. I'll let you know."

Although satisfied with her appearance, Trent lingered at the mirror, tugging at the green satin sash on her ivory gown, fussing with her hair, and applying a last dab of talcum. *It is important I be at my best,* she reflected intently. *Above all, I want to be perfectly composed. If Shareef Fargo or whatever he called himself, expects me to grovel for mercy, he'd be sadly disappointed. I would never give him that satisfaction.*

In truth, she looked forward to the test. She could almost forget the horrifying circumstances in the odd exhilaration aroused by the coming encounter.

Squaring her shoulders she moved to the door and rapped twice.

She covered her head with a shawl as she stepped outside—partially to protect her hair from the wind, and partially to avoid the nightmarish scene on deck.

With all her precautions, she was unprepared for the sight awaiting her inside the cabin.

The simple, sturdy furnishings in Captain Holbrook's quarters had been transformed into a vision of Oriental splendor. A large brocaded tapestry covered one wall and an ornately patterned rug graced the floor. The heavy mahogany desk that formerly dominated the room had been pushed into the far corner, in favor of the silken pillows strewn around a low silver table.

Its exquisite array of hand-tinted china bowls was artfully garnished by a bouquet of yellow roses, whose vibrant hue provided stark contrast to the dark figure seated nearby.

Hall Fargo was dressed in black, from his open silk shirt to his gleaming leather boots. Black, too, were his eyes, which glinted like ebony crescents beneath arched clouds. But darkest of all was his brooding smile.

Both bemused and cynical, it shaded his smooth aquiline features with an air of childlike curiosity.

"Presenting Lady Trent to his eminence, Shareef Hazar," the escort intoned.

Trent stroked her chin thoughtfully. "I believe we've met."

"So we have." He chuckled, rising to his feet.

"Hall Fargo at your service, milady."

"I fear your services are too dear for my purse."

His smile widened. "But it's precisely your purse that brings us together, fair lady."

"At least you're honest. I suppose that's a redeeming quality of sorts."

"Never confuse candor for honesty," he said, taking her hand. "Come, you must be hungry."

Fargo led her to the table and gently guided her to a pillow beside him. "I hope you won't find this overly uncomfortable. It's an old tribal custom. One shared by both the Romans and Egyptians. They, too, preferred to recline while they dined."

"How *intime*. You must be distant cousins. To which branch of the tree are you attached?"

His brows lifted in surprise. "Why, the Barbar tribe, of course."

It was Trent's turn to look surprised.

"Something wrong, milady?"

"Not really. It's just that one associates Barbars more with the art of pillage than civilized custom."

He regarded her pensively for a moment. "That's unfortunately true."

"Unfortunate for whom? From what I've witnessed, I'd say the reputation is well deserved."

"Without question it is," he admitted. "However, it's rather limited in scope."

"That may be the fault of the subject rather than the viewer."

"I'll let you judge for yourself. Surely a race that's developed such a sublime touch with food can't be totally uncivilized."

Trent was forced to agree. Each of the bowls contained a special delicacy.

As she sampled each dish, Fargo told her its name and how it was prepared.

An extensive knowledge of art, theater, history, poetry, and science, further spiced his conversation. In spite of herself, Trent found his company fascinating.

"There's something I can't quite understand," she said.

"About the honey sauce or the chicken?"

"Neither." She carefully set down her fork and looked at him. "Why did you save my life in New Orleans?"

His gaze didn't waver. "We Barbars consider it uncivilized to discuss business while dining. I'll answer such questions over coffee. Agreed?"

"Under the circumstances, I'm loath to disagree."

"Extremely commendable. Now you must venture an opinion of our native wine."

It was excellent. The tangy white vintage complemented the repast the way cream enhanced berries. In fact, dessert included rum-glazed fruit and strawberry crepes. By then, however, she felt disinclined to argue.

But the moans of the man she'd seen murdered haunted her festive humor.

"I've kept my share of the bargain," she noted, as Fargo's manservant poured coffee.

"And now it's time for your questions," Fargo said cheerfully. "Will you have more of this crepe?"

"Don't evade me, sir."

"Merely offering my hospitality."

His charm masks a multitude of mortal sins, she reflected, savoring the thick strawberry syrup inside the crepe.

"Why did you save my life?" she asked abruptly. "Was the encounter due to accident or design?"

"Accidents are but threads in Fate's tapestry. Pure chance spooked your horses that day."

"Is that why you forsook poker for piracy?"

His laughter rang truer than his reply. "That was a calculated risk, based on simple logic. Why settle for part of the plunder, when by going to the source, you win the entire prize."

"Do you really consider murder a game?" Trent said, eyes flaring with anger. "Let me remind you, sir, only gentlemen play games. Your Barbar logic is kin to that of a mad dog."

Fargo sighed regretfully. "Don't let your coffee get cold, milady."

Trent immediately regained her self-control. "Tell me," she said, lifting her cup, "which is your real name?"

"Shareef Hazar is my tribal name, and title. Loosely translated, it means 'Holy Avenger.'"

"Impressive. And how did you manage the translation to Hall Fargo?"

He ignored the scornful edge in her tone. "As a boy I was apprenticed to a British merchant and the ship's master took me under his wing. He taught me how to read, write, and speak English. I took his name—Captain Hall Fargo."

"A stolen name? That at least seems logical."

"Let's say it was inherited," he suggested, smooth features veiled by a polite smile.

"You must have inherited an extensive library, as well."

"I completed my education in Paris," he said curtly. "Is the coffee too strong?"

"Just to my liking, thank you."

"Any further questions?"

"Just one. What do you intend to do with us?"

His brows lifted slightly. "Why, hold you for ransom, of course."

"I suppose it will take weeks."

He reached out and gently stroked her cheek. "I promise you won't be bored."

The fleeting touch quickened Trent's pulse, and sent her thoughts racing.

He's nothing but a savage, she told herself. But she couldn't deny her galloping heartbeat.

"You place an exalted value on your hospitality," she said casually.

He leaned back, eyes narrowed pensively. "How much would you say you're worth? In terms of ransom, that is."

"You're the expert in such matters."

"Quite so. In that case, I would estimate one million in gold is dirt cheap for Lord Kiferson's firstborn daughter."

"I suppose I should feel flattered."

"Merely an accident of birth. Your half-sister Shan would have fetched a bit less. Your brother, a bit more—two million for Kevin, let's say."

"You're well informed of our relative value in the marketplace."

"It's to my interest." Fargo beckoned to his manservant. "We'll celebrate our imminent contract with a rare Barbar liqueur."

"I've nothing to celebrate." *Except for this marvelous repast I've nothing to celebrate,* Trent reflected, as the servant heated an ornate silver flask over the candle flame before pouring its contents into two gold cups.

"Then we'll drink to Hashib, who prepared and served this feast."

The dark-skinned aide grinned, showing his gold tooth, as Trent lifted her cup.

The golden liqueur tasted like absinthe and heated her body like cognac. "It's made with anis," she said, venturing another sip.

"You have a gourmet's palate," he murmured. "It's a blend of anis, distilled wine, and the resin of a cactus flower that blooms every ten years. The flower— and the liqueur—is called mejun."

Trent gave him a provocative smile. "Some pleasures are well worth the wait."

"After blending, the mejun is aged in wormwood casks for another decade, before it's mature enough to uncork."

"Patience is another Barbar virtue," Trent observed, dabbing her neck with a scented handkerchief as the mejun's warmth spread across her skin.

"Take care, milady," Fargo murmured. "Barbar virtues are as dependable as a roulette wheel."

"So I've noticed. But I would think you thought better of yourself than to squander your manhood as a cheap gambler and common thief."

He pondered the statement impassively.

"I'm flattered that you believe me capable of salvation."

"To be sure, you'll have to prove yourself. But in

time you'll regain public respect. And mine too," she added softly.

He stared at her intently. "You mean I might aspire to wed a lady of breeding?"

"A gentleman knows his place," she said, turning away. "No doubt you'll find a lady of suitable class."

"But never as beautiful."

The compliment stirred her emotions and she met his gaze. "How gallant."

He leaned closer, lips curved in a lazy smile.

"A gentleman is always direct."

He kissed her gently, his breath misting her senses like rain. Instinctively she lifted her mouth to drink. Then she felt his hand on her breast and jerked back.

"Have you no shame? Only a buffoon comports himself so basely for the amusement of servants."

"You presume too much, milady," he said calmly. "Hashib left us some time ago."

She glanced around the room, somewhat shaken by the aide's absence.

"You also err in your appraisal of me," Fargo continued. "I'm neither a cheap gambler nor a common thief. I'm master of this ship—and you're here for my amusement."

Trent stiffened. "I'm afraid it's too late for further amusement. If you'll excuse me, I'll return to my cabin."

"You'll be sleeping here tonight," he murmured, drawing her near.

The full impact of his words registered slowly. By the time her numbed brain grasped his meaning, she'd already succumbed to his embrace.

Icy panic splashed her reflexes and she twisted free. As she groped for support, her hand closed on a serving fork. She slashed at him wildly, forcing him back, then stumbled to her feet and pressed the sharp prongs against her own throat.

"One move, one word—and you forfeit a million in ransom," Trent hissed.

Suddenly his hand flicked out, and the fork exploded. The weapon flew from her pain-scorched fingers with a loud crack that left her dazed.

Trent reeled back toward the door until a burning hand seized her by the throat and she fell to her knees, gasping like a spent filly. Then she saw Fargo loom near and reared wildly. She flailed against the leather thong squeezing her neck, but he held fast.

"You need taming," he muttered, dodging a kick at his groin. With a swift motion he looped the thong around her wrists.

"Stop this!" she rasped, as the dark figure dragged her across the floor like a trussed lamb.

He paused to secure her bonds, then bent closer. His eyes smoldered like fuses, setting off spasms of alarm but she couldn't turn away.

"Now look what you've done," he said, finger lightly tracing her neckline.

She glanced down and saw her bodice had been torn in the struggle, leaving one shell-pink nipple exposed.

"You cowardly savage. Even a swine has more honor."

"Such calamities make equals of us all." His fingernail brushed her taut nipple like the tip of a feather. "Permit me to correct the imbalance."

With deliberate slowness, Fargo ripped the silken gown from her body. Face blank with shock, she lay completely still as his gaze wandered over her naked flesh.

Her arms were crossed above her head, thrusting

her ripe, hard-nippled breasts upward against the steep curve of her ribs. Shame flushed her translucent skin, making her seem like a statue carved from smooth, pink marble.

Without warning she sprang to life, and yanked the thong from his grasp.

Hissing with fury, she swung her bound hands. The thong whipped out and caught his shoulder, slashing through sleeve and skin.

Being weighted on both ends with sharp metal, the leather braid was a dangerous weapon—especially when wielded by a crazed witch.

Fargo ducked out of range, but she struck at him relentlessly.

Then he stumbled and she lashed out.

Too late, she saw him dart forward and snatch the thong in mid-flight. As he turned, she was jerked off-balance and fell heavily to her knees.

A sudden exhaustion numbed her bruised limbs, as he dragged her across the floor.

She felt herself being lifted and floated limply in space, suspended by a satiny cloud. She moaned softly as a feathery caress drifted across her naked shoulders. Her eyes fluttered open and she saw Fargo hovering close, watching her with falconlike intensity.

Disbelief and despair collided in her brain, jolting her awake.

She was kneeling on the quilted bed, nude body half-suspended by the thong knotting her wrists to the overhead post.

Completely vulnerable, Trent dangled before him like a strung trout, twisting to elude his loathsome touch.

Choking with frustration, she arched back and spat

in his face. "Damn your soul," she gasped, yanking at her bonds. "You filthy Barbar bastard."

His slap seared her mouth like a torch.

Trent sagged against the post, lips blistered by pain and mind boiling with panic.

"Oh, God, help . . ." she groaned, as he stroked her thigh. Then she clenched her teeth, unwilling to give him the satisfaction of her pleas.

She stopped struggling and resigned herself to his groping fingers. Separating mind from body, she retreated inward, leaving her limbs to hang passively.

Suddenly his moist lips covered hers, cooling the pain, but she pressed her mouth shut, refusing to respond or retreat.

He can take anything else, but only I can give up my pride. Trent repeated the thought silently. But he was patient, and kept kneading her quivering flesh until it began tingling with warmth. She shrank back as his lips gently plucked at her nipples, trying to smother the hunger prickling her senses.

Fargo took his time, fingers gliding in a slow, lazy circle from the tips of her breasts to the base of her belly. His restless hands fanned the need, smoldering under her trembling skin until it flared, devouring all restraint.

Writhing convulsively, she lifted her body to meet his touch. A husky moan rose unbidden to her lips as he eased away. She looked up and saw him tugging angrily at his shirt. The silken fabric shredded, he hurled the garment to the floor.

Then he hooked his breeches with one hand and ripped the tight pants from his hips.

His naked body was webbed with rippling muscles giving him the sleek, shadowy menace of a panther. Raw animal power bristled from his gleaming flesh as he reached out for her, eyes narrowed in a sphinx-like smile.

Trent shuddered when he seized her thighs, clawing helplessly against the fiery need licking at her will. She felt herself being lifted from the quilt and tried to resist, but he held her fast, easing her onto the bed. His moist skin steamed against hers as he forced her legs apart and suddenly her perceptions dissolved in a white-hot burst of agony.

The pain chopped through her resistance like a searing arrow of fire, tearing at her flesh until mind and body were consumed by rampant hunger.

"God damn you . . ." Trent sobbed, unable to quench the wanton greed gnawing at her senses.

His triumphant manhood filled her as she flung herself upward to meet his thrust, limbs thrashing feverishly. Then she was swallowed by a boiling spasm of pleasure that sucked her higher and higher until she cried out wildly at the peak of ecstasy, then fell back, drained.

"God damn you . . ." she repeated, voice choked by the feral stench of blood and lust. "God damn you to hell."

While silently, Trent cursed the whore's body that had betrayed her secret shame.

CHAPTER EIGHT

It was still dark when Shareef Hazar eased away from the soft white form curled beside him, and rolled out of bed.

He dressed quickly, then carefully moved to the door, taking care not to awaken the sleeping girl.

He was relieved to find the decks deserted. Most of the crew, as well as their prisoners, were asleep. Although the sea had calmed, the clipper was lurching unsteadily, and he climbed to the bridge for a report.

"Foresail not yet repaired," Hashib said apologetically. "Shall I round up a work crew?"

"It can keep till dawn. But I want this vessel fully rigged by noon, is that clear?"

"By noon it will be. What about the prisoners? Mustafa has been threatening to take their heads."

He scowled at the news. The crew knew he'd specified that prisoners be taken alive. However, Barbar custom decreed that warriors fly the heads of their vanquished enemies from the mast in tribute to their gods. Mustafa's threat was another gambit to test his power, but the matter couldn't be settled by a sword.

"Remind Mustafa that every head he takes cuts down our profit. The prisoners will fetch a good price in Tingis. From now on, anyone who kills a prisoner without cause forfeits his share of the sale."

"So be it," Hashib affirmed. "That should cork the whale's spout," he added with a grim smile.

The remark lightened his captain's brooding expression.

"He'll soon find another hole to blow through," Shareef Hazar said, ruefully.

Hashib was sympathetic, being one of the thirty-odd crewmen bound to him by blood. The rest were Barbars from alien tribes whose allegiance was determined by gold. Since their first day at sea, Mustafa had asserted himself as leader of the mercenary contingent, pursuing his scheme to wrest control of the ship.

But this prize had firmly established Hazar's authority and when they reached Tingis he'd be able to rally greater loyalty among the Barbar privateers.

"I'll be glad when we make port," he confided. "This run has yet to yield its wealth."

"I'll wager the American wench yielded her purse," Hashib mused slyly.

His grin faded when he saw the fury lancing Shareef Hazar's slitted eyes.

"Such speculation is beyond your limit," the chieftain warned, hand clenching his blade.

"Excuse my foolish error," Hashib said hastily. "I meant no disrespect. With your permission, sir, I'll go below and post orders."

Shareef Hazar's anger was blunted by regret as he watched the man depart. He knew Hashib had meant no harm. And he'd violated a basic precept of his station by bearing arms against a loyal tribesman.

That a chance remark about Lady Trent could ignite his emotions was even more disturbing. With astonishment, he realized the red-haired witch had gotten under his skin.

The knowledge evoked a sudden panic, like that of a strong man abruptly weakened by a strange disease. Then his will dispelled the thought.

Fate left him no margin for self-indulgence. Lady Trent was far more useful as a weapon than as a woman. Indeed, she'd proved her superior strength.

Or my own fatal weakness, he observed with steely detachment.

The girl was just raw bait—the Judas goat needed to attract the prey he'd been stalking since childhood. His life was dedicated to that one kill. And he would not be denied.

As dawn cracked the darkness like an egg, Shareef Hazar reaffirmed his vow.

Not love, nor laughter, nor respite from loneliness will ever be mine until I have fulfilled my quest. My only desire is vengeance, he intoned, watching the golden mist ooze across the sky . . . *and the head of El-Kifer.*

CHAPTER NINE

Trent dozed fitfully after he left the cabin, half-expecting him to return. Though her hands were untied she made no effort to escape. She listened to the steady creaking of the masts, thoughts drifting like a rudderless ship.

She lifted her head when the door opened and was vaguely disappointed to see the mate enter.

"Beg pardon, milady. It's time to go," he announced, staring intently at the ceiling.

Trent realized she was partially exposed and drew the quilt to her neck. "Time to go where?"

"Why, back to your cabin."

"Very well. Kindly wait outside," she said briskly.

The mate hesitated, then backed away, closing the door behind him.

All she could find of her gown was some tattered remnants, so she wrapped herself in the bulky quilt.

When she entered the cabin, Melba gaped at her in stunned silence.

"Are you hurt, missy?" she whispered, hands fluttering uncertainly. "What can I do?"

Trent shuffled to the bed. "Draw me a hot bath," she said softly. Melba sponged her clean, brushed her hair, creamed her chafed skin, and helped her with her dress in taut silence, as if fearful that some careless word might unleash an avalanche of hysteria.

Later, she was more concerned by Trent's mute, listless manner. Her mistress propped against the pillow like a porcelain doll, eyes fixed in a glassy stare.

Better to cry it out, Melba reflected grimly. *Tears wash out the poison*.

She remembered the numbing degradation she'd suffered on the slave ship. Then, she wanted to kill herself. However, Time had taught her that what she endured was a trifling concern. She held her peace, knowing truth was no remedy for Trent's despair.

"Can I get you something?" she ventured, unable to contain her anxiety.

"Perhaps some tea."

The request seemed to calm Melba's nerves.

Trent relaxed, as Melba performed the familiar task, grateful for momentary respite. Her friend's hovering apprehension had become a burden.

While Trent wanted to reassure her, there was no way to explain how she felt. Indeed the attempt might prove more unsettling than her silence.

How could she describe what it meant to be two people at once? To be split asunder, yet newly joined, like a bud bursting from a severed branch. For, while cast down in humiliation, she'd emerged reborn. Somewhere in the long night, she'd tapped the root of human love and discovered her destiny.

She was no longer Lady Trent, but a primal female, whose flesh pulsed with the rhythms of her mate.

Mistaking Trent's withdrawn mood for depression, Melba continued to minister to her. After coaxing her to eat lunch, she tucked a blanket around Trent's legs and sat beside the bed.

Later that afternoon Trent became restless. Melba was surprised to see her rise briskly and begin rummaging through her wardrobe. She pondered a long time before choosing a gown, then carefully selected appropriate jewelry. It was almost dusk by the time she was dressed.

She was still rouging her lips when Hashib entered.

"Beg pardon," he drawled politely. "I bring the captain's compliments."

"I'm not quite ready," Trent called from the vanity table. "Please be good enough to retire."

The mate shuffled his feet. "Beg pardon, milady. But the captain's invitation is for Miss Sanjin."

Melba gawked at him.

"There must be some mistake."

"No mistake, madame," the mate assured. "Are you ready?"

Instinctively Melba patted her hair, and glanced uncertainly at her simple cotton frock. Then she saw Trent's face in the mirror.

She was staring at her like a silver-eyed Medusa, face white with fury and lips drawn in a predatory grimace.

The reflection confirmed what Melba didn't want to believe. Her mistress had become a mortal enemy, who'd kill without compunction.

Unable to bear the malevolent gaze, Melba turned away.

"I'm ready," she said softly.

Though Melba left shawl and purse behind in her haste to escape, Trent's wrath buzzed at her senses like a cloud of hornets.

Her confusion was amplified by the exotic splendor of Captain Fargo's cabin. Feeling unkempt and out of place, she sat down stiffly, body tensed for sudden flight.

Fargo seemed to understand and patiently drew her out, asking questions about her life in America, and her girlhood in Africa. In passing, he displayed an uncommon knowledge of tribal ways.

"I noticed the man who brought me here . . . your aide . . . has circumcision scars," Melba inquired hesitantly. "Do Barbars have such rites?"

"Hashib is my first mate, as well as my tribal brother," Fargo explained, offering her a bowl of stuffed olives. "Hashib's mother is of the Masai nation and he was privileged to be initiated as a warrior. We also have rites of manhood; however, Barbars only scar themselves in battle. Will you have some champagne?"

Relaxed by his gracious manner and refreshed by the cold, sparkling wine, Melba slowly began to respond to him as a man rather than a master. Fargo was gentle, sophisticated, witty, and yet she could sense the primitive violence coiled beneath his smooth, aristocratic features.

"You have lovely eyes—like clear topaz," he said softly.

Melba smiled. "Thank you, sir. It's nice to know I have some jewelry on my person."

He stroked her cheek lightly with his fingertips. "A woman with wit as well as beauty is rarer than the Holy Grail."

"And as precious?" Melba asked breathlessly.

"Value is always a matter of demand," he murmured as he drew her close.

When he kissed her, Melba was engulfed by the animal energy pulsing from his body. She yielded to its power and pressed herself against him, drinking in the warm sweetness of his mouth.

Melba had learned the futility of resistance the night she'd been enslaved, but this night she had no desire to resist. She surrendered herself fully to the rapture drenching her body, naked flesh curling like an orchid in the monsoon rain.

The sudden memory of Trent's cold hatred flickered across her brain and she froze. Then a surge of pleasure swept her to a place far beyond thought, where nothing existed except the ecstasy flooding her senses, and the drumming of his heartbeat against hers.

It was quiet when Melba awoke.

Fargo was gone, but she knew he'd come back.

She could feel his presence, like some dark moon drawing the tide. As she turned, an unfamiliar object brushed her skin. Even as her hand reached to touch it, she realized what it must be. Dangling from a golden chain around her neck was a large topaz pendant, shaped like a teardrop.

Shortly before noon the mate entered Trent's cabin. She was still where he'd left her the previous evening.

Lady Trent didn't look up when he came in, but remained seated at the vanity table, her head bowed as if in prayer.

Thinking she was asleep, Hashib gathered Melba's belongings as quietly as possible, grateful that he'd been spared the ordeal of an explanation. He'd sooner swim with a shark than tangle with an hysterical wench.

Hashib had misjudged Lady Trent on all counts. She was fully awake and required no explanation. She knew he'd come to move Melba's things to the Captain's quarters. And while she'd been awake all night, she certainly wasn't hysterical. Nor in fact, was she praying.

Instead, Trent's entire being was concentrated on an oath. She swore to sell her immortal soul to whatever deity or devil who'd meet her price. All she asked in return was the slow, agonizing death of Shareef Hazar.

CHAPTER TEN

At an early age, Countess Evita de Medici learned that a woman's boudoir rendered all men equal. Her father was a dashing Italian nobleman who died with more honor than assets, and most of the latter went to pay his gambling debts.

Evita's mother, The Countess Ilsa de Medici, was of Russian descent and there were those who suggested that her title had been bought. If so, the expense had drained the family coffers because Ilsa received no financial aid from her parents.

She managed to salvage the Roman palazzo from the ruins of her husband's estate, but found herself shut out by her former friends. The noble matrons of Roman society were extremely scornful of foreigners, especially if they happened to be beautiful, young widows.

Her husband's family also displayed a distinct coolness toward wife and child after the funeral, and barely a year later, their contact ceased completely.

Ilsa tried to support herself by giving piano lessons and instructing the daughters of wealthy merchants in the social graces. To augment her meager income she rented out the lower rooms to an elderly duchess from France.

It was Madame Rouge who taught Evita to speak

French and sat with the little girl while her mother attended to her pupils. Evita came to love the eccentric old woman, besieging her "Tante Rouge" for fairy tales and chocolate cremes almost every day. Madame Rouge also taught the child the rudiments of sewing, reading, and writing during their long afternoons together.

The old woman had a number of nephews who visited her every week. On such occasions, she'd call Countess Ilsa and Evita to join them for tea. Afterward Madame Rouge would take Evita for a walk in the park.

When Evita was ten, the piano students seemed to dwindle in number while the size of Madame Rouge's family increased. About that same time Ilsa decided to send Evita to a convent school.

For the little girl it was a descent into hell. Discipline was quite harsh at the Catholic institution and the nuns focused special attention on Evita de Medici. She was forced to kneel in the chapel for hours, denied her food, and sometimes caned for the slightest infraction. Even worse, she was ostracized by her fellow students. Evita didn't understand why she'd been singled out until the next year. Her main tormentor was a plump senior named Flora Santini.

The girl delighted in baiting her with cruel insults and often incited the others against her.

Evita took sanctuary in religion, spending much of her time in the chapel or at devotional meetings. Her piety eventually won the nuns over, but Flora continued her taunting. Finally she devised a strategem to repay her enemy.

One evening after vespers she accosted Flora on the chapel steps.

"Why do you hate me?" she asked calmly.

As she expected, Flora seized the opportunity to berate her publicly. "Because your mother is a slut," the plump girl replied with a triumphant smirk.

Some of the other girls began to giggle.

Evita shrugged. "I don't understand what you mean."

"I suppose you don't know where babies come from?"

In truth, the scornful query took Evita by surprise. From the other girls' giggling she divined it had deep significance.

"Sister Louisa says the angels bring babies."

The reply evoked more giggles and she started to move away. Flora blocked her path, fists perched on her wide hips. "Are you really so stupid?"

Receiving no answer she proceeded to give a graphic description of human conception, to the great amusement of her classmates.

By the time Sister Louisa arrived, Evita was on the verge of nausea.

Evita had planned to accost Flora, knowing the girl wouldn't resist being the center of attention. She knew as well that Sister Louisa would be coming to keep their appointment, and witness Flora's bullying. However, she hadn't counted on hearing such vile profanity.

Then she received another shock. The nuns had decided to place Flora Santini on permanent chapel duty, which meant her punishment was merely a few hours extra work every evening.

Evita expected at least expulsion for the blasphemies Flora had uttered. She had even considered the possibility of excommunication from the Holy Church for such a grave offense.

Her astonishment soon curdled into outrage.

Nightly she appealed to God to strike down the sinner, and every morning she awoke disappointed. To make sure she'd made no error in addressing the Savior and His Saints, she turned to the library and began reading as much as she could about Catholic ritual. One day she discovered a reference to the Black Mass, where people actually worshipped the devil. Intrigued, she delved further and found fleeting mention in some of the more scholarly tomes. In one work of Papal history, she learned that a Pope had practiced Black Magic. Another work of comparative philosophy mentioned the crux of satanic worship: *Do what thou wilt shall be the whole of the law.* The author decried this as a licentious temptation to ultimate destruction.

However, Evita disagreed. To do what she willed, she didn't have to pray to anyone, including Satan. If she had to pay some forfeit, it seemed fair enough. Since Flora Santini had paid so little for her grave offense, she was willing to take the risk.

The next evening Evita left the chapel service early, complaining of stomach cramps. She went to her room and gathered her tools: a long piece of rope, two large balls of paper, and a book of matches.

The students were given a half hour of recreation after chapel, but Evita knew she really had fifteen minutes. At 7:15, the grounds would be completely deserted, and she'd have enough time to return before the proctor checked her room.

It was simple enough. She put one paper ball just inside the door and strung the rope between the two pillars at the head of the stairs. She placed the other paper ball halfway down the stone stairway, then struck a match. When the paper ignited she dashed up the stairs and set fire to the thick wad of paper inside the door.

Flora was sweeping the floor, her back to the entrance.

"Fire!" Evita shouted. "Over here!"

Having alerted Flora, she hid between two pillars.

The fat girl waddled to the door, stamped out the flames, then hurried to stamp out the small pyre further below.

She never saw the rope.

As Flora toppled headlong down the stone stairway, Evita moved out of the shadows.

Ignoring the bawling figure below, she untied the rope, and took it with her as she ran to the rear stairway.

The result was a mixed blessing.

Because Flora broke her leg she'd be forced to repeat the year. While Evita didn't relish the prospect of her company, she was satisfied that Flora had finally received just punishment.

Fortune spared Evita of further dealings with her adversary. During the August holiday, her mother revealed that she wouldn't be returning to school. Instead, Madame Rouge would see to her tutoring in French literature.

Evita was pleased but curious. When she asked Madame Rouge, the old woman shrugged. "Your mother is having money problems. Household expenses are criminal. But don't you worry, little countess, it will soon pass. It always does."

The old woman took a worn deck of cards from her cabinet and began dealing them out in a circle.

Evita remembered that Madame Rouge often consulted her cards, but until then she'd considered it a child's game.

She joined the old woman at the table.

"What kind of cards are those?" she asked.

"The Tarot, my child. But it's only for certain people who know how to read them."

"Do you think I could learn?"

Chuckling, Madame Rouge gathered the cards up and handed them to the girl. "Even I haven't learned in all these years. But you may try your hand."

As Evita shuffled the deck she recalled the dictum she'd gleaned in her study of Satanism. *Do what thou wilt shall be the whole of the law.*

Like Madame Rouge, she dealt the cards out in a circle, then studied them for a moment. Rather than trying to interpret the strange figures depicted on their faces, she merely recounted her own first impression.

"Momma isn't happy. And there's a bad man after her. She's going to get sick."

"What about the bad man?" Madame Rouge asked in a hushed voice.

"He's going to get sick, too. But not yet. Not like Momma."

The next day, Countess Ilsa came down with a fever. By the time she'd recovered, Madame Rouge had instructed Evita in the rudiments of the Tarot.

The girl was an apt pupil, and her sense of kinship with the old woman deepened with their shared secret. So much so that Evita dared ask a more personal question.

"*Chére tante,* how are babies born?"

While the old woman's explanation was sensitive, tender, and much more beautiful than that offered by Flora, it was essentially the same. Evita was wiser, but still curious.

When her mother recovered, Madame Rouge's

cousins came to pay their respects. Evita soon realized that they changed from week to week. One afternoon she returned to the palazzo on some pretense, and spied on her mother as she entertained their guest. Everything she saw confirmed Flora's devastating pronouncement.

Although Evita never mentioned the incident, she ceased attending mass. She became quite proficient at divining the future, however.

She foresaw the man who came into their lives and the havoc he would wreak on her mother. She also predicted Madame Rouge's illness.

Countess Ilsa's lover was a young playboy with blond hair and blue eyes, bent on destroying himself with absinthe and roulette. Unlike the other visitors, Ilsa received Baron Marcello Trenta in her private chambers and soon he was a permanent guest.

Ilsa lost her students and Madame Rouge's cousins stopped calling. There were loud, drunken arguments and violent fights. More than once Marcello beat her.

At such times Evita took refuge with Madame Rouge, and the two of them would conspire at ways to convince her mother to give up this profitless passion. Yet Countess Ilsa persisted, much to her detriment.

Baron Trenta's debts drained what little they had until there was scarcely enough for food. The violence became more frequent, and to make matters worse, Madame Rouge fell ill.

Knowing from experience she couldn't influence the future, Evita tried to endure the present. She was aided by repeated signs of her own success despite the disaster looming over the household.

The riches foretold by the Tarot exacted a great price. Madame Rouge became weaker, and though she sold her jewelry for doctors and medicine, they proved worthless. Despite their expensive treatment the old woman died.

The nightmare was compounded by Marcello's climactic fit of rage.

Since Madame Rouge's body was lying in state downstairs, Evita had nowhere to hide.

All through the night she huddled in her bed, listening to the drunken rantings of her mother's lover, too numbed by sorrow to get under the blanket.

Marcello started banging on something, and she dimly understood her mother had locked him out of her bedroom. Abruptly, it was quiet.

The silence penetrated Evita's thoughts like a warning shout. She glanced at the unlocked door, unable to rise and throw the bolt. Without warning, the door flew open and Marcello lurched inside.

"Your mother is a bitch," he declared, brandishing a half-empty bottle.

He stopped and peered at Evita.

"You're just like her . . . two of a kind."

His wine-sotted perceptions were quite sound. Though not yet sixteen, Evita had matured. She possessed the jade-green eyes; pouting, bow-shaped lips; and lush body that made her mother one of Rome's loveliest courtesans.

Marcello's bloodshot leer made her suddenly aware of the partially open dress that exposed her butter-smooth thighs.

Evita realized his intention an instant before he moved toward her. With a surprising surge of strength she pushed him back and rolled to her feet.

"Momma! Help!" she screamed, ducking away from his grasp.

A moment later Ilsa burst into the room, brandishing a knife.

"Don't touch her . . . filthy pig!"

The blade slashed his arm and he roared with fury. As he spun, the bottle in his hand clubbed the side of her skull.

The knife dropped from her lifeless fingers as she toppled back through the door.

Cursing, Marcello staggered after her.

Without hesitation, Evita snatched up the fallen weapon with both hands and drove it between his shoulders. Then her awareness splintered into darkness.

It was absolutely silent when she awoke, and everyone in the house was dead. Pure reflex guided Evita's actions for the next few hours—or perhaps the next few days.

With icy calm she packed her few belongings, then went to her mother's room and methodically gathered her valuables, including a hoard of gold scuti. To this she added Madame Rouge's Tarot cards. Before leaving, she impulsively searched through Baron Trenta's pockets. The impulse made her rich.

Marcello had a pouch filled with gold coins in his coat and a small sack of precious stones in his vest. Apparently he'd been lucky at the gaming tables.

Still acting on instinct, Evita left the palazzo and took the dawn coach to Naples. Upon arrival she booked passage to the south of France, on a merchant man leaving the next evening.

Fortunately she was able to board the ship immediately, sparing her the risk of going to a hotel.

"I pray you enjoy the voyage, madame," the steward said politely after showing Evita to her cabin.

"Call on me if you require anything for your comfort."

Though taken aback by his strangely formal manner, Evita was too exhausted for conjecture. As she prepared for bed, she happened to glance into the mirror and almost fainted.

Sometime during the night her thick black hair had turned bone white—making her seem like a woman of thirty.

Evita remained sequestered during the brief voyage to Nice and upon debarking, rented a secluded flat near the sea. Given the clear green water, radiant sun, and good food, she recovered her youthful bloom. But there was no remedy for the looming fear that haunted her dreams.

Of primary concern was establishing her innocence. News of the Countess Ilsa's scandalous death took weeks to reach Nice. When it did, Evita stepped forward and revealed her identity to the authorities.

She told the police she'd been sent on a sojourn to perfect her knowledge of French, and pretended to be devastated by the tragedy.

Word of her plight spread quickly. Within days the young countess was a *cause célèbre*. Evita found herself being courted by the best families on the Côte D'Azur. The most avid of her new protectors was a certain Marquis de St. Germaine.

An elderly widower who resided alone on a vast estate, the Marquis sought out the Countess de Medici and offered his hospitality for the length of her stay in France.

At first Evita declined, but urged by other respectable friends, including the prefect of police, she eventually accepted his invitation.

Evita enjoyed the heady whirl of attention, especially since the possibility of her complicity in the stabbing of Baron Trenta had been totally discounted by her new friends. As far as they were concerned she was a lovely silver-haired child victimized by her mother's infamy.

It was precisely her innocence that fascinated the Marquis de St. Germaine, and after a few days she lost her shyness and began calling him Uncle Rouber, which pleased him immensely. He was also pleased by her unusual knowledge of Catholic philosophy, being one of France's leading intellectuals.

Uncle Rouber personally assumed responsibility for her education. He started by buying Evita new clothes, instructing her in the fine arts of gracious living, and exposing her to the most fashionable people on the Côte D'Azur.

She responded admirably, displaying a charming wit without marring her innocent dignity.

St. Germaine invited her to spend Christmas in Paris. Having nowhere else to go—and no wish to leave her guardian—Evita accepted immediately.

Since it was still October, St. Germaine suggested that she read some of the works of the new school of philosophers and poets, of which he was a respected member.

Evita was stimulated by the sharply anti-clerical, highly libertarian views held by French scholars. She admired their scientific logic and bold declarations of artistic freedom, but most of all, she was intrigued by their intense mysticism, especially in the works of Baudelaire and the American Edgar Allan Poe.

In Paris she found that many others shared her

curiosity. She was introduced to the tomes of the alchemists, and the books of the magical arts that were forbidden in Italy.

Indeed everyone seemed to share St. Germaine's enthusiasm for his lovely protégé. There were many young nobles who courted her favor, but Evita only had time for one man—her beloved protector.

The sophisticated ambiance softened Evita's rigid view of human sexuality and after a New Year's Eve celebration at Versailles, she accompanied Rouber to his bedroom. Though nothing had been said by either of them prior to her decision, a mass of roses, an iced magnum of champagne, and two crystal wine flutes were arranged on the table.

"Have you been reading my thoughts?" she murmured, perching on the edge of the couch.

St. Germaine eased beside her and poured some wine. "I've found that love has its own language. Of course there's always the chance of misinterpretation. I've erred more than once and probably will again."

"It's hard to imagine you being wrong about anything."

While her reply was accompanied by a smile, Evita meant every word. Indeed, she lived by it.

St. Germaine had done everything, been everywhere, and influenced kings and philosophers alike during his distinguished career. He moved in the most select circles in France, numbering statesmen, artists, and scientists; students and seekers of every class and persuasion flocked to him. And they always found his door open.

He also exuded a strong physical magnetism that attracted almost every female who met him. Despite his gray hair, St. Germaine retained an animal vitality that belied his age. Since he ate no meat, and fasted frequently, his body was as lean as a greyhound's.

The impression of youthful vigor was amplified by his proud carriage and vibrant blue eyes. Deep lines scoring his gaunt, sun-bronzed features merely accentuated the fiery intensity lighting his gaze.

He lifted his glass and looked at her, as if pondering a scientific theorem.

"A toast to you, *ma chérie*," he said finally. "The loveliest heiress of the new age."

Evita touched her glass to his, then waited until the crystal chime faded. "To us, for without you there is no future."

"However well meant, it's obvious that your future extends far beyond mine," he confided with a small, sardonic smile.

"I'll never love another."

Evita's flat statement stayed his hand in midair. He glanced at her, then drained his glass. "That would be wrong," he said gently. "Tomorrow you'll be as far from today, as you now are from yesterday."

The flickering candles illuminated Evita's stark white hair and exquisite features like an angel's halo, but her green eyes danced to Pan's wanton song as she set down the crystal flute and slowly unlaced her bodice.

"If you can't be my future, I want you to be my present," she whispered, letting the gown peel away her plump, pink-tipped breasts.

With great patience and tenderness, St. Germaine initiated Evita into the ecstasies of womanhood. Hours later, while both lay entwined in blissful exhaustion, St. Germaine bequeathed all his remaining years to the ageless female nestled against him. But as

his sated flesh basked in her sensuality, his sleep was
webbed with foreboding.

The next two years were idyllic for both St. Germaine and his devoted mistress. They toured the capi-
tals of Europe, where Evita was entertained by the
powerful and wealthy.

And while most hailed the young beauty as the
new DuBarry, she remained aloof from their adulation, focusing all her attention on St. Germaine.

When they returned to France, St. Germaine made
plans to speak at a scientific congress, intending to go
to Reims alone, while Evita stayed in Paris. On the
eve of his departure she begged him not to go.

"I know your enemies await you," she declared.
"Have faith in me now, if never again—I implore
you."

St. Germaine stroked his clefted chin, coolly weighing her plea. "How do you know this, ma petite?"

"I saw it in my cards."

His brows arched slightly.

"Perhaps I should see these cards as well."

When she showed him the frayed Tarot, he immediately altered his plans.

The next morning St. Germaine's carriage departed
for Reims as scheduled, but all it carried was a letter
of apology.

The celebrated Marquis and his dazzling ward were
already on their way to a secluded villa near Le
Havre.

A week later they heard that St. Germaine's carriage had met with an accident. Both team and driver
were killed when a bridge collapsed outside of
Château-Thierry. Oddly enough a similar accident be-

fell Count Adhemar, who died in a rockslide while on his way to the congress.

Since St. Germaine and Adhemar were associates, and planned to announce the results of certain joint experiments, the coincidence seemed ominous.

Evita discovered many other strange things at the remote villa. For one thing, St. Germaine had a price on his head. The Vatican had offered a bounty to whoever succeeded in executing the French liberal, long considered one of the Church's most dangerous foes.

Indeed, some factions in France accused him of being a foreign agent.

All this came as a shock to Evita who thought she knew everything about her guardian. Then he revealed the truth of his experiments with Adhemar. St. Germaine had perfected the technique of hypnosis.

However, if the secret were made public he could very well be branded a warlock and burned at the stake.

Therefore St. Germaine deemed it best that they remain in hiding until matters settled. To while away the time, he began conducting experiments with Evita.

The girl's remarkable ability to foresee events in the Tarot cards proved to be only one facet of her talent.

With St. Germaine's guidance she acquired considerable knowledge of palmistry, astrology, and hypnosis.

In a few months they sailed to Cannes, and after gauging the political climate, decided to return to Paris.

If anything, St. Germaine's prolonged exile had enhanced his notoriety.

Accustomed to having his undivided attention, Evita suffered from the sudden loss. Worst of all, she fell victim to jealous anger whenever another woman flirted with him—which was often.

Especially galling were the persistent advances of Count Adhemar's widow. That Evita understood the obligation Rouber felt as her husband's colleague merely added to her frustration. Maria Adhemar had little need of sympathy, having already secured a replacement for her departed mate.

Her constant consort was a wealthy entrepreneur with vast holdings in the Carib Isles. But while most would consider Baron André Bouvier a treasure, Maria had the sensitivity of a shark.

For Rouber's sake Evita reined her emotions and pretended not to notice Maria's crude overtures.

Baron Bouvier seemed oblivious to his fiancée's flirtations, preferring the intrigues of high finance.

Taking full advantage of his lack of interest, Maria threw herself at St. Germaine at every opportunity.

Despite his cool response, Evita's resentment flared beyond control.

"I refuse to watch her vulgar display yet another evening!" Evita fumed. "You might consider my feelings once in a while. Surely we can refuse one dinner invitation. Or perhaps you find my company bland compared to that overripe widow of yours."

St. Germaine regarded her with bemused affection.

"I'm as fed up as you are. In fact I've arranged for us to take an extended holiday at Le Havre. Think you'll be ready to leave in the morning?"

"I'm ready now."

"I suppose I could send my apologies."

A pang of guilt deflated Evita's temper. "Perhaps we'd better go, and say our farewells."

"A brief appearance will suffice," he said, drawing her close. "We'll say nothing of our holiday and leave right after dining, agreed?"

Her kiss sealed the bargain.

The dinner was held at Baron Bouvier's luxurious residence. As always Evita found the lavish display of wealth vaguely disconcerting.

The guest of honor was the decadent poet Baudelaire, and for the occasion Bouvier had imported primitive totems and tropical plants from the Carib Isles, which endowed the marble rooms with brooding majesty.

In the muted candlelight, the effect was somewhat oppressive. Once or twice during the meal she caught Rouber's eye and he nodded wearily as if sharing her discomfort.

To be sure the decor seemed to stimulate the others, most notably the guest of honor.

With long, unruly hair falling to the shoulders of his rumpled black velvet coat, and eyes glowing like embers deep inside his gaunt white skull, Charles Baudelaire resembled a shaman at the tribal fires.

His melodic voice held the diners with its piercing vibrancy, as he expounded on the mysteries of existence.

The announcement that coffee would be served in the salon drew Evita from her reverie. She glanced around the shadowed room but St. Germaine had already left the table. Thinking he was making his excuses, she trailed the others into the salon.

Baudelaire's sinister aura seemed to pervade the dimly lit room and Evita peered impatiently at the door. Then she realized Maria was also missing from the group.

A sudden anxiety propelled her in search of Bouvier. She found him in the corner, chatting with a young woman.

"Ah, dear Evita," he said, taking her hand. "Isn't our poet devastating this evening?"

"Extraordinary. Have you seen Uncle Rouber?"

"I believe he felt a bit ill and retired to the library. Shall I show you the way?"

"Please don't disturb yourself," Evita said casually.

But as she moved to the door she was accompanied by a nagging apprehension. While reason suggested she wait for Rouber's return, emotion prodded her toward the darkened hall.

The library was empty and she was just about to return when she glimpsed a faint light from an adjoining door that was partially ajar.

Peering inside, Evita made out two blurred shapes, heaped on a chaise.

The wavering glow of a single candle rendered them indistinct for a few seconds. As her eyes adapted to the lights, however, they focused on an incredible scene.

Maria was crouched on the chaise like some sleek, pink-fleshed sow, her heavy breasts swinging like pendulums as she greedily rutted at the figure below her.

It took a long time for Evita to grasp that the man pinned between those obscenely quivering thighs was St. Germaine.

She lurched back, her mind reeling between disbelief and despair. Somehow she found a door to the outside and dove into the protective embrace of the night.

An hour later, when St. Germaine returned to the salon, Evita was sitting beside Baudelaire calmly discussing the merits of Shelley.

"An elegant poseur," Baudelaire scoffed. "Give me William Blake, Coleridge . . . give me divine visions."

St. Germaine caught Evita's eye and gestured.

Her answering smile was as remote as the North Star.

"Does anyone care for some hashish?" Baudelaire drawled, proffering a long pipe. "Or are you afraid to venture into the cosmos? Come, who will be my traveling companion this night?"

Evita turned. "I will."

Without hesitation she took the pipe and put it to her lips.

"We're all exiles on this earth. Yes, we're the outcasts of paradise searching for our destiny in the ruins of the past, while denying our dreams. And without doubt man's most sacred legacy is the power to dream . . ."

The acrid smoke enveloped her senses with tingling warmth and she felt her limbs relax. Minutes later she realized that St. Germaine had left, but it didn't matter. He'd ceased to exist the moment she'd seen him with Maria.

To her amusement, Countess Adhemar seemed quite upset by Rouber's abrupt departure. She fluttered about the room in confusion before descending on Evita.

"Poor Rouber hasn't been feeling well," she clucked. "Perhaps we should look after him."

"Even your wings aren't swift enough for that."

Maria looked at her suspiciously. "I fail to follow your meaning, child."

"I thought you knew," Evita said innocently. "Uncle Rouber has gone to his villa at Cannes."

"He didn't . . . I mean, *I* didn't know," the countess sputtered. "When will he return?"

Evita shrugged. "A week or so."

As she took another puff of Baudelaire's pipe, Maria hurried to the door.

Knowing she had all the time in the world, Evita slowly stood up and drifted to Baron Bouvier's side.

"Will you join me?" she murmured, tilting the pipe toward him.

Bouvier sighed and reached out.

"What man could refuse you anything?"

It took Maria forty-eight hours to discover she'd been duped. By then it was too late. When she returned Baron Bouvier had already departed for Marseilles with Evita. They were wed a few days later on a galleon bound for the Orient.

Evita's new husband shared many traits with her former guardian. Like St. Germaine he was past middle age but endowed with the vitality of a twenty-year-old. Bouvier had the same craggy features and his blue eyes shone like newly tempered steel.

In truth his jet-black hair and extroverted personality made him seem younger than St. Germaine. In time, however, the resemblances were to blur.

While St. Germaine was a scholar, Bouvier was a hedonist. Unlike Evita's protector, her husband dedicated himself to power, rather than philosophy, amassing wealth and courting pleasure with equal dedication. He also devoted himself to pampering his young wife and gratified Evita's slightest whim. At first she indulged herself like a greedy child.

She developed an insatiable appetite for expensive finery, priceless art, and beautiful young men.

Being preoccupied with his various enterprises,

Bouvier was frequently away, leaving Evita free to pursue her amusements.

Her search for fresh diversion spanned two years and four continents. If anything, Bouvier encouraged her amorous interludes and made no pretense of concealing his own affairs with certain well-born ladies of varying distinction.

One in particular was the beautiful and long-married Princess Ruspoli of Italy.

Evita knew that Crista Ruspoli entertained her husband when he was called to Rome—which was often—but remained indifferent to the liaison.

However, Princess Ruspoli's sudden visit to Paris stirred her curiosity.

With mild anticipation, she accompanied André to a private reception in honor of the princess.

Though impressed with Crista Ruspoli's vibrant beauty, Evita was quite a bit more intrigued by Crista's eighteen-year-old son. In her estimation Sergio Ruspoli was a fair bargain in exchange for her husband!

The boy's dark, sensual eyes and angelic features could have been drawn by daVinci, while his limbs had the languid grace of an Egyptian god.

To Evita's annoyance, Crista jealously protected her eldest son.

Evita could sense Sergio's response to her subtle flirtation, but was frustrated by his mother's repeated intrusions.

After dinner Crista whisked her son off to the billiard room with the other males, where he'd be safe from further temptation.

Of course, the Princess pretended to be charmed by her young rival and invited her to dinner the following evening.

Later, as Evita prepared to retire, André visited her chambers.

"How did you like the princess?" he asked casually, pouring a glass of cognac.

"Extraordinary woman. I'm looking forward to our little dinner."

"I'm glad you hit it off so well. The princess wields a great deal of influence in Naples, and I'm negotiating for an important charter."

"Be sure I'll cultivate her friendship," she said, returning to her mirror.

He shrugged and sipped his cognac. "Young Sergio is quite a handsome boy."

"I found him irresistible," she murmured. "No wonder his mother dislikes sharing him. Hopefully she'll be more generous tomorrow night."

"Didn't you know? Sergio's off to England tomorrow."

"That's hardly sporting of Crista, considering her attachment to you."

"If you're really interested, I might be able to delay his departure."

After pausing a moment to consider, she began brushing her hair.

"I appreciate the gesture, darling, but why bother? Crista won't let him out of her sight."

He moved closer to the vanity. "Suppose while we're enjoying brandy I managed to arouse Crista's passions. She could hardly deny you under the circumstances."

"If Sergio takes offense, you'll forfeit more than your precious franchise," Evita reminded him, watching her husband with narrowed eyes.

"He'll be as willing as Crista, with the proper encouragement."

"What makes you so confident, darling?"

"A professional secret, my pet."

Evita set down the brush and went to her writing desk. "I also have professional secrets," she declared firmly. "We'll soon know what profit this game holds for you."

She took the cards from a drawer and began dealing them out.

"Did St. Germaine teach you the Tarot?"

Since they'd rarely spoken of Rouber in three years of marriage, Evita was surprised by the question.

"My aunt gave me these cards," she said softly. "But no one taught me to read them."

That night the Tarot augured well, promising abundant returns for their venture.

"I'll be more than pleased to aid you, dear husband."

He stroked her cheek. "You'll have to exert your powers in my behalf more often."

"If you share your professional secrets," Evita said, putting the deck aside.

"Very well," he whispered as he nuzzled her ear. "Lesson one: don't drink wine or eat veal at Crista's table."

It proved sound advice. When the four of them retired to the drawing room, Evita noticed that Crista's face seemed flushed. Sergio's agitation was also evident.

"Are you feeling well?" Evita whispered, taking his hand.

Her touch seemed to rouse him, and he smiled lazily, eyes glassy in the candlelight.

"Quite well, thanks."

Then he blinked, as if trying to clear his vision.

She glanced up and saw Sergio's mother sprawled

on the couch. Crista was moaning huskily as André kissed her.

Evita caressed Sergio's arm and felt him respond seconds before he turned. She drew him close and began to feed on his sweet flesh.

As predicted, the interlude yielded bountiful rewards. Bouvier's hold on Princess Ruspoli gave him the leverage he needed to secure his charter. In a few months, his holding doubled, then quadrupled, until he had the largest fleet of slave vessels in Europe.

The affair also sated Evita's restless quest for pleasure. She took more interest in André's business ventures. As he'd requested, she employed her skill with the Tarot in his behalf.

And as agreed, he revealed a secret trove of rare herbs, drugs, and poisons from every corner of the world.

Belladonna, poppy, datura, hashish, coca, khat, hemp, snake venom, deadly mushrooms and berries, narcotic flowers that induced sleep, and aphrodisiacs that aroused wanton passions . . . Bouvier recorded every formula with the zealot's precision.

He instructed Evita in their uses with the same care, and within another year, their combined efforts inflated their power. Bouvier's fleet was surpassed only by Lord Kyle Kiferson's magnificent flotilla of merchant clippers.

In fact, only Lord Kiferson prevented Bouvier from seizing total control of the trade routes.

However, every ship he'd sent to attack Kiferson's vessels had been lost.

Then Evita advised a move to the far south.

Having learned to rely on her precognition, André established a stronghold in Tingis.

Located on the northern tip of Africa, at the mouth of the Gibraltar Straits, the outpost was the richest slave market in the world. Fortunes were made and lost overnight by the speculators in human cargo.

Once ruled by the Barbar tribes, Tingis had become a free zone where survival was the sole law.

Unencumbered by social conventions or the threat of public condemnation, André and his devoted young wife gave full rein to their desires. They built a palatial fortress crammed with treasures, and entertained kings, cutthroats, and adventurers of every allegiance.

Still the Kiferson fleet limited Bouvier to the slave trade. And wealth was merely the means to a more sublime ambition.

In time, Evita gave him the weapon he needed.

Bored with her usual diversions she went out to tour the gambling houses that edged the native quarter. Although accompanied by her guards and an entourage of friends, she found the evening dull.

Then she saw the dark figure standing at the roulette wheel, and her senses bristled.

Though he stood at the center of the crowded table, the other patrons kept their distance, attesting to their respect—or fear.

Far more impressive was the animal intelligence radiating from his finely chisled features. He seemed like a silk-furred panther among a mob of baboons.

However, Lady Luck eluded him that night. As Evita neared the table she saw he was down to his last thousand-franc chip. With a careless flick he tossed it on number twenty-two.

The croupier spun the wheel.

"Vingt-quatre rouge," he called as the ball settled into the slot. "Twenty-four red."

The young gambler regarded the board impassively, then turned to go.

" I believe you dropped this, sir."

His brow furrowed when he saw the gold chip in Evita's hand.

"Beg pardon, milady?"

"I found this chip on the floor," she explained trying to conceal her excitement.

He gave her a faint smile. "I'm in your debt."

"It's easily discharged, I assure you."

He bowed and gestured toward the table. "In that case, milady, perhaps you'll sweeten my luck by choosing a number."

Evita scanned the squares embossed on the green felt and placed the chip on twenty-one.

Never before had she been so intent on the roulette wheel. The single chip represented the greatest risk she'd ever taken. If she lost, she'd lose him as well.

"Vingt et un, noir," the croupier droned.

"Twenty-one black." He pushed thirty-five gold chips on the winning square, and raked in the rest.

After calling for the cashier, the young gambler regarded Evita with a rueful grin.

"You must tell me your system."

"I merely picked your age."

"You were three years in advance," he said, pressing a five-thousand franc note in her hand. "However, you deserve a commission."

"How generous of you," she said coolly.

"Please don't mistake my offering for gratitude, Countess Bouvier."

Evita's eyes narrowed. "You have the advantage."

"Hall Fargo at your service, milady. Perhaps you'll

allow me to show my appreciation with a bottle of champagne."

"I don't see why not. We can join my friends in the dining room."

"I'm afraid the vintage offered by this establishment is of mediocre quality," Fargo said regretfully.

Evita shrugged. "Wherever you suggest then."

As they left the gaming house, two armed men fell in step behind them.

Fargo paused and gave her a questioning glance.

"My bodyguards," she assured him.

"I pray you never need their skills."

She understood his meaning a few minutes later. They had just descended the stairs and were walking toward a waiting carriage when one of the guards gave a sharp grunt and toppled to the ground. Before the other could draw his sword, two men leaped out of the shadows. One pointed a pistol at them, while his companion retrieved his knife from the fallen man's back.

"Hand over jewels and money quick," the thug rasped, jabbing his pistol at Fargo.

Suddenly his eyes bulged and the pistol flew from his grasp—followed an instant later by his severed head. As it wobbled crazily along the ground, the other thief started to run but was cut down immediately by a flashing broadsword.

When Evita recovered her composure, there were three dead men strewn across the street, and three armed savages glowering at her.

Fargo said something in a strange tongue and the men nodded. Then, as swiftly as they'd appeared, they vanished into the shadows.

Fargo glanced at the dumbstruck bodyguard.

"We won't need you any longer. Take care of your comrade."

Later, while enjoying an excellent wine in a secluded bistro, she understood what had transpired.

"Those men who rescued us were my own bodyguards," Fargo explained.

"They're certainly efficient."

"They're Barbars," he said, as if that alone made everything clear.

"Part of your crew?"

"I am their king."

He said it so casually that the words didn't register immediately.

When they did, Evita didn't question their veracity.

She'd known from the first moment that the dark, smooth-featured gambler was special.

What she found astonishing was his comparative youth. At eighteen he had the self-assured dignity of a patriarch.

She was also acutely aware of his primitive sensuality.

"Have you never found a queen?" she mused playfully.

"I'm wed to my destiny."

His grave tone muted Evita's smile. "Which is . . . ?"

He lifted his glass. "To the destruction of our enemies."

"One man's enemy is another's ally," she reminded.

"I have but one enemy—the traitor who calls himself Lord Kiferson."

Evita slowly raised her glass to his.

"To our common goal," she whispered.

His ebony eyes seemed to probe her thoughts.

"What is Lord Kiferson to you?"

"He's my enemy, isn't that enough?"

"Not quite. But you wouldn't understand our uncivilized code."

"I don't understand why you're wasting your time in gaming parlors," Evita snapped. "Or is that part of your Barbar code as well?"

"It takes money to launch a warship."

"I have money."

His scowl didn't waver. "What would you consider ample return for such a sizeable investment?"

"I want . . . you."

The words echoed through the quiet as Fargo sipped his wine. Then he flung the glass aside and reached out for her, exploding the silence with a surge of roaring excitement that swept Evita on a long, turbulent voyage beyond ecstasy—from which she never returned. . . .

CHAPTER ELEVEN

Although the Tarot cards favored the mission, Evita's apprehensions mounted rapidly when Fargo failed to appear on schedule.

She was comforted by André's confidence and relied on him for sustenance during the long vigil.

Three days later she sighted the clipper's sails rising over the horizon, and her anxiety gave way to expectation. André, on the other hand, exhibited a marked nervousness as the ship approached, putting extra guards around their estate. He also posted a small army on both sides of the port, fearing a possible attack.

Despite his warnings Evita met the clipper in port, being too impatient to see Fargo.

Indeed, she'd seen little enough of him in the past two years. During that time he'd caused a great deal of damage to Kiferson's merchant vessels. But this was the sweetest prize of them all. Not only had Fargo seized Kiferson's most valuable clipper, he'd taken his eldest daughter in the bargain. And Lady Trent was worth a hundred ships.

A twinge of jealousy disturbed her thoughts as the carriage neared the bay. She'd heard the girl was beautiful and no doubt Fargo had exercised his right of conquest.

Evita was doubly dismayed when she boarded the clipper.

First by Lady Trent's exceptional beauty, which transcended her disheveled state. And then by the exotic black wench who shared Fargo's cabin.

"I thought this was to be a private meeting," said Evita.

Fargo didn't bother to rise.

"Presently, milady—when I conclude my obligations here."

"Obligations to whom?"

"Why, to my crew of course. And my investors."

His indifference sparked Evita's temper. "Tell the bitch to get out. I want to speak to you alone."

"Permit me to introduce Miss Melba Sanjin," he said calmly.

Evita's eyes didn't waver. "Then I take it you've broken our compact?"

"A Barbar honors all debts," he said, tone edged with scorn. He nodded at the black girl, and she quietly left the cabin.

"You're in a foul mood for one who's just received her bounty," he remarked, moving to the sideboard. "Wine or cognac, milady?"

"Who is that black slut?"

He filled two glasses with cognac and returned. "Miss Sanjin is my mistress."

"At least Barbars ply their betrayals openly," she observed, masking her shock with a sarcastic smile.

"One can't betray a married woman," he reminded. "Our contract didn't specify ownership, but mutual consideration."

"Now you talk like a lawyer."

"Better not to talk at all, milady, since we know what we want of each other."

His soft voice set off an avalanche of conflicting emotions.

"Don't think you can toy with me," she fumed.

Fargo smiled and eased into an armchair.

"In truth, milady, that's exactly what I hoped to do."

With a great effort of will she turned and took a step toward the door.

"Come here."

As she glanced back her anger was smothered by lust. Fargo was stretched out like a sleepy panther, watching her with hooded, red-flecked eyes.

She wanted to leave, but his gaze held her fast. Even more compelling was the sensuality exuding like musk from his supple flesh.

Drawn by its scent Evita slowly moved to the chair. The feral desire clawing at her senses stripped away all pretense of resistance.

Fargo knew why she'd come. And she reveled in his power.

"Take off my boots."

His husky voice devoured her thoughts.

She sank to her knees, aware of nothing except her convulsive hunger—and the wild beating of her heart as it thrashed against her ribs like a trapped bird.

Melba suppressed an impulse to visit Trent's cabin. Instead, she bided her time in the officer's dining room, with a pot of tea. She knew it was too late for reconciliation. At least for her. She'd never compromise her love for Fargo.

Of greater concern is his white-haired consort, Melba reflected. *Obviously, she is my rival, not Trent.*

Melba's anxieties multiplied with her second pot of

tea. She felt helpless against the powers exerted by the countess. A stroll on deck helped console her. The ship was anchored in a shimmering green bay, edged with blue and white houses with gilded domes. The beach was adorned by a necklace of great ships bobbing placidly in the sun, while a number of smaller boats clustered around the captured clipper.

Melba forgot her fears as she watched the strangely costumed tribesmen unload the clipper. It seemed both alien and familiar—like some dream she'd had many times before.

It was almost dusk when Fargo's visitor departed.

By chance Melba was descending the stairway when the countess appeared on deck. For a moment the woman stared at her, then continued briskly toward the gangplank.

That woman told Melba more than she wished to know. The woman's bloodless face was glazed with triumph, like some white-haired vampire who'd just feasted on its prey.

CHAPTER TWELVE

It was dark when they came for Trent.

Two armed men ushered her off the ship, put her in a closed carriage, and escorted her to new quarters.

She saw the gold-domed dwellings gleaming in the moonlight as she debarked, but the carriage had drawn curtains. When they arrived, however, Trent glimpsed a dim cluster of lights braiding the glimmering water far below. Then she was taken inside and deposited in a large room furnished with tapestries, carpets, and pillows, upon which reclined a number of unsmiling females.

"Is there anything to eat here?" she inquired briskly.

The women glared impassively.

Trent repeated the question in French and one of them nodded. "You'll be fed," she assured her with a smirk. "But first you'll have a bath."

Before Trent could respond, the two guards entered with a large porcelain tub filled with hot water. The tub was fitted with silver wheels enabling them to roll it easily into place.

"I don't require a bath," Trent said firmly, thinking of the bag of jewelry hidden beneath her skirt.

The woman snorted. "You'll learn to do as you're told."

She said something to the others in a guttural tongue and they laughed.

Trent ignored them and settled down on the far side of the room.

Eventually a guard came in with a tray of food. He glanced questioningly at the unused tub and the woman across the room made a remark which seemed to amuse him.

Their derision was lost on Trent, who intently sampled her repast. She found both the cuisine and wine quite pleasant and consumed the contents of the tray with considerable relish.

When she looked up she saw four female faces watching her.

This time it was Trent's turn to laugh. "You look like four painted crows," she giggled.

They looked at her blankly. The woman who spoke French smiled at her. "Feel better, my dear?"

"Quite well, thank you. But tell me—what is this place?"

The woman rose from her pillow and approached Trent. "This is the seraglio of Shareef Hazar."

The name pierced her mind like a nail.

"Are you hostages?"

"He is our king."

Trent looked at her with undisguised contempt. "May he be cursed."

The woman shook her head. Like the others she had exotic features accentuated by heavily shadowed eyes and red lips.

They were similarly attired as well, in sheer silk blouses and pantaloons that barely veiled their bodies. The woman with Trent was taller than the rest, with Amazonian proportions and an arrogant manner.

"You'll learn child," she grunted. "If you live that long."

Trent's reply was lost in the sudden warmth that engulfed her body. She looked up in confusion and saw the woman's features blur. Then a sudden chill shivered across her skin.

"Let me help you, dear," the woman murmured, tugging at Trent's dress. "You'll feel better after a nice warm bath."

It was true. Despite Trent's feeble protests, she felt refreshed by the scented water and allowed herself to be scrubbed, toweled, and perfumed without further resistance.

She felt exhilarated as the woman helped her dress, and was vaguely aware of the silken garment veiling her flesh.

The guards entered some time later and wafted her through a long series of corridors until they reached the blazing sunlight. Surprised that the night had passed so quickly, Trent reclined on a satin couch and closed her eyes.

A large shadow floated across her senses. Trent blinked and saw a massive shape, blocking out the light. Before her vision adjusted, a foul odor smothered her perceptions.

Dimly she realized that the blazing light was actually a large chandelier, but she couldn't distinguish if the giant looming over her was man or ape.

His touch jolted her awake. The stench stuffed her throat like an oily rag as she struggled to push him away. She felt his hot breath on her face and twisted desperately.

Suddenly Hall Fargo flashed into view far beyond

the light—his features more loathsome than the stinking giant squeezing her breasts. She tried to scream but the fetid darkness swallowed her up before she could utter a sound. . . .

CHAPTER THIRTEEN

Fargo hadn't been eager to dine with the countess. However, he couldn't afford to offend her.

His reluctance stemmed from his Barbar code which scorned excessive lust, vanity, or greed as signs of weakness, while Evita celebrated vice the way other women prayed.

During the feast, her husband cast a blind eye to her open infidelity, being preoccupied with the dazzling young Nubian girl he'd purchased that week.

"Why didn't you invite your little slave girl?" Evita purred, pressing her half-bared breasts against his arm.

He reached for his goblet. "I thought you'd provide sufficient entertainment."

"And so I have."

Something about her self-assured smile disturbed him, but he suppressed his doubts. *Evita's decadent ways were Count Bouvier's problem after all,* he reflected coolly.

Throughout dinner they enjoyed music provided by Asian dancing girls, and over cognac Evita unveiled her surprise.

"This is for you, my king," she said huskily, lifting her glass.

Fargo glanced at Bouvier, but he was whispering

something to the Nubian beauty, while his hands stroked her thigh.

One of the dancers across the room lowered the chandelier, illuminating an empty couch.

A moment later two women entered, dressed in traditional harem garb. The tall one was his own tribal concubine, Dezda. But it took a moment for him to recognize his hostage. Lady Trent seemed drunk and leaned on her companion for support as she shuffled into the room.

"Who authorized you to have my prisoner removed from the seraglio?" Fargo muttered sharply.

Evita's green eyes narrowed. "I thought Kiferson was your enemy."

He hesitated, knowing she was testing him. While he'd captured a rich prize, he still needed Evita's gold to arm the clipper for battle.

It isn't my concern what she intended to do with Lady Trent, as long as the wench retained her market value, he speculated. *All things considered, it was wise to humor Evita's whims.*

"I don't like anyone superseding my authority," Fargo said calmly.

The answer satisfied her doubts, and she leaned closer. "It won't happen again."

Lady Trent was obviously in a stupor. Knowing the countess's talent for narcotic potions, Fargo diagnosed the girl's condition.

"What did you give her?" he muttered.

"Oh, just a pinch of poppy, and a dash of belladonna spiced with special herbs."

As Fargo sipped his cognac he noted that Count Bouvier had stopped nuzzling his companion and was staring expectantly at the scantily clad hostage on the couch.

Evita also exhibited marked signs of anticipation, as did the young Nubian who leaned forward in tight-lipped fascination.

But an odd reluctance continued to cloud Fargo's mood. As a Barbar he disdained torture unless necessary.

His regrets were shattered by shock when Mustafa entered. The giant warrior's naked flesh quivered like a hairy mound of pudding as he lurched toward the couch and began pawing at Trent's body.

Evita purred with excitement when the girl tried to fight off her massive attacker, who drew back in confusion.

He recovered immediately and exerted his strength to render her helpless against his greedy fingers.

"Stop it."

Fargo's husky command jerked Evita's attention from the struggle. She glared at him, bosom heaving breathlessly.

"You sound like a jealous lover."

"I speak as Shareef Hazar, master of the pig who dances for your pleasure. He is under my command. Do you understand? Now you stop it or I will."

"He's right, you know," Count Bouvier declared, rising from his pillow. "I'll take care of this."

"We don't want to weaken discipline, do we?"

Evita left the question unanswered as her husband ordered the sullen warrior to leave, and helped Lady Trent sit upright.

She glanced at Fargo, her face rigid with anger.

"Are you satisfied?" she spat venomously.

Fargo was gratified by Bouvier's support, but gravely concerned about Evita.

"I'm not at all satisfied," he confided with a rueful smile.

"I'm at your disposal," Evita snorted. "What more do you require?"

His smile faded and he drew her close.

"No more than what I came for," he murmured, mouth warm against her ear.

Then he felt her anger dissolve in a steaming surge of lust that fogged his senses like a scented mist.

Need smothering his reason, he tore at her clothes, no longer heeding the watchful eyes around them—and only dimly aware that he too had been drugged.

While Count Bouvier rarely opposed his young wife, they were too near victory for needless risk. If anything, he wanted Kiferson's destruction even more than Fargo. *I'll even sacrifice Evita if need be*, Bouvier admitted to himself, as he assisted their groggy hostage to her feet.

"No . . . leave me alone . . ." she mumbled.

"It's all right, milady. Don't be afraid."

She gaped at him blankly.

"Who . . . ?"

"I'm Count André Bouvier," he whispered. "I want to help you."

"Thank you . . ." She sank against his chest, unable to finish.

"Just lean on me," he urged.

". . . must . . . escape . . . help me . . ."

It amused André to play the white knight. Especially since the deception opened a wealth of opportunity.

His mood clouded when he looked back and saw Fargo embracing his wife. *They may as well take their pleasure now*, he mused grimly. *Victory was far*

*from certain. Few men could boast of having bested
El-Kifer.*

"My . . . father . . ." the girl rasped. "Lord
Kifers . . ."

"Don't worry. I'll contact your father," Bouvier assured, guiding her to the door. "You can trust me, milady . . ."

CHAPTER FOURTEEN

"Believe me, I want to help."

Moss Radcliffe gave his guest a sympathetic smile and lowered his voice. "If it's a matter of money, depend on us."

His son Gavin nodded emphatically. "Anything."

"I need armed ships and fighting men," Kiferson said, voice edged with contempt.

Radcliffe sighed and shook his head. "Even if I could press a crew into combat duty, it would make my other ships vulnerable to attack by the British or the French. They'd welcome an excuse to take over the slave trade. And that's not all—what you propose could touch off a war along the African coast."

"Those Barbar savages would run amok and sink every ship in the straits. They don't like white men."

That's why they won't barter slaves for a livelihood, Lord Kiferson observed privately.

"We don't even know if Lady Trent's been kidnapped," Radcliffe went on. "Did you receive a ransom demand? After all, your clipper may be delayed."

"*The Mercury* was sighted outside of Tingis," Kiferson said firmly. "I'm expecting a message any day now. Few vessels on the trade routes are as swift as my clippers."

Radcliffe averted his eyes from Lord Kiferson's icy

gaze. "Of course, of course. Magnificent fleet . . ."

Gavin nodded. "I adored Trent's boat."

"Trent's boat happens to be a ship."

His tone left no doubt that he considered the error inexcusable.

"Uh, Gavin, perhaps you'll excuse me while we discuss some confidential matters," Radcliffe said hastily.

"Of course, Father." He turned to Lord Kiferson and stretched out his hand. "Shall I see you at Julie Devon's ball this evening?"

Kiferson ignored his hand. "I think not," he said quietly. "Unlike you, I've nothing to celebrate. And nothing further to discuss."

Father and son gaped at each other in stunned silence, as the powerful, golden-maned figure strode from the room.

"There's nothing I can do," Paxton muttered. "What's more, as your lawyer I must warn you that what you propose is against the law. As a federal official I can *assure* you that neither the Navy nor the State Department will sanction a private campaign. They have their hands full with Mexico acting up, and those fool Texans talking about a republic."

Judge Paxton swallowed some bourbon and grimaced.

"As your friend I say it's a damned shame. Be different if Stephen Decatur was still alive. He'd have a fleet of frigates on the high seas before they took roll call. He was a man . . . not like these blasted pantywaists . . ."

Kiferson shrugged. "The eulogy is touching, but it won't solve my problem."

"Seems to me you've got to risk it," Paxton drawled, scratching his goatee. "But beware, every slaver from here to the Congo will be gunning for you, if you try to attack Tingis. The money from those flesh markets rolls right into Capitol Hill."

Kiferson's gold-flecked eyes dimmed at Paxton's words.

Despite his distinguished record, he'd be branded a criminal if he threatened the inviolate temple of profit.

He also realized he had no choice.

Civilized law was as dependable as a paper shield. If he didn't defend his ships now, they'd eventually be destroyed.

Only the loyalty of his Barbar tribesmen offered real hope for Trent's rescue. But until he received news of her fate he was bound to a land where human lives were sold like sides of beef—every day except the sabbath.

While Melba was granted freedom to come and go, she never left the walled estate. She knew it was safe to walk the streets of Tingis; no one would dare try to harm Shareef Hazar's mistress. And yet she was afraid of the violence bristling beneath the exotic spectacle. She was also afraid of losing any opportunity to see her lover. Fargo spent most of his time with Countess Bouvier.

It doesn't matter, Melba told herself, as she strolled through the terraced garden behind the house. And yet, it did matter.

Someday, he'll tire of me and I'll lose everything— including my freedom, she brooded. *At least Trent will go home once the ransom is paid.*

Still, she harbored one fervent hope. Fargo had promised to take her on a voyage when he returned.

And Melba knew she'd risk anything for those few weeks.

I'll finally have the chance to prove my love, she mused, pausing to pluck a pink rose for her hair.

A blurred movement froze her hand in midair.

As she peered through the thick bush, she heard a familiar voice and realized it was Evita Bouvier.

"I want them both out of the way," the countess muttered angrily. "And you—why did you take his part the other night. Do you find the wench attractive?"

"Her beauty is enhanced by her ability to lure Kiferson to his death," a male voice replied. "I admire Shareef Hazar for the same reason. As far as I'm concerned, his fascination will end when he's blasted Kiferson out of existence. After that you may dispose of him or his mistress at will. Lady Trent will die with her father if that's any comfort, my pet."

Evita's voice smoldered with hate. "It's the black bitch I want."

The reply ignited Melba's panic and she began to tremble, fearful that she'd be discovered.

"Be patient, dearest," the man replied. "All things will come with Kiferson's death."

His low tone faded into Melba's booming heartbeat, as they drifted away. She remained crouched beside the tangled rosebush for long moments, not daring to move until she was certain they'd gone.

It took much longer to recover from the shock.

She returned to her room and remained in bed for the rest of the day, refusing to eat or drink.

Sometime after midnight she started sifting through her muddled thoughts, and by morning realized that her only hope of survival was escape.

She also realized it was impossible. Everyone in

Tingis knew and feared their monarch, Shareef Hazar.

There's no other choice, Melba reminded herself, preparing herself for the flight.

After breakfast she instructed the serving girl to lay out fresh clothes and draw a hot bath.

But when it came time to call for the carriage, Melba lost her courage.

In an effort to calm her nerves, she went out to the garden and gazed at the golden hills of Spain just across the straits. For a wild moment she thought of trying to swim across, but she remembered Fargo describing the strong currents that propelled heavily loaded ships at great speed through the channel. In passing, he'd mentioned that no man had ever made the swim from Africa to Europe.

I might make it with a small boat, she reflected, pacing back and forth. *Someone might ferry me at the right price.* She had some gold coins and the small hoard of jewelry Fargo had given her: an emerald ring and matching bracelet, a diamond ring and necklace, a strand of pearls, a heavy gold bracelet, a ruby-studded watch on a gold chain, emerald and ruby earrings . . .

Surely love's precious plunder will buy a few miles passage—and my life, she speculated grimly.

It was easier planned than performed.

The main obstacle being the fear of what would happen if news of her intentions filtered back to the countess. There was no way of knowing who could be trusted among such vermin.

"Isn't it a lovely morning?"

The question pierced her thoughts like a sliver of ice.

It was the voice of Evita's companion.

She looked up and recognized Count Bouvier's gaunt features.

"I'm sorry if I startled you, my child," he said, beaming at her.

His paternal manner made it difficult to believe he was the same man who'd been casually conspiring to kill her.

Exerting all her control Melba forced herself to smile. "I must have been having a daydream."

"Quite understandable, considering the view."

Melba ignored his insinuating tone.

"I've never seen anything so beautiful," she sighed, "not even in New Orleans."

"You should visit the port," he confided gravely. "I've seen you walking through the gardens every day, and while I'm very proud of my flowers, Tingis is one of the wonders of the world. You owe yourself at least one tour of the marketplace while you're here."

While I'm alive, you mean, Melba corrected silently. Aloud she said: "Oh, I couldn't. I'd be lost in two minutes for sure."

"I'd be delighted to be your guide."

Her heart leaped at the offer, but she pretended to be uncertain. "It's too great an inconvenience."

"Not at all, dear child. I'm leaving shortly to settle some business. It would be a pleasure to have you along. I've looked forward to becoming better acquainted."

"It would be foolish to overlook such an ideal opportunity," Melba conceded. "I'll be waiting for your call, sir."

"We can leave immediately if you wish. Do you have everything you need?"

"Perhaps my parasol . . ."

Bouvier gently took her arm. "Never fear, my child," he murmured, guiding her toward the gate. "We'll buy you the finest parasol in Tingis."

Even with a fine carriage driven by swift thoroughbreds, the trip took almost an hour, and Melba realized how invulnerable the mansion was from attack.

She also discovered why Bouvier suggested the little jaunt. He plied her with questions about her life in America, being particularly interested in Lord and Lady Kiferson.

One of the first skills a slave had to master was how to say nothing and still appear responsive. When they reached Tingis, her escort knew little more than when he started.

While still polite, his smile seemed dimmer and his mood less festive.

True to his word, he took Melba into the walled marketplace where he purchased a brocade parasol with a carved ivory handle from a Chinese merchant with long, pointed fingernails.

While brief, the tour proved highly informative. Their quick stroll confirmed Melba's original fear. Every boatman, sailor, stevedore, and wharf rat along the docks tipped his hat as they passed. She'd never be able to slip through Bouvier's network of informants.

The maze of alleys connecting the inner markets offered less hope.

Even if she managed to elude pursuit, one of the many slave dealers would surely scoop her up.

As might anyone with an eye for profit, Melba observed. Every male in the quarter seemed to have a few slaves in tow, like prosperous squires showing off their dogs.

Bouvier's abrupt departure added to her dismay.

"Forgive my haste," he implored, his smile both regretful and remote. "But I'm already late for my appointment. Choose whatever trinket you fancy, and have it charged to me. My carriage is also at your disposal whenever you wish."

As Melba watched him disappear into the crowd, she was acutely aware of being alone. Her brain reeled with dizzying panic, as if she were lost in a hostile jungle. Instinctively, she hurried back toward the waiting carriage.

But before she reached the pier, a vaguely familiar figure darted out of the shuffling mass of people.

"Miss Melba, don't you remember?" he exclaimed. "It's me—Django—from aboard *The Mercury*."

Memory collided with alarm and she jerked back. "We mustn't be seen together," she whispered hoarsely.

"Follow me. Nobody will see us."

Reassured by his confident manner, Melba trailed a few paces behind.

He led her to a sparsely populated area behind the main square, and ducked into a side street. When Melba turned the corner, however, she saw that the long, twisting passage was empty.

Fighting back a surge of fear, Melba took a few tentative steps along the secluded street.

Django's husky voice leaped out of an open doorway. "Stop right there."

Melba paused, blinking nervously. Though she heard him clearly, he was concealed by the shadows.

"Pretend you're looking for some doodads," Django suggested.

Melba glanced around and saw the shop window nearby. She moved closer and stared at the gaudy array of jewelry displayed inside.

"Tell me what happened," he muttered. "Quickly, girl."

"We're being held for ransom. That is—Lady Trent is being held, by the Barbars."

"Who's their leader?"

"A man called Shareef Hazar. But Count Bouvier is behind it all. He plans to betray Lord Kiferson."

"Betray him how?"

"When he comes to claim Lady Trent, he'll be attacked," she said impatiently. "You must help me find a small boat—anything that can get me to Spain."

"No way to get out of here 'cept they let you," Django rumbled. "Not alive, anyway."

"Then we're doomed," she said softly.

"Take heart, Miss Melba. I'll be makin' port in time to warn Lord Kiferson."

"Pray God you do."

"You best be gettin' back."

"Where do I go?" Melba hissed, suddenly unsure of the direction she'd taken.

"Bear left till you reach the wide street, then left again. Now get."

Repeating the terse instructions over and over, she hurried away. When she reached the outer market, her anxieties suddenly evaporated. If Django relayed her warning there was still a chance. So long as Lord Kiferson stayed alive all of them—Fargo included—were safe from Countess Bouvier's treachery.

Buoyed by the thought, she slowed her pace to admire the richly costumed tribesmen and veiled women flowing into the market.

CHAPTER FIFTEEN

Django brought Kiferson the information he sought. He recognized the black sailor as a member of Captain Holbrook's crew and ushered him into the library.

"She's alive, sir," Django blurted. "They're holding her someplace outside Tingis."

Kiferson filled a goblet with his finest cognac and handed it to him.

"How did you escape?"

Django flashed a proud grin. "I was in the brig, sir—on account of your daughter."

A deep swallow of cognac helped unfold the rest of his story. . . .

Apparently the first shell tore a large chunk of timber from the hull. Django was thrown clear by the blast and when he recovered, found himself bobbing in the sea, arms wrapped around a splintered plank. He could hear the terrible screams aboard *The Mercury* and began paddling frantically away from the ship, before the sharks came to feed on the dead.

A Corsican galleon fished him out of the water the next day. They debated whether to sell their find, but Django's culinary skills convinced them he was more valuable as their cook.

The captain was so impressed that on reaching

Tingis, he personally secured Django a berth on a slaver bound for New Orleans with the next tide.

Having twenty-four hours liberty, Django took a stroll around the bustling marketplace.

He'd barely left port when he spied Melba.

"She say it's a trap," he declared as Kiferson refilled his glass. "Hazar and this Bouvier fellow plan to attack when you bring the ransom. And maybe they got help aboard your own ship."

Kiferson's eyes glinted like ice-tipped darts. "What sort of help?"

"Funny how it come about," Django said, lowering his voice. "When I got on board that slaver—the *Virginia Star* by name, I chanced on another of me shipmates."

He leaned back and shook his head sadly. "Old Harry Daws was a damn fine carpenter. Cap'n said so himself. Now they got his poor black ass on the slave block. Suppose he lucky at that," Django mused, draining his goblet.

"Get to the point man," Kiferson snapped. "What the devil did he tell you?"

"Way old Harry got it figured, somebody chopped the lines on *The Mercury* before she got hit. He was on the repair crew and swears they been cut clean."

"Cut by who?"

"That's what I said. An' old Harry give me a funny smile. Then he tell me what few wasn't butchered, was sold off. 'Cept for one man. And *that* man was sittin' at the Captain's table swillin' champagne, and spendin' gold eagles like they was farthings. I saw him myself, sir. It was the third mate—Grady, sure enough."

"If that's the case, it won't be long before he comes calling."

"Beg pardon, sir?"

"If Grady is indeed our traitor, he'll be carrying the ransom message," Kiferson said, voice as quiet as a razor.

Third mate Grady paused frequently to refill his whiskey glass as he recounted his harrowing experience.

"It was brutal what they did," he declared indignantly. "Only reason I'm alive today is because they needed somebody to deliver this ransom note."

Kiferson took the sealed envelope without comment.

" 'Course you can rest easy about your daughter," Grady assured. "They're keepin' her safe and sound, bein' as how she's so valuable."

Lord Kiferson glanced at his son, who sat silently to one side. "Mr. Grady is amazingly well informed, don't you think?"

"He should be commended," Kevin said softly.

"I keep my eyes open," Grady gloated, reaching for the decanter.

"Perhaps you can tell us something about Shareef Hazar."

Grady seemed startled by the suggestion. "Hear tell he's some Barbar freebooter out of Tunis," he muttered, avoiding Kiferson's icy gaze.

"And this Count Bouvier?"

Grady glanced at him warily. "Can't say as I know the name. 'Course, I can ask around if you like."

"I'd appreciate that."

"Well I suppose you'll be havin' your hands full until you turn over the bounty," Grady sighed, setting down his empty glass. "God knows this mess has left me destitute."

"Be sure I intend to show my gratitude," Kiferson said curtly.

"Much obliged, Cap'n," the mate wheezed. "I've had it rough."

"I'm putting you back on the payroll immediately, so you needn't worry."

"What payroll is that, Cap'n?" Grady asked suspiciously.

"Why, of course you'll want to be on board when we ship out for Tingis."

The mate lurched to his feet. "I can't do it. Not after what I been through. I'm a sick man."

"Nothing better than the sea air to get you back in shape," Kiferson reminded affably.

"I'm looking forward to it," Kevin interjected.

Grady's eyes flicked toward the door. "Time I be gettin' back to me wife," he rasped.

Kevin started to rise, then saw his father's warning gesture and settled back in his chair.

"I'll think over what you said about shipping out," Grady stammered, as he edged away. "May God be with you," he added, fumbling for the knob.

What remained of his dignity crumbled when he opened the door.

He blinked at the two black men blocking his escape, then fell to his knees, squealing hysterically. He was still blubbering as Django and his mate, Harry Daws, hauled him off like a sack of overripe melons.

After Grady had been disposed of, Kiferson turned to his son. "Be prepared for many surprises on this cruise."

Kevin pondered the cryptic remark. "I'll do my best, sir."

"You always do," Kiferson noted. "However, this is much more than a baptism of fire."

"I'm not sure of your meaning," the boy said hesitantly.

Kiferson gave him a fleeting smile. "This, my son, will be your baptism of blood."

CHAPTER SIXTEEN

Trent learned many things during her weeks of captivity—the first being self-defense. On waking from her drugged sleep, she realized the Amazon, Dezda, had stolen the pouch of jewelry hidden beneath her skirt. She waited a few hours until she'd recovered fully from the effects of the potion; carefully studying her quarry.

Dezda, tall and lithe, seemed to dominate the other three members of Fargo's tribal harem. They waited on her as if she were a queen, cringing at her frequent outbursts of temper. They paid scant attention to Trent, which well suited her purpose. At midday she dined alone, but that evening she joined the others at the communal table.

Dezda seemed delighted by her presence.

"Feeling better, little one?" she asked in French.

"I'm still weak. I must have eaten something that disagreed with me."

The woman said something that made the others laugh.

"You seem to have quite a wit," Trent observed, as she filled her plate.

Dezda scowled. "Maybe you're the one who's funny."

The other women grinned at Trent with ill-disguised anticipation.

"Fascinating, perhaps, but hardly funny. At least, not to civilized Christians."

Trent continued eating while Dezda ruminated over the remark.

"I suppose you're one of those pampered hens who can't boil tea and think they pee perfume," Dezda sneered. She added something in her own tongue that evoked fresh peals of laughter.

Trent paid them no heed, intent on their glowering leader. "I know a filthy thief when I see one."

"You'll apologize for that."

"You're beneath apology," Trent said calmly, slicing a piece of bread.

The woman pushed herself erect. "I'll teach you respect," she snarled.

Without hesitation Trent tipped the food-laden table, flinging it against the Amazon's legs, as she scrambled to her feet.

With equal swiftness Dezda smacked the heavy tray aside, and lunged at her, while the others scattered for safety, squealing in panic.

So quick was her reaction that she didn't see the knife in Trent's hand until it was too late.

She jerked back but her weight pulled her into range of Trent's weapon. Even so, she managed to deflect the blade with her forearm and twist away from another jab. When the flurry subsided, she was unscathed except for a long slash from elbow to wrist.

Ignoring the wound, Dezda warily circled the crystal-eyed madwoman who kept jabbing at her with the bread knife.

Unlike most well-bred ladies, Trent had learned

the rudiments of fencing during childhood, and wielded the short blade with authority.

It seemed a draw, with Trent unable to penetrate the tall woman's sweeping fists, yet skillful enough to keep her from attacking.

But Dezda had skills of her own. She feinted, then leaped clear of Trent's thrust, throwing her off balance. Before she could recover, Dezda grasped the metal-tipped thong binding her waist and tugged it free. Her arm lashed out like a shiny red snake, spitting blood across Trent's face as the whip cut into her flesh.

Pain-numbed fingers stubbornly clutching her weapon, Trent lunged at Dezda, but fell back when the braided thong cracked between her breasts. Stunned by the searing burst of agony, she blindly hurled her knife at the giant female, then scrambled back to the wall.

With a triumphant snort Dezda gave chase, hefting the weighted thong. Searching wildly for a weapon, Trent saw the knife lying far beyond her reach. At the same instant she glimpsed Dezda's arm coiling back to strike.

As Trent ducked, she instinctively grabbed the thick fringe edging the carpet and yanked with all her strength.

The narrow rug shot out from underneath Dezda's feet and she flew backwards, arms flapping for balance. Her skull smacked the floor a split second before her huge body crumpled into a lifeless heap.

Trent dove for the fallen knife and scooped it up, eyes rolling toward the women huddled nearby.

They shrank back at her threatening flourish of the knife, and she returned to her dazed adversary. After jerking the braided thong from Dezda's grasp, Trent pressed the blade into her soft throat. When the sharp point pricked her skin, Dezda's eyes popped open.

"Now give up the jewels or I'll slit your gullet," Trent rasped, digging the point deeper.

Dezda nodded frantically. "Under my bed . . ."

After that she had no trouble with the other women in the seraglio. Indeed, they became quite friendly, and in a few days started teaching Trent a few words of their strange language. They taught her other things as well, such as how to wield the metal-tipped thong she'd taken from Dezda, and the art of throwing a knife. Despite their alien ways she felt an odd kinship with the Barbar women. But she never forgot her vow of revenge. Every day she reaffirmed her hatred of Shareef Hazar by honing her newly acquired skills with knife and whip. And every night she prayed for the chance to use them.

She was disappointed to discover that Fargo never visited his tribal concubines, preferring the company of Count Bouvier's wife. She also learned that Melba languished in solitary splendor while her paramour was preoccupied with the countess.

Although she bore no grudge against her former handmaiden, Trent felt a surge of exultation at the news. Only the announcement that her father had agreed to the ransom demands gave her more pleasure.

"I implore you to delay this venture," Evita repeated, straining to control her exasperation.

"As I explained before, milady, to delay would only lend Kiferson time to strengthen his hand."

"Can't you understand? The cards show we've been betrayed. This mission bears a curse, I tell you."

Fargo heaved a long sigh and idly ascertained the clarity of his wine against the candle flame. "Cards . . . curses . . . I'd expect such jabber from that Nubian wench, but from you . . ."

He let the words drift into perplexed silence.

Evita glanced appealingly at her husband. "Surely *you* can testify to the Tarot's power to forewarn."

"The cards have spared me countless misfortunes," Bouvier conceded affably. "I've learned to rely on your instincts as sounder than my own," he added, giving her an appreciative smile. "Quite frankly, if it were I about to confront so formidable an enemy, I'd wait at least twenty-four hours. There's not much Kiferson can do while he's anchored off Safi."

While irrefutably sound, Bouvier's logic failed to temper Fargo's impatience.

"As you said, it's I who pay the piper."

"Heed that you don't pay more than you bargained for," Evita snapped. "You've already been too careless with your affections."

"I take it you refer to my mistress." Fargo's brows lifted slightly.

"I mean that treacherous black slut," Evita said softly.

"You have proof of her treachery then?"

"Your own Dezda provided that for us."

"I'd sooner trust in tea leaves," Fargo snorted. "My tribal concubines are mere adornments. To take them seriously, one would have to be deluded, or desperate."

"Right now I'm *both*," Evita declared, voice taut with emotion. "I'm deluded by your bone-brained stupidity—and, desperate to save you from rushing headlong into a trap."

"Exactly what proof did your confidant provide, milady?"

"The black wench visited Tingis a few days ago. Apparently to meet a confidant of her own caste—a common seaman I believe, *Negro* of course . . ." she added with emphatic satisfaction.

"What of it?"

Evita pursed her lips into a smug pout. "The seaman sailed for New Orleans the very next morning. *Obviously* it was a tryst."

"I'm most sorry to disagree with you, my pet."

Both of them looked at Bouvier, who was regarding his snifter with a bemused smile.

"You see, it was I who insisted that Miss Sanjin accompany me that day. She was quite reluctant, in fact. No, my dear, I think our young king's assessment of Dezda's intelligence is accurate in this case. Most likely the girl chanced to be accosted by some lout."

"And the cards?" Evita demanded.

Bouvier acknowledged her point with a courtly bow. "I certainly cannot dispute the reliability of *your* intelligence, my dear. I'm living tribute to your extraordinary power."

Evita turned to Fargo. "Reconsider, I beg you."

"Rather than waste time in conjecture, suppose we make a simple wager," Fargo suggested, with a sly smile.

"You risk your life."

Her stern reminder failed to impress him.

"That we all risk upon waking every morning."

"Philosophy isn't your forte."

"But gambling is, milady. Have you no sporting blood? After all, a wager is a sign of faith. Surely you have faith enough in the cards to accept my contract."

"I'll *consider* your offer, at least," Evita snapped.

"Then consider this: if your warning proves true, I'll give you full command of the next mission."

"Hardly a bounty," she observed coldy. "With you dead, I inherit command by right of succession."

"With me dead, my warriors will choose a new king. You inherit only the war."

"Then your wager is doubly faulted."

"My men will obey my orders posthumously. For one mission. Fair enough?"

Evita shrugged. "If I can't prevent you from this disastrous course I may as well profit from it. Your wager is accepted."

"Splendid. Now let's drink to your loss."

"Why waste wine on the inevitable?" Evita said, touching her glass to his.

"Let's drink that you'll survive to carry out my orders."

CHAPTER SEVENTEEN

While Kevin Kiferson had served under his father's command on many voyages, he found this cruise vastly different.

For one thing, his father's ship was manned by fierce-looking savages who spoke a strange guttural language. Equally astonishing was their outstanding seamanship. Using their own unorthodox methods of navigation, they kept the huge clipper moving toward Africa at better than twenty-two knots. But most curious of all was their overly respectful manner toward him, and their outright reverence of his father. To be sure, their obedience went far beyond ordinary ship's discipline, even taking into account the military nature of the voyage.

Along with their regular duties there was a three-hour training session with weaponry every morning, rain or sun. Kevin learned how to handle a cannon, throw a dagger, fire a variety of pistols, and fell an enemy in unarmed combat. Since he served as an officer, he was in his father's company much of the time. However, he was treated like the others in every respect. What Kevin couldn't grasp was why the others treated him differently. The sole exception to their diffidence was during the training periods.

The crewmen, he soon discovered, were Barbar

tribesmen who took great pride in their fighting prowess. They made little distinction between practice and combat, and more than once Kevin was cut or bruised as a result of their enthusiastic instruction.

However, he soon learned to hold his own in their mock battles, and as they neared their destination he'd become a feared opponent, especially with dagger and sword. He'd also learned to communicate in their alien tongue, even so far as to adopt some of their customs, such as that of exchanging weapons to seal a friendship.

When Kevin admired a shipmate's bone-handled dagger, he was surprised when the man presented it to him. Uncertain whether to accept or return it, he sought his father's counsel.

"The gift is a sign of respect," Kiferson explained. "You should be complimented. A Barbar values his blade more than gold. The only way to honor Gediz's gesture is by offering something of similar worth to yourself."

After some deliberation, he chose to give Gediz a set of matched derringers with silver grips. From then on, the seaman appointed himself Kevin's official guardian.

It was Gediz who taught him how to navigate the swiftest currents in order to coax maximum speed from their ship.

Though *The Trojan* was heavily armored, it carried nothing but stores and ammunition in its massive hold, making it quite buoyant. Together with the clipper's streamlined design, this served to give them an incredible rate of passage. In less than sixteen days they were off the western coast of Africa.

By then Kevin felt at ease with the fierce crewmen. Indeed, with his bronzed skin, long sun-bleached hair, and loose-fitting tunic, he seemed like one of them. Kiferson kept the ship close to the coastline as they sailed north toward Tingis, avoiding the trade routes.

But two days away from their destination, he gave the helm to Kevin and instructed him to head for shore.

It was dawn, and the sea was veiled by a fine mist that limited visibility. As they neared the coast, Kevin saw a towering wall of cliffs looming above the choppy waters.

He glanced at his father, who stood calmly nearby.

"Steady as she goes," Kiferson grunted. "Mind the reefs."

Straining to see through the haze, Kevin made out a line of jagged black rocks some fifty yards ahead. He gripped the wheel tight, fearing the currents would drive them into the barrier.

"Steady now," Kiferson murmured. "Heel to port and slip through the opening."

The narrow passage between two large boulders seemed barely wide enough for the clipper's hull. Holding his breath, Kevin nosed the prow into the opening. Then he felt a powerful current grip the ship as surely as a giant hand, guiding it past the reefs into a placid bay, half hidden at the base of the cliffs.

A number of vessels were anchored in the bay, and as they neared shore, Kevin saw the domed houses scattered across the rocks like small blue eggs.

He also saw the people crowding the shore. Surprisingly, the waters were quite deep, enabling the clipper to tie up at the main dock. As they weighed anchor, the waiting crowd swarmed over the ship, greeting the crew members with much laughter and shouting. Kevin was overwhelmed as the brightly robed women and turbaned warriors embraced his father, kissing his hand. The youth was more astonished when one of the women greeted him in that manner.

He looked up, face reddening with embarrassment.

Kiferson smiled and gently clapped his son's shoulder. "Welcome home, young prince."

Kevin shook his head as if dazed. "I don't understand."

"This is where I was born," his father said quietly.

"I am Kahlil el-Kifer, king of the Barbar nation—and these are my people—as they are yours."

It took some time for Kevin to fully comprehend his words. He accompanied his father ashore and sat beside him at the joyous feast that celebrated their arrival.

That night Kiferson told Kevin the story of his secret past as head of the Barbar marauders. He revealed how he'd abducted Lady Trevor Weymouth for ransom, but ended up marrying her instead—after helping the American naval hero, Stephen Decatur, rid the straits of a renegade armada of pirates.

With peace restored, the Barbar tribes assumed the role of policing the straits, enabling commerce to flow freely to the New World, and the Weymouth–Kiferson shipping empire to prosper. In turn, a share of these profits was divided equally among the tribesmen.

Unfortunately, with the opening of the trade lanes, slavery spread its tentacles and quickly took hold on the northern tip of Africa. With slavery came corruption, and the Barbar tribes drew back from the vice-ridden ports of Tingis and Safi. Some retreated as far as the Atlas mountains that separated the Sahara from the rich markets of Marrakesh, and preyed on the slave caravans.

These mountain Barbars took no prisoners on these

raids but always set free the captive blacks being transported to the auction block.

Others at the feast, who were able to speak English, recounted stories of his father's daring exploits when he was the most feared marauder on the Barbary Coast. However, what impressed Kevin most was their devotion to their king. And whether it was a mother seeking his blessing for her child, or two litigants asking for his judgment, El-Kifer served them all.

As the tribal fires ebbed, Kiferson turned to him. "We can leave in the morning if you wish."

The statement left Kevin confused.

"My wish is to carry out our mission."

"Of course. However, since we're a week early, you have the honor of choosing our course for the next few days—as a reward for your outstanding display of seamanship this morning." He added, with a casual smile, "I'm proud of you."

Kevin's throat swelled and he nodded; he was unable to speak. Finally he managed a few hesitant words.

"I'm proud to be your son."

Kiferson's gold-flecked eyes glinted in the fire light.

"We're agreed on everything except your choice of action—perhaps a shakedown cruise to the Canary Isles would suit you."

"If you don't mind, I think I'd prefer to spend this time with my new family," Kevin said quietly.

It was the answer his father had hoped to hear.

Many celebrations followed, as Kevin was formally initiated as a Barbar warrior. His friend Gediz acted as his sponsor during the ceremony, and later instructed him on the subtleties of dealing with Barbar maidens.

"Very stubborn . . ." Gediz warned. "No use fight . . . do what they want till they get marry. Then man is cap'n . . ." He flashed Kevin a meaningful grin. "But if they want you . . . no use fight . . . enjoy . . ."

Kevin soon discovered what he meant. Barbar women were allowed to take lovers before marriage and were quite uninhibited about making their preferences known.

To be sure most of them were quite comely and very curious about visitors. Both Kevin and Gediz were amused by the predicament of one non-Barbar crewman, who interested a few ladies.

The crewman, called Django, was most vigorously pursued by a large-breasted maid with braided hair, and thick legs, who unleashed a blaring stream of insults at anyone who dared compete for his affections. Her constant badgering forced Django into hiding, but she relentlessly hunted him down. Wherever he went, Rauna was only minutes behind him.

However, Kevin's amusement evaporated when he found himself being courted by three exceptional, and insistent, young females. Having been raised a gentleman, he found their aggressive attentions disturbing, but was unable to avoid all three. He was only mildly relieved when the field narrowed to two: a tall, graceful maid with long chestnut hair and cool green eyes called Aja; and Gyn, whose softly curved body and smoldering gaze melted his resolve. Completely disconcerted, he turned to his friend for advice.

"I say before . . . if they want you . . . no use fight . . . *enjoy*," Gediz urged cheerfully.

"I've come that far," Kevin confided. "What I can't decide is which one. Aja is sublimely beautiful, but Gyn is so sensual."

Gediz shrugged. "Man love one girl . . . he make enemy in other one . . . man love two girl . . . he make two friend . . ."

Kevin followed his advice with gratifying results, but he was relieved when they finally sailed.

After a few hours at sea, the mood sobered. Although little was said, an ominous tension hovered over the clipper as it raced toward their rendezvous.

Safi was a large port a few miles south of Tingis, which guarded the Atlantic entrance to the straits. Like Tingis it was an important link in the slave trade. And as such, an ideal place for an ambush. "They'll be expecting us to arrive from the west instead of south," El-Kifer told his officers. "We've got to take every advantage to prevent being trapped. Order double-watch at battle stations until we're off Safi."

Hazar didn't try to attack *The Trojan*, as Kifer's unexpected arrival prevented him from deploying the small Barbar vessel anchored in a small cove. Kifer's lookouts spotted the ship as soon as they neared the rendezvous point, much to Hazar's frustration.

As was customary, both ships remained at a safe distance while two emissaries went out in small boats to finalize the arrangements.

The presence of the Barbar craft complicated the negotiations immediately. Finally, Hazar's agent rowed back to his ship and returned with his consent to have the unauthorized vessel removed.

As it sailed away, the two representatives settled down to the details of their transaction.

Hazar had arrived aboard the captured *Mercury*,

and through his glass El-Kifer could see that the clipper had been refitted as a war cruiser with heavy cannon amidships and light cannon on deck. Like *The Trojan*, the ship's prow and masts had been armored, as well as the lower part of the hull. And like his ship, *The Mercury* rode high on the waves like a great white-winged bird poised for flight.

The emissaries wrangled through the morning, but by afternoon had agreed on a method of transfer.

A small boat manned by two men would ferry Lady Trent to *The Trojan* while at the same time two men would carry a chest containing one million dollars in gold to *The Mercury*. That way each side would have hostages while the goods were being certified. When the money was counted and Lady Trent reunited with her father, the hostages would return to their respective ships.

The Trojan lowered its boat first, but El-Kifer had his men wait until he saw a red-haired woman appear on deck, and approach the rail.

"That's Trent," he muttered under his breath.

She was obscured from view by a huge warrior who stepped in front of her as a boat was lowered over the side.

El-Kifer watched as the warrior lifted Trent in his arms and climbed into the boat.

He continued observing every move intently as the boat began moving toward them.

"Proceed!" he called out.

On the order, his own boat started across the wide expanse of water separating the clippers. *The Trojan*'s craft was equipped with a sail, while Trent was transported in a double-prowed rowboat which was somewhat slower. As a result they crossed closer to *The Mercury*.

Trent's craft was still lumbering through the waves as the ransom boat neared its destination.

Cursing the delay, El-Kifer watched the two men pulling at the oars while the red-haired figure huddled near the stern. Then the boat dipped and turned, giving him a clear look at her face.

"Damn them," he exclaimed loudly. "That's not Trent! It's some blasted trick!"

As he spoke, Hazar's seamen dropped the oars and hurriedly lifted a mast that had been hidden under their feet. Within seconds they had the mast secured, the sail unfurled, and were heeling swiftly toward *The Mercury*. At the same time the Barbar gunship hove into view, swimming across the water like a hungry shark.

The deception had been perfectly timed, Hazar exulted, watching his gunship emerge from the cover of the setting sun, just as the boat bearing the ransom money came near.

The boat carrying Lady Trent's substitute had already turned and was rushing back to safety. *The moment the ransom is secured they'll attack,* he calculated, eager for the final kill.

"Battle stations—load and prime!" he shouted.

His attention was diverted by an odd sight.

One of the sailors on *The Trojan*'s boat dove into the water and headed back to his ship with the long, powerful strokes of a practiced swimmer.

Curious that his mate stays at the rudder, Hazar mused, fixing his glass on the small boat. Then he saw why.

The man was bound, gagged, and locked to the helm with a chain. Though the man's face was contorted with fear, Hazar recognized his turncoat—third mate Grady.

He also noticed that the brass chest at Grady's feet seemed to be burning.

Even as it dawned on him that the brightly sputtering flame was a fuse, Hazar was in action. He leaped from the bridge, grasped a line, and swung to the lower deck. *The Trojan*'s boat was only a few yards away when Hazar grabbed a rifle from an astonished warrior and fired.

Some other warriors nearby lifted their weapons, but Hazar's shot was sufficient.

The brass ransom chest suddenly erupted into a white-flamed volcano, spewing burning fragments of wood and red-hot metal over the deck. Shrapnel felled a few men and shock stunned the rest as the blast shook the clipper, unleashing a huge wave that crashed against the hull.

Brain ringing, Hazar scrambled to the stairs. When he reached the bridge he found the helmsman leaning dazedly on the wheel, while the first mate struggled to get up. Pushing the helmsman aside, Hazar took the wheel and heeled toward *The Trojan*.

"Ready guns!" he roared.

The distant thunder of cannonfire rolled across the water and he looked up in time to see the boat carrying his decoy lift up and shatter—blown to bits by a direct hit. An instant later Hazar's gunship opened fire but, being out of range, its missiles fell short.

As the smoke from *The Trojan*'s guns faded, he saw two Barbar warships dart out from behind the large clipper, like a pair of winged scorpions.

"Heave to! Full sail to the wind!" Hazar bellowed, spinning the wheel to put his ship on a diagonal course calculated to intersect that of his gunship.

The quick maneuver saved them both. On seeing his retreat, the gunship turned as well, joining *The Mercury* at the apex of an inverted "V."

Both ships opened fire at their pursuers as they converged, continuing the salvos as their wakes extended into a wide "X" pattern; the deadly crossfire caught one of El-Kifer's cruisers amidships and the other circled back for survivors. *The Trojan* gave up the chase soon after.

Although *The Mercury* and the small gunship escaped undamaged, Hazar was far from grateful.

The bitch was right, he reflected bitterly as the lights of Tingis emerged from the moon-glazed sea. *I played right into El-Kifer's hands—and lost my birthright on a fool's wager.*

CHAPTER EIGHTEEN

Though dismayed to find herself still captive, Trent found comfort in Hazar's defeat. She was also pleased to learn that Dezda had perished in the exchange while trying to decoy El-Kifer.

To be sure, she saw little of the fray after she appeared briefly on deck, having been spirited back to her cell, while the red-wigged Amazon boarded the ransom boat in her place.

Trent was thrown to the floor when the explosion jolted the ship. She heard the booming cannon-fire outside her windowless cabin, but days passed before she learned what transpired.

On reaching Tingis she was returned to the walled estate, and imprisoned in a dank, airless dungeon.

After thirty-six hours a few slices of salted bread and a cup of water were pushed through a slot at the base of the metal door. Being ravenously hungry, Trent quickly devoured the meager repast. In a short while she became thirsty but her calls for more water went unheeded.

She was roused some time later by a loud clanking outside her cell and she moved to the door.

"Blyss . . ." she groaned, using the Barbar term for water.

In response, a metal cup was shoved through the

slot. Trent gulped down the contents then suddenly spit it out.

"It's salted . . ." she croaked, hurling the cup against the door.

"Miss Trent—is that you?"

Her senses bristled at the familiar voice.

"Can you hear? It's me . . . Melba."

Trent pressed her face against the door.

"Did the ransom arrive?"

"It was a trick. They never meant to free you. But your father found out."

"How did he know?"

"I warned him."

Melba's terse statement penetrated her thoughts like a cool rain. "Bless you for that," she muttered.

"They plan to kill us when they get the money," Melba said woodenly.

"Both of us?"

"Yes."

"You've got to help me escape."

"No way I can do that now."

"At least get me some water."

"You don't understand, Miss Trent. I'm locked up . . . just like you."

"But why?"

"Hazar drugged my wine. I told him everything."

His name coiled around the silence like a snake.

They continued to talk until Trent's increasing thirst made speech impossible. Her lips were cracked and her tongue swollen, making it difficult to breathe.

She drifted into a feverish sleep, mumbling incoherently as eerie dreams tumbled through her brain.

Melba's screams pierced her delirium like broken glass.

Trent lifted her head as the agonized shrieking

grew to a mad crescendo and shattered, disintegrating into a soul-shredding shriek that was more animal than human.

"Stop . . ." she croaked, pounding the door.

Unable to squeeze any more words through her parched throat, she sagged to the ground trying to shut out the gibbering howls of pain filling the darkness.

Despite the constant sounds stabbing her senses, she was consumed by her rabid need. Desperately she crawled across the floor to retrieve the cup she'd thrown on the dim hope of finding a few drops of salted water left inside.

There was nothing but the heart-rending sound of Melba's cries of agony.

Will shriveled by thirst, she slumped against the door and waited to die. Then she felt something damp between her fingers and looked down.

Her hand was covered with grimy fluid. Without hesitation Trent licked it clean then crouched on all fours to lap up the moisture trickling under the door. A stench filled her nostrils but she greedily sucked at the wet earth until her tongue and lips were drenched—mewling hoarsely as she nuzzled the ground for more. While slightly saline, the liquid eased her raw throat like oil, allowing air to flow into her lungs.

She was still on her knees when the door opened.

The sudden brightness forced Trent to look away and she scrambled to the wall. Squinting into the glare she made out two large shapes. She shrank back as one of them moved closer, but an iron fist clamped her arm and dragged her out of the cell.

Trent blinked, trying to clear her vision. She focused on the blurred mass in the center of the floor, but when her vision cleared her mind crumbled.

Melba was in the center of the room.

Although her hands were bound behind her back, her feet dangled free—straddling a smooth, cone-shaped pole jammed between her legs. Greasy strings of viscera spewed from the ragged gash in her belly like a tattered apron, while gore covered her body from groin to ankle.

She seemed to be running in midair—head flung back and limbs splayed convulsively—as if trying to escape the thick red prong spearing her flesh.

Eyes bulging Trent gaped at the glistening ooze trailing from Melba's impaled torso to the open cell.

A surge of nausea boiled up in her throat, bubbling through her anguished scream as she realized that she'd slaked her thirst with Melba's blood.

CHAPTER NINETEEN

Hazar took only a few sips of wine and nibbled reluctantly at the sumptuous repast, unwilling to fall victim to one of Evita's potions.

The bitch has become even more arrogant, if that is possible, he fumed, watching her slap the serving girl for some infraction.

It's my own doing, he reflected dourly. *If I hadn't been so pigheaded ...*

As he had a thousand times before, he left the thought unfinished.

"You seem troubled, my pet," Evita said, leaning closer. "Don't you feel well?"

He ignored the mocking note in her tone. "I'm wondering why we delay our mission. Each passing day affords El-Kifer further advantage."

Evita caressed his cheek. "You'll learn to trust me one day."

"Never as well as myself."

Annoyance flickered across her smile.

"You have a tendency to misplace your faith, as evidenced by your paramour's betrayal."

The biting reminder cut off further discussion.

Evita glanced at her husband. "André trusts my judgment. Don't you, darling?"

Her question drew Count Bouvier's attention from

the young Nordic girl seated beside him. "Implicitly, *ma petite*. You have a rare sense of timing."

"You've proved your prowess," Hazar conceded with a rueful smile. "If anything, I'm anxious for an encore."

She smiled and leaned closer. "Soon my king. El-Kifer has no choice but to accede to our demands—if we insure his daughter's return. But once aboard his vessel she's fair game. Suppose you were to intercept *The Trojan* at the mouth of the straits?"

"Suppose he takes another route?"

"We'll make sure he can't."

Hazar stroked his chin thoughtfully. "When does the Tarot suggest we contact El-Kifer?"

"I dispatched a messenger to Safi, this afternoon."

His expression relaxed and he filled his goblet with wine. "*That* I consider cause for celebration . . ."

"Then you'll be fascinated by our after-dinner entertainment."

Two things stayed Hazar from swallowing his wine. He recalled Evita's affinity for potions and recognized the barbed edge in her tone.

"No doubt it will be a revelation."

"Actually more of a reformation," she purred, eyes narrowed like an ivory cat.

Although Bouvier had turned to his blond companion, Hazar sensed he had one ear turned to his wife's conversation.

The old shark seems to be waiting for something, he mused, trying to fathom Evita's cryptic remark.

After dinner Evita insisted he join her in a special toast, and to prevent deception he ordered a bottle of rare cognac brought from his quarters.

"Such an occasion deserves a special indulgence,"

he explained, as they awaited the servant's return. "After all, the cognac took fifty years to ripen."

"Your patience shows admirable improvement," Evita observed dryly.

He carefully uncorked the bottle. "Indeed I'm eager to hear your toast."

"I propose we drink to Barbary justice," she intoned. "Be it swift, sure, and sweet."

Though still uncertain of her drift, Hazar drained his glass.

"And now, if you'll all follow me . . ." Evita said, moving to the door.

Bouvier remained intent on soothing the Nordic girl's fears. Having just been acquired in a deal that sent the Nubian to a plantation, she was understandably confused. The glazed shine in her wide blue eyes suggested she'd been drugged to insure her docility.

The girl swayed awkwardly as they walked through the hall, her limbs wooden. She stumbled and fell heavily to the floor before Bouvier could catch her.

When Hazar paused to help him haul the wench to her feet, Evita whirled angrily.

"Let her be," she ordered. "There's not much time."

As she unbolted the door leading to the cellar, Hazar moved to her side, alerted by the urgent note in her voice.

But it was too late.

A gut-wrenching shriek of raw agony jolted his awareness and he froze, neck hairs bristling. The Nordic girl jerked upright, her narcotic stupor fractured by the frenzied screams.

Then he noticed the self-satisfied pout twisting Evita's features. Her hooded, half-closed eyes and taut smile gave her features a demonic cast as the anguished screeching rose in intensity. She seemed to be enthralled by the sounds, head cocked like a music lover at a concert.

As if to answer his questioning glance, she gestured toward the door. "Your precious bitch sings her farewell aria."

Brain reverberating like a bell tower, Hazar lurched down the stairs, instincts pealing an alarm his reason refused to accept.

All the horrors he'd witnessed during his violent career hadn't prepared him for what awaited him at the bottom of the stairs.

Never had he seen anyone be so brutally maimed and yet survive. Melba's body seemed like a cracked egg impaled by a sharp pencil. Torrents of blood streamed from the yawning wound in her belly, drenching the floor with a gleaming red carpet.

At the same time, his stunned perceptions registered the presence of an animal-like female kneeling inside an open cell while a giant figure loomed over her.

"She'll taste the price of betrayal before she goes free," Evita rasped, voice muffled by Melba's incessant wails.

Her smug tone splashed his senses like ice water.

"You had no right."

Something crossed the corner of his vision and he glimpsed Mustafa moving toward him.

"You forget our wager," Evita said scornfully.

Hazar glared at her. "You won command of a single mission—not my throne."

Before she could reply he'd drawn his sword and was spinning to meet Mustafa's charge.

The massive warrior swung his ax as easily as a toothpick as he shuffled closer, eyes shiny with anticipation. The blood smearing his chest testified to his participation in Melba's torture.

But Hazar was more concerned with Mustafa's grime-encrusted feet. He kept them in focus as he feinted, and leaped back from Mustafa's vicious chop.

The force of the warrior's swing carried a half step too far. He never recovered from that momentary imbalance. The instant he staggered, Hazar lunged, driving his sword under Mustafa's outstretched arm. The blade punctured his thick flesh like an ice pick sliding into butter.

The warrior slowly collapsed, jaw sagging in disbelief as the Barbar chieftan yanked his sword free and in the same motion swung toward Melba. Again his blade darted out and suddenly it was quiet.

Melba slumped forward, head dangling loosely as if bowed in gratitude for her merciful release.

But Hazar didn't linger, moving swiftly to the figure kneeling in the cell. So intent was he on his purpose that he barely noticed the oily red splotches staining Trent's mouth. Nor did he take heed of her struggles as he grasped her wrists with his free hand and dragged her to the stairway.

Evita made an attempt to block his escape until the tip of Hazar's blade nicked her throat.

"You're insane," she shouted, scrambling back to Bouvier's side.

Of all of them, the count seemed the most calm.

"You go too far, my friend," he said regretfully. "Stop and consider the consequences of this day's work. You've broken your solemn word . . ."

"It was you who broke faith," Hazar corrected. "No one usurps the authority of a Barbar chieftan. The woman's death dissolved our pact. From now on, I'll handle this my own way."

"'The black slut betrayed you!" Evita shouted frantically. "Can you deny your tribal code? The only honorable satisfaction for treachery is death!"

"A Barbar warrior takes no honor in the torture of women," he snorted. He lifted Trent like a sack of meal and draped her over his shoulder.

Evita glanced at her husband, but the count made no move to impede the abduction of their precious hostage.

"Hazar, stop . . ." she muttered hoarsely, clawing the air in frustration. "You can't do this to me . . . to yourself . . ."

The only response was the measured tread of his footsteps on the stairs.

She whirled to face Bouvier, green eyes pale with fury. "Don't stand there—we've got to stop him!"

"Do you propose to incite a civil war here in Tingis? That would surely afford El-Kifer an ideal opportunity."

"You can't let him escape with a million dollars in gold."

"The money means nothing."

"I suppose El-Kifer means nothing to you as well."

"On the contrary, my pet. The fact is, he means so much to me that I decided some time ago to insure against just such an emergency."

Evita heaved a long sigh of relief. "Then you'll retrieve the Kiferson wench after all. You had me worried for a moment."

"I'm afraid Lady Trent is beyond our grasp," Bouvier confided with an apologetic smile. "However, she's not necessary any longer."

Exasperation frayed her patience.

"You talk in riddles!" she exclaimed contemptuously. "Like an old fool."

His mild reply was tipped with venom. "Take care, my pet, lest you forfeit the game."

"Forgive me, darling," she said hastily. "It's just that I'm too upset to understand what you mean. Please enlighten me if it's possible."

"Very well, riddle me this. Why pursue the daughter when her mother is close at hand?"

"Why indeed?" Evita reflected, her doubts fading into a slow smile.

CHAPTER TWENTY

Shan had never felt so alone.

The news of Trent's capture seemed to make them all vulnerable, as if some crucial moat had been breached. Indeed, even the familiar nooks and crannies on the Kiferson plantation had assumed sinister dimensions.

With Lord Kiferson and Kevin away, she felt defenseless, despite the small army of guards, servants, and field hands on the estate.

Lady Trevor also seemed apprehensive, although few might notice. She executed her duties of overseer of the large plantation without displaying any emotion. However, Shan could see signs of deep strain in her beloved foster mother.

Pale blue shadows circled her crystal eyes and she spent much of her time in the house, foregoing her daily tours of the estate on horseback. She also became short-tempered when confronted by routine problems.

For this reason Eubert was reluctant to deliver his message.

When the elderly driver reached the estate, he sought out Shan before speaking to her mother.

He found her on the rear veranda, tending to her flowers.

"Beg pardon, Mis' Shan. But there's somethin' I got to ask."

Shan nodded and went on trimming a thick rosebush. "Ask it, by all means."

"Well, you see, I took Charlie and Dickens for a little workout, and broke a wheel on the road. We was halfway to New Orleans so I just kept on goin' to the liv'ry in town."

"You know very well you weren't supposed to leave the estate without Lady Trevor's permission," Shan chided gently. "But I suppose under the circumstances it'll be all right," she added, knowing Eubert's weakness for his prize stallions. Since Trent's departure he hadn't had much opportunity to show them off.

"Thank you, Mis' Shan," he said, after a moment's hesitation.

"You're welcome."

He remained where he was.

"It'll be all right," she repeated, with a reassuring smile. "I'll explain it to Lady Trevor."

Eubert nervously fanned himself with his white top hat. "Well, you see, there's something else."

Her smile faded. "Such as what?"

"Well . . . er . . . Mis' Millicent Devon saw me while I was waitin' in front of the liv'ry. And she give me a note to bring her."

"I can understand why you came to me first," Shan muttered. Her foster mother was quite upset by Julie Devon's sudden friendship with Trent's fiancé. She'd been seen everywhere with Gavin and local gossip hinted that Trent's capture had sullied her virtue.

"Lady Trevor won't be pleased," Shan sighed. "Not even by a courtesy note."

"Er . . . thing is that it's more in the line of a

courtesy *call*. I let slip that Lady Trevor don't leave the house much, and she jumped like a jackrabbit. Didn't hardly say howdy 'for she was writin' out an invite. Mis' Millicent say she drop by come teatime."

Shan put her shears aside, face clouded with worry.

"You do have a serious dilemma."

"Does *deelemon* mean you won't help me explain?"

"It certainly means I won't like it," she declared, moving to the door. "Come along, I'll do my best to ease the blow."

It proved scant protection.

"You had no business being on that road," Lady Kiferson fumed, glaring at the crestfallen driver. "No one is to leave these grounds without my permission."

"Yes'm, that's for sure. I only thought to work the team properlike," Eubert mumbled, avoiding her gaze.

"Two weeks work behind a plow should help you remember to follow orders."

Face stricken, he looked to Shan but she shook her head sadly and turned away.

"That will be all, Eubert," Lady Trevor said crisply. "Report to Mr. Brandt for further instructions."

"Poor Eubie. He'll be desolate without those horses to fuss over," Shan said as he carefully closed the door behind him.

"It's because of his precious stallions that we're forced to suffer Millicent Devon this afternoon," Lady Trevor reminded acidly.

Shan was forced to admit the driver's folly had had dire consequences.

"Perhaps I could convey your excuses."

Lady Trevor crumpled Millicent's note and tossed it into the wastebasket. "That would really give her something to crow about. No, dear, I've got to see the woman to save face—even if it does cost me a pound of flesh."

Millicent Devon drove away from the Kiferson estate with much less than she'd wanted. Lady Trevor had received her graciously, but never once lowered her guard. While careful to avoid mention of her daughter Julie, she made it clear that she considered Gavin Radcliffe's behavior beneath contempt.

In fact, so skillfully did she conduct the conversation that Millicent didn't realize that she'd been insulted until long after she'd left the mansion.

The nerve of that woman, calling Gavin a witless whoremonger, Millicent raged. *What, pray tell, does that make my Julie?*

Her angry question spilled over into speech, causing the driver to turn.

"Beg pardon, Missus?"

"Mind your driving, Walter," she snapped.

"Sorry, missus, thought you spoke."

"Can't you go faster?"

Heeding the contentious edge in her tone, the driver whipped his team into a gallop.

The horses responded well, pulling the enclosed carriage smartly along the empty road.

As well they should, considering the lightness of their load, Millicent observed smugly. It gave her great satisfaction to know the reason why the carriage traveled so swiftly.

Not even Walter knew that little secret, she gloated, rummaging for her cosmetics case.

Not the driver, nor the men guarding Lord Kiferson's estate were aware that the spaces beneath the passenger seats were hollow. Nor were they aware of the fact that both spaces had been occupied when they passed through the gates, and were now empty— their human cargo having slipped out of the carriage while she enjoyed tea with Lady Kiferson.

Millicent barely had time to freshen her rouge and brush her hair before the carriage turned onto the side road leading to Jason's lodge.

Jason Dean was sitting in the main room of the hunting cabin, his boots propped on a table and a whiskey glass balanced on his chest.

"How did it go?" he grunted.

"Just as you said it would. Nobody was the wiser— that cretin Walter didn't even notice the difference in weight."

"Old Moss will be pleased."

"Moss Radcliffe's approval isn't why I'm here," she said with a coy smile. "Are you pleased with me as well?"

He lifted his glass in mock salute.

"Your beauty is pleasure enough for me."

Millicent moved to the couch, fingers tugging at her laced bodice. "I believe there's time to show me the full extent of your gratitude," she whispered.

"Thank God she's come and gone," Lady Trevor said fervently. "Another minute with that vulture and I might have done something unseemly."

"I thought you handled her quite nicely," Shan murmured.

"The ordeal is over, at any rate."

Shan gave her a sympathetic smile. "What would you like for dinner?"

"That woman dulled my appetite, I'm afraid."

"You must try to keep your strength up."

"I'm strong enough for the Millicent Devons of this world."

"We have much more formidable foes these days."

Shan felt a pang of regret when she saw her mother's pinched expression.

"Why don't you rest?" she suggested gently. "I'll fix us both a little snack."

Lady Trevor nodded and sank wearily into an armchair. "That would be nice. It's been a long time since I tasted Barbar food. Kahlil is probably sick of it by now," she added, gazing into space, as if expecting her husband to appear.

Shan was also lost in thought as she walked to the kitchen. The long weeks without any word had worn down her spirit and she knew her mother's suffering was more intense. After all, she had the responsibility of carrying forth Lord Kiferson's domestic and business affairs, despite her personal anguish.

Not many men, and fewer women, could bear such a harsh burden.

Shan's reverie was cut short by a number of odd circumstances.

The heavy silence struck her immediately, as did the fact that the house seemed deserted. At the same time she felt that someone was in the kitchen with her.

A flickering movement crossed her splintered vision and she whirled.

Then she saw two shadowy figures floating toward her, and everything became clear.

But before she could scream the blackness smothered her perceptions.

CHAPTER TWENTY-ONE

The two men had little trouble evading Lady Kiferson's household guards once Millicent Devon smuggled them inside the gates.

They emerged from the secret compartments inside Millicent's carriage and concealed themselves behind the stables. After she departed they began working their way toward the main house, pausing every few yards to make sure they weren't being observed.

Their caution was a mere formality in this case. The few sentries on duty used neither bloodhounds nor torches to aid their intermittent patrols.

The intruders, on the other hand, were professional kidnappers, having trained for their calling with the Congo slavers. When they reached the rear of the house they readied their weapons, but that too was a formality. The kitchen door was unlocked, making it easy to overpower the cook.

One man stood guard at the entrance while the other bolted the rear door, then stored the cook's bound body in the pantry. Although he wasn't quite finished when the housemaid entered the kitchen, his partner required no assistance. Not until leaving the pantry did he realize there was another unconscious hostage to bind, gag, and conceal.

Fortunately he managed to put the maid away in

time for the next arrival. The butler was broad-shouldered and bull-necked, enabling him to absorb the first blow. Too stunned to cry out he lurched forward and nearly avoided the second assailant's club.

Fearing his quick recovery, the two men bound and gagged him securely. Because of his weight, it required both of them to carry the butler's unconscious form into the pantry, exposing them to discovery by another visitor.

Little was known of Kiferson's staff, so they had to rely on chance to carry out the next phase of their mission.

As luck would have it, one of their objectives walked right into their arms. With Kiferson's foster daughter secured, they had only to wait for an hour or so. If Lady Trevor didn't become curious about the whereabouts of her daughter or maid, they would go up after her. Odds were, she'd be alone.

They were correct on both counts. Within thirty minutes Lady Trevor entered the kitchen. Despite their advantage, however, she almost eluded capture. Her reflexes pulled her back the instant she saw the strange figures. She even managed to run halfway to the front stairs before being brought down, kicking and clawing like a tigress. During the brief struggle she started to scream, but it was too late. Mouth stifled and limbs bound, she was hauled to the pantry like the rest.

They paused long enough to pick up Shan and make sure the others were tightly bound. Then they slipped outside, bearing their captives to a dense grove of trees behind the mansion.

There they untied Shan's ankles and helped her stand. "If either of you wenches tries to run we'll make it hard on the other," Shan's warder muttered, passing his long blade before her eyes. "Do you understand now?"

He waited until both women nodded assent, before loosing Lady Trevor's bonds.

She waited to follow Shan into the darkness, dismayed by her captors' confidence and efficiency. They had left two dark cloaks in the grove, which they draped over both of them, to conceal their bound hands and gagged mouths.

They patiently made their way through the gardens to the stables.

Sudden hope skipped through Trevor's heartbeat when she heard voices drifting above the muted shuffle of hooves.

As they crept nearer, she saw a white-clad figure standing near the stalls.

Her first impulse was gratitude when she realized that Eubert had defied orders to stay away from his beloved stallions. But it soon became apparent that had he obeyed, her kidnappers might have been foiled.

One of them remained with the two prisoners while his companion crawled closer to the elderly driver. His approach caused the horses to stamp and wheeze nervously, but Eubert calmed them down instead of taking heed, and was clubbed and trussed before he knew anyone was there.

Although Eubert hadn't unharnessed the team, they were difficult to handle. Both stallions began to kick when the assailant sought to lead them to the carriage.

To expedite the problem, they pushed the carriage closer to the stall, and loaded the two women onto the vehicle. Trevor's captor began to retie her ankles while his partner hitched the team. Both men found their tasks impossible to complete.

The stallions struggled fearfully against the intruder. Their violent bucking shook the carriage, preventing the kidnapper from binding Shan's ankles. He'd scarcely knotted Trevor's bonds, when the stallions reared high, jolting the coach hard enough to toss its occupants about like tenpins.

Cursing, the kidnapper scrambled out to aid his harried companion. In his haste he neglected to latch the door and as the stallions reared again, Shan kicked it open and dropped to the ground.

Her bound hands threw her off balance as the carriage tipped to one side. She pitched forward and rolled wildly, tumbling head over heels into a shallow ditch.

Being intent on subduing the horses, the assailants didn't notice her departure. By the time they did, Shan had twisted free of the unwieldy cloak and crawled deeper into concealment.

While Trevor's captor was able to stop his charge from diving out of the carriage, his frantic search failed to retrieve Shan.

"She's slipped us!" he muttered urgently.

Abruptly he turned, hurried to the stall, and dragged the still-dazed driver outside.

He revived Eubert by drenching him with a bucket of water, then cuffing him sharply. Having gained the old man's attention, he pulled him over to the carriage and showed him the bound female inside.

"Anybody catch us we kill her—then you. Hear that?" He underscored the question by drawing his blade across the driver's throat.

Eubert nodded emphatically, eyes wide.

Satisfied he understood, the kidnapper bent down

and cut the ropes from his hands and feet. He left the gag in place until the driver had the stallions hitched and ready. Then he climbed onto the front seat and pulled Eubert beside him.

Lifting his knife to the old man's ear, he casually slit the gag open. "Now get those blasted nags movin'," he rasped, jabbing the blade into Eubert's ribs.

The stallions responded immediately to his familiar touch. They cantered briskly to the gate, paused briefly while Eubert exchanged a few words with the guards, then broke into a gallop that didn't slacken until they reached their rendezvous.

Despite their swift escape Lady Trevor was hoping against hope that Shan would rouse pursuit in time to run them down. She nurtured the hope until her captors transferred her to a waiting ship, and she felt the long swells of open sea pounding in the darkness.

CHAPTER TWENTY-TWO

Although Count Bouvier was quite pleased with the capture of Kiferson's wife, Evita remained apprehensive.

"She's trouble, I tell you. I can feel it."

"Do you suggest I send her back?" he inquired mildly.

"I suggest we mend our differences with Hazar," Evita declared.

"But *ma chère petite*, it was you who insisted . . ."

"I was mistaken," she said flatly.

"Then perhaps you're mistaken again," he observed with a patient smile. "What do the cards advise?"

Evita shrugged and looked away. "I don't know. Ever since the Kiferson woman arrived they've been clouded somehow. As if covered by a dark veil."

"Hazar's defection has made you overwrought, my pet."

She glanced at him sharply. "I don't discount that possibility. Nor can I ignore the demands of my senses."

"It must present quite a quandary. However, it doesn't help us trap El-Kifer."

"What if I were to ask you to turn her over to Hazar as a gesture of friendship."

"I would refuse."

"Don't you see? You're being as stubborn as he was. Please, André, don't ignore my warning."

"My dear child, I didn't ignore your warning—that's why I arranged for Lady Trevor's visit. But you admit yourself that you're confused in this matter. After all, you read Hazar's misfortune in the Tarot," Bouvier reminded, taking her hand. "Perhaps his departure has affected you more deeply than you care to admit."

She pulled her hand away. "Hazar is an impetuous fool. But we need him. Listen to me, André. With our forces divided Kiferson will have half an enemy to contend with."

"Or twice as many," Bouvier pointed out. "That's why it's important we strike quickly. Should we fail, Hazar will finish the job. His quarrel is with El-Kifer remember, not with us. Take heart, *ma chère*, he'll come back one day. Where else could he find such a rare combination of devotion and beauty?"

She shrugged off the compliment. "What are your plans, then?"

"Lady Trevor will write a letter to her husband, asking that he come to a certain address in Cape Tarifa, on the Spanish side of the coast. Barbars are hated there, so he'll have to go with only a handful of men. Unlike Hazar, I'm free to operate in Spain."

"That might work," Evita conceded. "If the wench writes the letter. My hypnotic potions will make her hand too unsteady to hold a quill."

Count Bouvier's eyes seemed like distant glaciers.

"When I apply my methods, Lady Kiferson will embrace that pen."

*   *   *

Lady Kiferson proved to be a worthy adversary. Refraining from any hysteria she endured starvation, whipping, lack of sleep, thirst, or threats. All failed to convince her to write the invitation to her husband.

After thirty-six hours, Bouvier was forced to take over the task personally. He was also forced to admit that he relished the encounter.

Face-to-face with the red-haired witch after all these years, Count Bouvier brooded as he descended the stone stairway. *It's fitting that I've been called to perform the exorcism.*

When he entered the deserted dungeon he saw Lady Trevor chained against the wall, her white flesh striped with dark lash marks. As he neared he was struck by the invulnerability of her beauty to the ravages of time and torture. Her chiseled, aristocratic features and supple body retained their youthful vibrance despite almost two days of deprivation.

She still has the firm breasts of a twenty-year-old, Bouvier marveled, nudging her awake with the razor-tipped cane he carried.

She lifted her head, and blinked at him—more curious than afraid.

"It's a pleasure to see you, milady."

At the sound of his voice Lady Trevor's crystal eyes flashed with recognition.

"Flaubert! I should have known . . ."

"How could you? Philippe Flaubert has been dead for twenty years or more," he reminded.

"Because only a swine such as yourself would be capable of such heinous acts."

"Or a swine like the Barbar raider who took you hostage."

Trevor snorted. "A Barbar wouldn't stoop to tor-

turing women—only a coward like Count Philippe
Flaubert!"

Although they were alone, it disturbed him to hear
her contemptuous cry. Count Philippe Flaubert was
still wanted for murder, treason, and piracy in England and America.

"You shouldn't speak so badly about your ex-fiancé,
my dear," Bouvier chided softly.

"That was my father's error, not mine," she spat.
"Thank God I was spared such humiliation!"

"That remains to be seen," Bouvier said, gazing at
her naked body with a small smile. "You certainly
have ripened with age, my dear. It would be a pity to
mar such loveliness for such a trivial request."

She met his gaze without shame or fear. "I don't
consider my husband's death trivial."

"And your own?"

"You wouldn't kill such a precious hostage. Especially with the letter unwritten."

"Your confidence leaves me little choice." He
sighed, casually lifting his cane. The razor tip sliced a
thin red crescent on her ivory breast.

"I don't care what happens to me," she muttered.

"We could start by cutting off a finger, or perhaps a
foot," he speculated. "Then you'd still be able to
write the letter."

She tossed her head back and glared at him.
"You'll have to kill me."

The intensity in her tone assured Bouvier she was
telling the truth.

He thoughtfully tapped his stick against his thigh,
then moved to a large, cloth-draped box standing
nearby.

"This may give you pause to consider," he drawled
affably.

As he pulled away the sailcloth covering, Trevor saw that the object was a large cage, about ten feet square, which was divided in half by a solid slab of metal. One section was empty, and the other housed a dark, squirming mass that resembled a fur-covered jellyfish.

Bouvier twisted a lever at the side of the cage and a small panel in the metal divider slid open. Almost immediately a piece of the jellyfish broke away and slithered through the opening.

Unable to suppress a gasp of horror, Trevor gaped at the plump rat scuttling around the empty cell. The beast was the size of a small dog, with sleek brown fur and pointed fangs. Scenting blood, he stood on his hind legs and leaned against the wire-mesh wall, peering at her with feverish yellow eyes.

Bouvier closed the connecting panel. When he smiled, his triangular face, glittering eyes, and sharp teeth bore a marked similarity to the creature at his feet.

"A few hours with one of my pets might make you eager to comply. If not, we'll allow a few companions to join him. In time they'll either convince—or consume you, milady."

"Better they eat my flesh than allow it to serve you," Trevor said hoarsely, staring at the rodent.

A faint tremor in her voice betrayed her uncertainty.

The triumph spreading across Bouvier's smile made it clear he'd heard it too. And for the first time, the proud, flame-haired aristocrat shrank back, her shackled limbs sagging with terror.

CHAPTER TWENTY-THREE

The enforced delay after *The Trojan*'s skirmish with Shareef Hazar gave Kevin an opportunity to extend his education.

He'd passed his first test as a Barbar warrior, having been aboard the vessel struck during the battle. Slightly wounded by a chip of shrapnel, Kevin managed to pull one crewman free of a burning mast that had him pinned to the deck.

Kevin's quick action prevented the man's death, earning him the respect of the entire tribe. Most impressed were the young women, who vied for his attention with unabashed enthusiasm.

He learned how Barbar maids nursed a wounded warrior, and found Aja especially eager to provide lessons. She taught him the phrases of endearment, and age-old customs of courtship, as well as some delightfully original variations.

After a week of Aja's fascinating tutelage, Kevin began to entertain the notion of granting the sloe-eyed beauty permanent tenure.

His friend Gediz advised him to wait a bit longer.

"Girls, like cream," he declared, "get sour after few months."

"Not Aja, she's too sweet," Kevin said dreamily, gazing across the sun-speckled bay.

"Got you churned up good."

Before Kevin could object, he glimpsed a small white speck on the horizon.

"It's the courier ship," he said breathlessly. "Maybe there's news of my sister."

Gediz sat cross-legged on the rocky ledge, calmly puffing on his long pipe as the speck expanded like a tiny balloon.

Abruptly, he tossed the pipe aside and sprang to his feet. "Not message ship," he grunted. "Too big."

Though hampered by his wounded leg, Kevin was only a few steps behind the Barbar seaman as he raced down the steep path.

The villagers responded immediately to their alarm—women herded the children to safety, while the men took up battle positions.

Two vessels were dispatched to guard the entrance to the bay, fanning out on either side of the barrier reef.

The warriors' vigilance relaxed once it was confirmed that only a single small craft approached, it being impossible for a large vessel to penetrate their natural defenses. They waited while the ship paused outside the jagged rocks rimming the bay's mouth, and lowered a boat.

A few minutes later they abandoned their stations and hurried to the pier.

Despite her exhaustion, Shan's emotions were stirred by the familiar cries that greeted her arrival.

However, the shouting ebbed when she stepped on shore—stifled by her worn, somber face and funereal demeanor. The tribesmen moved aside to let Shan pass, silently contemplating the reason for her unexpected return to her birthplace.

El-Kifer knew why she'd come the moment he saw her. "Something's happened to your mother," he exclaimed, grasping her shoulders. "Is she all right?"

Shan stared at him. "I don't know. They captured her a week after you left. I escaped somehow," she added woodenly.

"Where is she?"

"Last news I heard before sailing was that she'd been taken aboard a slave ship."

His fingers tightened. "Then they weren't Barbars."

"Two white men," Shan muttered. "I didn't have much time for observation."

Relaxing his grip, he guided her toward the ramp leading to his blue-domed castle. "You must be tired, my daughter," he said gently. "We'll discuss this in detail after you've had a hot bath and some strong herb tea."

Although Shan had managed to elude her captors, it took her a long time to make her way to the gate and alert the guards.

Leaving the others to form a posse, she hitched up the buckboard and raced to New Orleans for help. She wisely sought out Judge Paxton, who immediately ordered roadblocks on all major arteries and dispatched a county-wide dragnet for Lady Trevor's abductors.

The effort failed to uncover the kidnappers but it did prevent Eubert's death—and in doing so, provided the only clue to Lady Trevor's fate. A search party found her coach wandering on a back road, with the driver unconscious, blood soaking through the crude bandage binding his knife wound.

The searchers rushed him to an infirmary, then contacted Judge Paxton. Moments after receiving their message, he was driving to meet them, with Shan at his side.

"I jes' play possum," Eubert confided proudly, as the doctor stitched the wide gash beneath his ribs. "The first time he stab me I drop off the coach and lay still. I don't move a hair—even when he kick me."

He winced as the needle lanced his torn flesh and sucked eagerly at a half-consumed bottle of bourbon. "Yessir, I don't move a hair," he repeated, smacking his lips.

"Yes. We understand," Judge Paxton said patiently. "Can you recall what happened to Lady Kiferson?"

"Like I said, I lay real still. Didn't see nothin' but dirt for a spell. Then I heard 'em movin' off and I open my eye a crack. That's when I see they left the horses by theyselves, so I start crawlin' over to the coach."

Shan wrung her hands nervously as the elderly driver took another swig of bourbon.

"It was pretty dark out there," he continued, wiping his mouth, "so nobody see me 'cept Charlie and Dickens—and they stay quiet while I climb up and grab the reins. Once I holler, though, they snap up and start to fly . . ."

He lifted his bottle in salute. "Ain't nobody can catch them boys once they in the wind."

"Forget that and tell us about my mother," Shan said sharply.

"Surely, Missy. I was just comin' to that part. Like I say, when I get atop the coach, I see they's a ship drawin' shore, and them two is waitin' with Lady Kiferson. That's when I give my boys the boot."

Eubert leaned on the pillow, as the doctor swabbed

the sutured wound. "I must've passed out 'round then. Can't recall what happened till they found me. But like I say, ain't nobody catch them boys once they . . ."

"Damn your horses!" Shan exclaimed. "What kind of ship was it? Sailing vessel—paddlewheel . . . Think, man, we're wasting time!"

Both doctor and patient blinked at her in surprise.

"Uh, well, Missy . . ." Eubert drawled. "You know I ain't no sailor man. But I do seem to recall strongly, it was a slaver—like the one brought me."

Judge Paxton sent a few marshals to cover the docks, but Shan knew further search was useless.

"I must warn my father," she said crisply. "Help me arrange passage."

"But, my dear, we don't know where he is."

Shan's gaze didn't waver. "I know where to find him. Just get me a ship."

On her insistence, Judge Paxton drove to Lord Kiferson's business office to make the arrangements. Unfortunately, the office manager had gone home for the day.

"It's past office hours," the clerk explained. "I'm only here because we've got a ship sailing to Valencia with the tide."

"Spain—that's perfect," Shan declared. "All they need make is a slight detour."

The clerk seemed horrified by the suggestion. "Oh no, I'm sure that's out of the question."

Shan glanced at him coldly. "Please inform this gentleman of my identity."

"Miss Kiferson has the full authority of her father," Judge Paxton assured.

"Mr. Timwell is the office manager," the young

man said firmly. "He has sole authority to issue shipping orders."

"Well get him then," Shan snapped.

The clerk frantically looked to Paxton for help.

"I'm sorry, sir . . . I don't know where he lives. And it's urgent I complete this manifest."

"You dare tell me what's urgent?" Shan exploded. "My mother has been kidnapped, you idiot. Nothing is more urgent than my sailing on that ship, do you understand?"

He looked at Paxton questioningly. "Kidnapped?"

The Judge nodded grimly. "We believe she was taken aboard a slaver. I'm sure there's no need to tell you Mr. . . . ."

"Er . . . Gaines, Malcolm Gaines," the young man blurted.

"Well Mr. Gaines, I'm sure you appreciate why it's imperative we contact Lord Kiferson. And why this must go no further than this room."

"Depend on my discretion, sir. I've never discussed Lady Trent's capture with outsiders," Gaines confided earnestly.

"Then I put it to you as a gentleman, Mr. Gaines. Surely you're well enough acquainted with official procedure to prepare shipping orders."

"I can write up the papers, of course. But they're not official without Mr. Timwell's seal."

"And where is Mr. Timwell's seal?"

The young man glanced around the office as if searching for an exit. Then he squared his shoulders and met Paxton's steely gaze.

"The top drawer of his desk," he said in a strained voice.

Shan grasped his hand. "Then you'll help me reach my father?"

"I'll do my best," he mumbled, skin flushing with confusion.

His uncertainty remained evident as he drew up Shan's orders, and he paused every few moments as if wrestling with his conscience. Finally he fetched Mr. Timwell's seal and carefully dipped a stick of blue wax into the candle flame.

"That makes it official," he sighed, pressing the seal into the soft wax. "At approximately 0100 the ship *Indigo* sails for Valencia with two passengers."

"You're mistaken sir," Paxton said hastily. "I'm not sailing with Miss Kiferson."

"No sir, I am," Gaines explained, with a sheepish grin. "Mr. Timwell made it quite clear that if I ever issued shipping orders again I would be discharged—no matter how extenuating the circumstance. So you see, I have no choice but to plead my case to Lord Kiferson."

The master of the *Indigo*, proved to be as inflexible as Mr. Timwell. Although the orders gave Shan authority to alter the ship's route, Captain Bundy refused to honor her request.

"It's out of the question," he grumbled, gnawing furiously at his pipe. "Safi is a Barbar port. We'd be hacked to pieces before we weighed anchor."

"Safi is a free port," Shan corrected. "Trade ships come and go from there every day."

"Slave ships, maybe. Not honest merchant vessels, like the *Indigo*. Sorry, m'am, I'm bringing this ship to Valencia as originally ordered."

"You forget my father owns this ship."

"That he does—but while this ship is at sea my word is law." Bundy declared, jabbing the air with his pipe. "That will be all, madam."

The captain was exaggerating the extent of his

power. After coming so far, nothing could deter Shan from her goal.

"If only I had a gun," she fumed, relating the incident to Malcolm.

"That's easy enough," he said, reaching under his shirt. "Judge Paxton kindly presented me with a bon voyage gift."

Shan studied the double-barreled pistol for a moment.

"We're indeed blessed by providence."

"To be sure," he snorted, taking her remark in jest. "All we lack is musket and cannon."

Shan gingerly lifted the gun. "Only one man's word rules this ship," she reminded, aiming at an imaginary foe.

Malcolm's objections were easily overcome.

More difficult was finding an opportunity to execute her plan. Captain Bundy was rarely alone and never received visitors in his cabin.

Again, it was Shan who hit on a solution. She cornered Captain Bundy on the bridge and requested his advice on a serious personal matter.

"I want to get married," she confided. "To Mr. Gaines."

"I suppose it can be arranged," he grunted. "Now if you'll excuse me . . ."

"It may present a problem," Shan said, lowering her voice.

He glared at her suspiciously.

"What sort of problem?"

"I'm pregnant."

"Then marriage is the proper solution to your problem," he assured, suddenly preoccupied with cleaning his pipe.

"The problem is that Mr. Gaines refuses to accept that solution."

"He won't marry you, eh?" Bundy growled indignantly. "Come with me. I'll see to it that he honors his obligations aboard my ship."

Captain Bundy remained in conference for the rest of the afternoon. Finally he called the first mate to his cabin.

The mate was surprised to find Captain Bundy in an armchair, swaddled by blankets, while Malcolm sat behind a nearby desk, puffing a cigar.

He was even more astonished by Bundy's statement.

"Due to my sudden illness, I'll be confined to quarters until we reach port," he said tersely, mouth pressed in a disgusted scowl. "Until then Mr. Gaines will convey my orders. Is that clear?"

It wasn't at all clear, but the mate knew better than to ask questions. "Aye, aye, sir," he replied, coming to attention. "I'll inform the crew."

Malcolm removed the cigar from his mouth and gestured at the sailor. "While you're at it, inform the helmsman to change our heading to ten degrees east by southeast."

The mate glanced at Bundy. "That will take us near the Barbary Coast."

"I'm well aware of that, mister," the captain barked. "Do you have some objection?"

"Ten degrees east by southeast," the mate repeated, backing hurriedly toward the door.

When he had departed, Shan emerged from the curtain just behind his chair, and brandished the pistol.

"You were wise to follow orders so well," she commended. "One false word and I would have blown your head off."

Bundy gave her a contemptuous glare as she adjusted the blanket around his tightly bound limbs. He didn't bother to tell her that being shot was far less of a threat than the fear that someone would discover he'd been outwitted by a woman.

CHAPTER TWENTY-FOUR

"On reaching Safi, we gave the entire crew liberty," Shan explained. "Then Malcolm stood guard over the captain while I went ashore. It didn't take long to round up a Barbar crew. We left Bundy behind with the others, and set sail to find you."

El-Kifer smiled. "You did well, my daughter. Even to maintaining the secrecy of our tribal stronghold."

Shan shrugged off the compliment. "What plan do you have for Mother's rescue?"

"Until we know where she is, there's nothing we can do but wait."

She looked away, disappointed by the answer. Her disappointment swelled to frustration as the days passed without progress. She took advantage of the idle time to reestablish her ties with the Barbar tribe, but even that proved fruitless. Although she'd been born in the secluded coastal village, Shan realized the years in America had made her a stranger.

Indeed, young Kevin seemed more at home among the fierce tribesmen than she did.

While loath to admit it, even to herself, he had matured considerably since leaving New Orleans. No longer shy, or awkward, Kevin carried himself with the calm, self-assured dignity of a Barbar prince.

She was vaguely disturbed to find he'd also outgrown his boyish crush on his stepsister. The realization that quite a number of young ladies now basked in the glow of his affections added to her discomfort.

Kevin thrived on the attentions lavished on him by the adoring maids, displaying a marked affinity for Barbar mating customs.

She pretended to be indifferent to his amorous liaisons until it became clear that he'd become particularly attached to a certain maid, Gyn.

For this reason she found a number of excuses to be alone with him.

"Perhaps you can advise me on a private matter," she suggested during a family lunch.

"Of course. What sort of matter?"

She glanced around the crowded table. "If we discussed it here it would no longer be private."

She took him to a sheltered garden hidden below the cliffs that protected the Barbar village.

"I've spent a lot of time up here, but I've never sighted this place."

"What do you do up here that's so fascinating?" Shan inquired, settling down on a moss-cushioned rock.

"Just think, look out at the sea, dream a bit . . . Nothing more exciting than that."

The sun was balanced on the rim of the horizon, and its rays tinted Kevin's long sea-bleached hair and golden eyes with a coppery aura. For a moment he looked like his father, then he turned and his bronzed features became those of another person—someone Shan didn't know.

"You said you needed some advice," he reminded with a bemused smile.

The smile was all too familiar.

"What's so strange about that?" she demanded.

"Since you never valued my advice before, I'm merely curious," he said mildly.

"You were never a Barbar before."

He shrugged, as if conceding the point. "How can I help you?"

Shan's violet eyes wavered. She picked up some flowered strings of moss and began braiding them, in the way Barbar women did when they pondered serious matters.

"While you were away, a gentlemen asked me to marry him."

"Do I know him?"

"I don't believe so," she said coolly, dismayed by his casual response.

"Why is his proposal a problem?"

"He doesn't know of my Barbar heritage," she said.

Kevin acknowledged the dilemma with a wry smile. "Until he does, there's no problem."

"You mean I shouldn't tell him?"

"I mean you don't know how he'll react until you tell him," he said firmly. "Don't sell him short before testing his true worth. Surely no man—or woman—is worth marrying who's more concerned with the past than your future together," he added, taking her hand.

She let his fingers linger, then slowly drew her hand away. "There's something else—you see, this gentleman is quite a bit older than I am."

"By how much?"

"At least twenty years," she ventured, intent on his reaction.

He pursed his lips thoughtfully. "That would make your friend about forty-five. Seems suitable enough."

"I'm not yet twenty-five," Shan reminded. "But no

matter, in fifteen years I'll be in my prime, but he'll be at the threshold of old age."

Kevin smiled at her. "If you love him, there'll be no problem with the gap in years."

"Can you be sure he'll love me?"

"I'm sure you wouldn't have a fool for a husband," he grunted, glancing away. "How could any man ignore such fortune in his declining years?"

"Would he be so fortunate in his youth?"

Kevin looked up, gold-flecked eyes gazing into hers. "Even more fortunate for the added time to spend with you," he murmured.

Shan responded shyly, when his lips brushed her mouth. While she'd invented her mythical suitor to probe Kevin's feelings, she wasn't prepared for the violent surge of her own emotions. But as she yielded to his kiss, the crack of gunfire rattled across the cliffs.

Even as she sighted the black shape outlined against the waning sun, Kevin was scrambling toward the path.

When they reached the village, the first ships were putting out to sea to head off the intruder. A small group of tribesmen, headed by El-Kifer, stood on the rocks above the bay watching the alien vessel approach.

The black-sailed ship paused while some distance away, and contacted the two reconnaissance vessels. In a short time it proceeded slowly toward the barrier reef, under close escort.

That it was a Barbar vessel became clear as the craft neared. Why it had come was another question.

El-Kifer had boarded his own ship by the time the vessel sluiced past the barrier reef and entered the placid bay.

Cautiously pinning the strange craft between the

reefs and his cannon, the Barbar chieftain waited while two men lowered a small boat and began rowing to shore.

"No wonder they negotiated the rocks so easily," El-Kifer remarked as a white-haired man waved from the rowboat.

"Why, it's Akmad," Kevin exclaimed, recognizing the elder statesman of a neighboring tribe. The patriarch had made a diplomatic visit when they first arrived. "No doubt he's come to pay his respects to Shan," the youth speculated, glancing at his father.

El-Kifer kept his narrowed eyes fixed on the boat pulling alongside his ship. "Judging from Akmad's choice of companion, this isn't a courtesy call."

"Who is he with?"

"I've never met the man. But if the descriptions I've gathered are accurate, Akmad's guest is Shareef Hazar—the jackal who kidnapped your sister."

CHAPTER TWENTY-FIVE

After ending Melba's agony with a merciful stroke of his sword, Hazar dragged Trent out of the dungeon. Pausing only to swing her limp body over his shoulder, he hurried through the hall, blade ready to strike down anyone who tried to prevent his escape.

Surprisingly, Evita didn't call for help, and he left the house without encountering any guards. Hashib and a few crewmen were quartered near the stables, enabling him to enlist their help. Within minutes they had spirited Lady Trent from Bouvier's fortresslike estate, and were galloping toward their ship.

The Mercury's speed took them out of range of any possible pursuit, but Hazar didn't shorten sail until they neared the Canaries.

He dropped anchor in a deserted inlet, then took stock of his crew and stores.

Of sixty-one warriors aboard the clipper, eighteen were in Bouvier's pay. Another hundred-odd members of Hazar's tribe were still in Tingis, along with both of his gunships. *The Mercury* had plenty of food in the hold but only enough powder to fire six salvos from their twenty-one cannons.

Unfortunately, his resources proved more abundant than his options.

As a Barbar he was fair game for the Spaniards; as

El-Kifer's enemy he was an outlaw to the tribes on the Barbar Coast; and by breaking his pact with the Countess Bouvier he'd lost his stronghold in Tingis, along with a powerful ally.

Though he still had access to Safi, the slave port just south of Tingis, so did El-Kifer. The port was more difficult to defend, and lacked the support of Count Bouvier's private troops which left Hazar only three alternatives.

He could turn over his hostage and use the ransom to finance his vendetta or simply return Lady Trent to Evita and beg forgiveness, or launch an immediate attack on El-Kifer.

The first and second offended his sense of honor, but the last choice defied all reason. *Without supplies or sanctuary I'll be courting certain disaster,* Hazar brooded, pacing the moon-glazed deck. *I can't sacrifice my warriors for the sake of pride. My sacred trust as their tribal chieftain is more precious than my personal honor. The safest, most profitable course is to exchange Lady Trent for the gold.* And yet it seemed an admission of defeat. As long as he held her hostage, El-Kifer was helpless. His daughter was their safest shield right now.

How long we can afford the luxury remains to be seen, Hazar speculated. *My tribesmen are depending on that prize to feed their children, while I quibble over my pride.*

But even this harsh admission masked a deeper, more devastating truth.

He didn't want to lose her.

Neither his vow, nor Melba's recent, tragic death could smother the animal hunger she aroused.

However, Lady Trent made no pretense of her own feelings.

"May God curse your soul as a cowardly murderer," she ranted, as he entered her cabin. "You loathsome Barbar scum!"

"I'm pleased to see you're in good health."

"I'll never feel in full spirits until you are dead," she spat vehemently.

He arched his brows in mock surprise. "Even after I rescued you from Countess Evita?"

"You lie as easily as taking a breath. *You're* the one responsible for my imprisonment. I saw you butcher Melba with my own eyes. It's something not easily forgotten."

"You know not what you see," he sighed.

"I know you for a killer of helpless women."

"But do you know who you are?" he replied, offering her a glass.

She struck the glass from his hand, spraying wine over them both. "There's your answer, Barbar pig."

Instinctively Hazar cuffed her, sending her back a few paces. Regret evaporated his rage, when he realized she'd always hate him for his act of mercy.

Does she think I enjoyed killing a woman who loved me so well? he reflected bitterly.

The answer to his question was painfully evident. Lady Trent's crystal eyes blazed with contempt and her jaw was clenched defiantly as she crouched on the floor, flame-ribboned hair tangled around her chiseled features.

Then his regrets were swept aside by a rage of desire. He moved close and grabbed her wrists, pulling her erect.

She kicked and clawed relentlessly as he pressed his mouth against her neck, then suddenly went limp. Her body sagged like a stringless puppet, yielding completely to his will. Only her eyes remained ani-

mated, dancing with hatred as he caressed her unresisting flesh.

Passion drained by the emptiness of his conquest,
Hazar let the lifeless figure slip from his grasp and
stepped back. He gazed at her intently before he
turned away and strode to the door.

By the time he reached the bridge he'd come to a
decision.

"We're weighing anchor," he announced curtly.
"Chart a course for Essouira."

Hashib squinted at him. "Essouira belongs to El-
Kifer's tribe. They're too many for us."

"Don't worry, my friend," Hazar muttered. "Only
one of us will fight this battle."

The Mercury's appearance caused an immediate sen-
sation in the Barbar village. A fleet of gunships sailed
out to meet their visitors, weapons ready despite the
large white flag flying from the clipper's mast.

Indeed, the gunships blocked the clipper's path until their leader took a small force of warriors aboard
the strange vessel.

"Why do you come here?" Akmad barked, when he
saw Hazar. "We have nothing to discuss with the enemy of El-Kifer."

"I've come to claim my right as a Barbar prince,"
Hazar replied calmly.

Akmad shrugged. "Your title died with your father."

"Then I've come to reclaim my birthright."

"What charter do you offer?" the white-haired patriarch demanded, his sword sweeping toward Hazar's
crewmen. "The loyalty of these thieves and va-
grants?"

"These men are Barbar warriors," Hazar said

coldly. "And their charter is beyond question. But with your permission I'll give you something more tangible."

Akmad nodded, but warily kept his blade cocked as the black-clad renegade strolled across the deck.

Hazar found Lady Trent stretched out on the bed when he entered. Without a word he lifted her up and carried her outside.

Trent gaped at the armed savages surrounding crew and ship with a dazed, disbelieving expression.

"Here is my charter," Hazar said, roughly setting the ivory-skinned girl down, as one might exhibit a chicken to a suspicious customer. "I offer El-Kifer's daughter to substantiate my claim."

Akmad's occasional grunts punctuated the silence as he inspected the merchandise. After a few moments he dropped to one knee and kissed her hand.

"Child of El-Kifer, welcome," the white-haired chieftain rasped.

Trent was almost as startled by his halting English as his unexpected gesture.

"Don't touch me, you filthy Barbar cur," she exclaimed, snatching her hand away.

She whirled to face Hazar. "What is this old fool talking about?"

"Take care, milady. Even Akmad's loyalty to your father has limits."

"You talk in riddles. What can this wizened savage possibly have in common with my father?"

"Blood, for one," Hazar murmured, eyes glinting like black diamonds. His cool, steady gaze cracked Trent's confidence and she glanced at the scowling patriarch.

"You're all insane," she whispered hoarsely.

Hazar shook his head. "It's *you* who have lost touch with reality," he corrected with a wry smile.

"Your father, the eminent Lord Kiferson, is known to these tribesmen as El-Kifer, king of the Barbar nation. Which means that you too are a Barbar savage, milady—and blood heir to our tribal code."

CHAPTER TWENTY-SIX

"Shareef Hazar invokes his right of charter as a Barbar prince," the wizened patriarch intoned after exchanging salutations with El-Kifer. "He has petitioned my intercession as his witness."

Kahlil stared at Akmad, ignoring the black-garbed figure standing alone at the edge of the dock. "Who credits his claim?"

"Your daughter."

His terse reply shook the powerful chieftain's composure. "Where is she?" he rumbled, squinting at Hazar.

"She is well," Akmad assured hastily. "She will remain aboard our ship until this matter is settled."

Kahlil's fingers slowly released the hilt of his sword. "So be it. I abide by your judgment."

"Thank you, my brother," Akmad said with a slight bow. "Do you consent to be bound by Shareef Hazar's challenge, under the ancient law?"

"I do."

"Then so be it. Let it be known that Shareef Hazar petitions for his right according to the code. He hereby challenges El-Kifer, king of the Barbar tribes, to a trial by combat—and offers as charter his hostage, his ships, and his birthright as son of Ben Rashad."

As the white-haired patriarch completed the announcement, Kahlil finally understood why Hazar was waging his guerilla campaign.

Kahlil had overcome Ben Rashad's massed troops in much the same fashion years ago.

And no doubt for the same reason, he speculated grimly. *To avenge his father's death during that bloody struggle.*

"What is my forfeit?" Kahlil inquired aloud.

"The price of your daughter's ransom, and your crown."

"So be it."

Having accepted the terms, all that remained to discuss were the weapons.

"As challenged party, yours is the choice," the old man declared.

Kahlil glanced at Hazar, mouth pressed in a tight frown.

"Let it be cold steel."

"What are they talking about?" Kevin demanded, as a hushed murmur rippled through the crowd.

Shan leaned closer. "Shareef Hazar has demanded a trial of combat. If he loses, Trent will go free and his warriors will swear allegiance to El-Kifer. If he wins, your father forfeits the ransom money, and his crown," she explained breathlessly, violet eyes clouded with apprehension. "Should he defeat El-Kifer in a death duel with Barbar daggers, Hazar will become our king."

Marrow chilled by the thought, Shan gripped his hand tightly for comfort. She was further depressed to find that Kevin scarcely noticed her touch.

Like all the other tribesmen, he was intent on Akmad's preparations for the ritual contest. After inspecting each man's blade and person for concealed devices, the patriarch carefully bound their left wrists to a thong, perhaps three yards in length.

"Objection!"

The spectators strained to see who'd interrupted the ceremony.

"Objection, I say!"

At the second cry the crowd parted, allowing the petitioner to approach Akmad.

"It's your friend, Gediz. . . ." Shan hissed, watching the muscular youth stride forward.

Akmad's wrinkled features pursed as if scenting an unpleasant odor. "What is *your* objection?"

"Simply this. *When* El-Kifer wins"—Gediz paused for emphasis—"only Hazar's life is forfeited. Yet his warriors depart with the secret of El-Kifer's stronghold. Who can say they won't use it for vengeance one day?" he asked, sweeping an accusing finger toward the strange Barbar ship.

A muted buzz of assent stirred the crowd, until Akmad lifted his hands for silence.

"There is only one member of Hazar's tribe aboard my ship," he said firmly. "The rest remain in Essouira, with *The Trojan.*"

"Cannot *one* take advantage?" Gediz persisted.

Unable to deny the loud reaction provoked by his logic, Akmad halted the proceedings while a boat was sent to fetch Hazar's aide.

If anything, Hashib's enforced presence seemed to bolster the challenger's will. Hazar flashed his tribal brother a brief grin as Akmad secured the knot on his wrist.

The rules of combat were simple.

The battle area was a large clearing bounded by the pier on the west, and a sheer cliff on the north, while spectators walled off the remaining two sides.

Both combatants were armed with daggers, and bound together by a long, braided thong. Akmad waited until the thong was stretched tight between them, before giving the signal to begin.

Then the old man nimbly moved to the sidelines, his function completed. The duel would end automatically, when one of the two men was dead.

The spectacle seemed oddly dreamlike to Kevin.

The setting sun washed the sky with crimson tints which dimmed the flickering torches at the edge of the clearing. Within minutes, however, the flames bloomed against the darkness, casting shadows across the looming rocks.

The two men circled each other slowly, blades glinting in the torchlight. Although El-Kifer was taller and more powerful, Hazar had the quickness of a hummingbird. The dark, slender figure darted from side to side dodging, feinting, and thrusting his knife with blurred rapidity. His golden-maned foe parried with equal swiftness, large frame perfectly balanced.

He stalked his leaner opponent patiently, unblinking gold eyes fixed on Hazar's dagger.

The renegade exhibited similar caution, gaze nailed to El-Kifer's fist. Abruptly Hazar leaped back, his free hand jerking at the thong.

Momentarily jostled off stride, Kahlil swung his body around, spinning back in time, to slash Hazar's exposed forearm. The sharp blade hooked through his sleeve, and dug into his skin, staining the black silk with the duel's first blood.

It was far from the last, however, as Hazar dipped under his thrust and countered with a lightning jab that punctured Kahlil's side. While minor, the wound magnified the need for caution.

Kahlil kept the thong between them taut, and his

blade cocked defensively, while Hazar constantly shifted direction, staying well out of striking range. When Kahlil lunged, the renegade danced away, narrowly avoiding a severed jugular. A moment later Kahlil stumbled and Hazar leaped forward.

Hazar attacked with incredible speed, feet barely skimming the ground as he swooped down for the kill. Even more amazing was his abrupt recovery in mid-stride when he realized he'd been tricked. As El-Kifer sprang, Hazar was already scrambling back to safety. At the same time he yanked desperately at the thong binding him to the blond-maned chieftain.

His explosive reflexes transformed certain disaster into near victory.

The watching tribesmen uttered a low moan of warning as El-Kifer stumbled forward. Kevin sucked in his breath when he saw his father dodge Hazar's slash only to become entangled in the thong. El-Kifer fell heavily, head jerked back by the braided leather noose twisted around his throat. Then he sprawled forward on his face, giving Hazar a perfect target for his blade.

The renegade crouched beside his fallen foe, arm cocked to strike the final blow.

A collective sigh rippled through the silence as Hazar slowly stepped away, allowing El-Kifer to free himself.

"I do not kill my enemies from the back," the black-garbed renegade declared. "Nor will I throttle an opponent in a knife duel. So do I honor my father's name, and my sacred birthright as a Barbar chieftain."

"You honor your own name as well," El-Kifer observed as he regained his footing. The two men moved into starting position, and when the thong was again stretched between them, began to circle.

El-Kifer feinted left, then dipped his shoulder to the right.

This time Hazar's snake-swift reflexes worked against his purpose, causing him to lunge too quickly.

The instinctive reaction left his flank exposed to El-Kifer's thrust.

But even off-balance, Hazar somehow managed to parry the thrust with his arm. It merely postponed the inevitable however, since he couldn't completely avoid El-Kifer's blade.

The force of the thrust sliced a deep gash in Hazar's bicep, causing him to drop his weapon.

He staggered back, hands raised to ward off another blow, but it never came.

El-Kifer stepped back and gestured toward the fallen dagger. "I do not kill a defenseless man," he said softly.

He waited while Hazar picked up his knife and readied himself before resuming their deadly combat.

It was no contest. Hazar's wound hampered his ability to raise his arm and his fingers were too greasy with blood to grip the dagger.

With a blurred movement El-Kifer yanked at the thong, tripped his opponent, and sprang, pinning Hazar's wounded arm with one knee, while digging the point of his blade into the renegade's throat.

"One last bargain," El-Kifer muttered. "Your life as ransom for my wife. Yield man—or die!"

"Since I know nothing of your wife, you'd best kill me."

"If you don't value your own hide, heed that your brother's life is also forfeited."

El-Kifer punctuated the reminder with his dagger.

"The man you want is Count Bouvier. That much should ransom my friend," Hazar added, teeth clenched in pain.

"Lead me to this Bouvier and you both live."

Shareef Hazar calmly met his gaze. "You ask me to betray my father?"

"Your father is dead. And so are you unless you choose. You've gambled and lost. There's no profit—or honor—in refusing a fresh deck."

Hazar looked away. "The ante's too high. You betrayed my father. That's a debt I can't forgive."

"I attacked Ben Rashad," the golden-eyed chieftain admitted, "but I did not betray him. He died through the fortunes of war. Instead, you squander your life for an empty pot."

"Can you prove what you say?"

"If I'm lying, would I want you alive to find me out?"

The soft-spoken question penetrated Hazar's hostility. "I've no reason to protect Bouvier," he conceded. "I can lead you to his stronghold in Tingis. But I can't guarantee your wife will be there."

"Fair enough," El-Kifer grunted, retracting his blade.

"Mark this well before sheathing your dagger," Hazar declared, eyes like ebony barbs. "Should I find you've lied about my father's death, I'll not rest until he's avenged."

El-Kifer stood up and slipped his knife into the scabbard at his waist. "I'll take that risk."

The bronzed chieftain turned to Akmad, who was standing nearby. "And now I claim my right of conquest. Bring my daughter to me."

The white-haired patriarch immediately dispatched

Hashib and one of El-Kifer's warriors to fetch Lady Trent.

As they rowed swiftly to the Barbar ship anchored near the reefs, the waiting tribesmen began jabbering excitedly, anxious for their first glimpse of the Barbar princess.

Their anticipation was shattered by confusion when the pair returned. Hashib leaped onto the dock and flung himself at El-Kifer's feet.

"The responsibility is mine alone. It was *my* duty to stay with her. Kill me, but spare Shareef Hazar . . ."

"The princess is gone," the oarsmen reported breathlessly. "They've taken her off the ship."

El-Kifer glanced sharply at Akmad.

"Do you think I betray you?" the patriarch asked quietly.

"Only a fool enters a lion's cage without the doorkey," El-Kifer observed grimly. "And you're neither a fool nor a traitor."

"Father, look!"

At Kevin's shout the two men cast their gaze past the youth's darting finger.

As they peered through the darkness the clouds veiling the sky parted, and the moon's ivory glare spread like a sudden smile, illuminating the ship far across the water. Having weighed anchor unnoticed, while everyone watched the ritual combat, *The Indigo* was in full flight, its sails bobbing like runaway horses, as it raced toward the silver-capped horizon.

"But who's taken her?" Akmad demanded.

His question was lost among the shouts of the warriors stampeding to their ships.

CHAPTER TWENTY-SEVEN

While Lady Trent needed no more than Melba's vicious murder to prove Hazar was insane, she found it difficult to believe an entire village could be demented.

Yet what else can explain their incredible delusions concerning my parentage? Trent mused, as she brushed her shimmering tresses. *Only a lunatic would insist I'm kin to a tribe of savages. Since these people are little better than beasts they're easily misled,* she concluded, turning her attention to more crucial matters.

The detour to the Canary Isles had skewed her reckoning slightly, but Trent calculated they were somewhere on the northwest coast of Africa, approximately three days sail from Tingis. She was also sure that if she made her way back to Bouvier's villa, the count would grant her sanctuary.

Hazar's violent farewell made it clear that he'd severed relations with the count and his young wife.

No doubt the countess was the real reason for Bouvier's liaison with the Barbar chieftan, Trent speculated. *Maniac and murderer he may be, but there's no denying Hazar's effect on women.*

It was more a confession than an observation.

It shamed Trent to acknowledge the animal lust

aroused by the renegade's touch. *Had he persisted a few moments longer when he visited my cabin, I might have succumbed to his advances,* she admitted bitterly, unable to condone her corrupt weakness. *Whether princess or lady, I'm no better than any common Barbar slut out there.*

Compared to her treatment in Hazar's dungeon, the villagers accorded her royal care, Trent conceded, noting the basket of fruit, bottle of wine, and bowl of flowers that graced her bedside table.

She knew that one of the women would respond immediately to her call, and do her utmost to satisfy the slightest whim.

I hold every privilege of my rank save that of freedom, Trent brooded, as she prepared to retire. *The best way short of a bullet to destroy Hazar is to escape. He'd be denied a million in ransom—and lose much more in reputation.*

Trent recognized the fierce pride of the primitive warriors and knew loss of respect would topple Hazar's rule, more surely than armed troops.

The weeks she'd spent with his Barbar concubines served her in good stead. Her ability to speak their strange tongue, and her mastery with dagger and lash especially impressed the females, and overcame their primitive hostility. Indeed, after a few days Trent began to feel a warm sense of communication with the tribeswomen, who by that time were completely captivated by her vibrant charms. But while moved, Trent sought some way to use their adulation to aid her escape.

Before she found the opportunity, however, Shareef Hazar and the white-haired chieftain called Akmad escorted her to a sleek gunship with black sails. She remained confined to her quarters for the next twenty-four hours while they traveled in a southerly direction along the verdant coastline. Though well-treated during the voyage, Trent sensed an undercurrent of tension girdling the ship.

The feeling intensified when they dropped anchor. Peering through the barred window, Trent saw they'd stopped in a placid, cliff-walled bay. They remained there until dusk, and judging from the hollow silence pervading the vessel most of the crew was ashore.

Her toilette completed, Trent blew out the candles, but as she pulled the brocade coverlet from her bed the flicker of distant fires danced across the darkened cabin.

The ship turned lazily in the breeze, enabling Trent to glimpse the torches dotting the rocks, and the shadowy mass of people gathered along the docks.

She also saw a few crewmen huddled at the rail, watching the proceedings ashore with rapt intensity.

As her eyes adjusted to the gloom, she made out the contours of another ship anchored outside the reefs. Then Trent recognized the galleon and her thoughts soared with hope. It was *The Indigo,* one of the prize merchants in Lord Kiferson's fleet. *Which suggests that my father is here,* Trent speculated, heart booming in the darkness.

At first she merely intended to satisfy her curiosity with a simple ruse.

She knocked loudly on the door until a crewman answered, and demanded some food. Although vexed that he was missing the spectacle on shore, the tribesman hastily complied with her order.

She was waiting at the door when he returned, and asked for a bottle of wine.

The warrior's reluctance was plainly evident in his

disgusted scowl, but Trent had expected him to be annoyed. In fact she'd counted on it.

As she expected, the crewman neglected to lock the door when he went to fetch the wine. He thrust the tray in her hands and hurried off, anxious to rejoin his companions at the rail.

His oversight enabled Trent to get a clear view of her surroundings, including the Kiferson ship.

The Indigo's proximity to the Barbar ship stirred Trent's thoughts. That the few crewmen guarding her were totally preoccupied with the torchlit event on shore ignited a sudden impulse. *If only I can keep him from locking the door,* she reflected, taking the handkerchief from her sleeve. She tore the gauzy cloth in half, rolled it into a tight ball, and stuffed it into the bolt socket.

Knowing her only weapon was human nature, Trent waved at the crewman as he neared the cabin.

"Is there any fruit?" she cooed, giving him an apologetic smile.

To her elation, he firmly rejected the notion of a third trip. "No fruit," he muttered. "Boat not come with supplies."

Without waiting for her comment he gave her the bottle, and slammed the door.

As Trent hoped, in his haste to return to the fascinating spectacle, the crewman neglected to use his key.

Normally it made little difference, since a spring bolt automatically secured the lock, but the balled cloth Trent had stuffed in the door socket prevented the bolt from closing.

It was that simple.

Trent slipped outside, and crept to the deserted

stern, climbed over the side with the aid of a rope, then paddled noiselessly toward the reefs.

Though the dark, choppy water afforded excellent concealment, Trent negotiated the channel between the rocks with extreme care, realizing she could easily be dashed against the boulders by the swirling currents.

Once past the reefs, however, she swam swiftly toward *The Indigo*, vowing with each stroke to drown herself, rather than be returned to Shareef Hazar.

Malcolm Gaines felt abandoned. For reasons unknown to him, he wasn't allowed to leave the ship—and was left with a handful of warriors to await Shan's return.

Malcolm had overcome his initial distrust of the fierce tribesmen Shan had recruited in Safi, but not the resentment caused by her indifference. Although his esteem for Lord Kiferson's foster daughter had deepened during the voyage, Shan studiously ignored his devoted attentions.

And yet, despite his unrequited affection for the dark-haired beauty, Malcolm had never felt better. The weeks at sea had trimmed the fat from his sturdy frame and supplanted his sickly office pallor with glowing color. The loss of his paunch made him seem taller, his bronzed skin accentuated his blue eyes and his shaggy sun-bleached hair gave his studious features a romantic flair.

For this reason Lady Trent didn't recognize him immediately.

Indeed, Malcolm also found her sudden appearance quite unsettling. He gaped at the water-soaked creature who'd just emerged from the dark sea like some ivory-skinned mermaid, his mind unable to grasp the evidence of his senses.

"Do you speak English?"

Her brisk tone pulled his scattered thoughts together. Malcolm squared his shoulders and came to attention.

"Certainly, milady. What do you require?"

"You know me?" she demanded.

"Of course, Lady Trent. I'm Malcolm Gaines, your father's, er . . . chief clerk. I sealed your shipping orders on *The Mercury*."

A flicker of surprise crossed Trent's features.

Though only three months had passed since she'd tricked her way aboard the clipper, it seemed more like three lifetimes.

"Who's in charge?" she asked crisply.

Malcolm glanced around the empty deck. "Why, er . . . I suppose I am."

"Then issue orders to weigh anchor immediately. We must get out of here before they find out I've escaped."

"But milady . . . that's impossible."

"I should have known. You're in league with these cutthroats."

"Oh no, you . . . you don't understand . . ." he stammered, stunned by the accusation.

"It's *you* who don't understand!" she exclaimed sharply. "This isn't a blasted counting house, it's a Barbar stronghold. When those savages find out I've escaped, all hell will break loose. I don't know why you're here but I *do* know you'll never see New Orleans if you tarry much longer."

Malcolm opened his mouth to speak, then clamped it shut, frantically trying to comprehend what was happening.

As he stared at Trent's matted hair and streaming wet face he suddenly realized she was naked—or so it seemed to his addled perceptions. For, while clad in a shift, the thin, water-soaked fabric clung to her body like transparent skin, outlining every detail of her ripe flesh.

"While you stand gawking, sir, our lives stand forfeit!" Trent snapped, eyes flashing like metallic whips. "If we're not underway in ten seconds, I'll give the order myself!"

Malcolm blinked and started edging toward the bridge, too mortified to protest. His embarrassment so amplified his confusion that he neglected to mention Shan's presence ashore.

When he finally remembered, it was far too late.

CHAPTER TWENTY-EIGHT

"Wait, damn you! Stop him, somebody . . ."

El-Kifer's cry was trampled beneath the rising babble of tribesmen rushing to their boats. Cursing, he pushed through the mob, golden eyes fixed on Hazar.

Before he could overtake him, however, the black-garbed figure leaped into a small boat and started rowing toward his ship. Despite a wounded arm, the renegade's powerful strokes propelled him through the choppy water as swiftly as a Toledo blade slicing an omelet. Even before reaching the ladder, Hazar was roaring at the crew to haul anchor—and of the six vessels harbored in the bay, his was the first to pursue *The Indigo*.

Indeed, his swiftness brought the chase to an abrupt halt.

"The reefs you blasted fool! Mind the reefs!" El-Kifer bellowed as the renegade nosed his vessel into the narrow channel.

No sooner did his warning fade, when he saw Hazar's ship tilt sharply to one side. Its sails slapped the water, then jerked upward at an awkward angle, reeling and flapping like a drunken albatross.

An instant later he heard the rapid chatter of

cracking timber as the jagged rocks chewed into the hull.

"He should have waited!" the chieftain groaned, pounding the wheel in helpless rage.

Clearly, his anger was justified. By rashly attempting to navigate the reef-strewn passage, without benefit of experience, Hazar had damaged much more than his ship, for now the foundering craft clogged the channel's mouth, smothering all hope of catching *The Indigo*.

The trailing ships were forced to lie idle, while the tribesmen worked to dislodge the wrecked vessel sealing them inside the bay.

The darkness further hampered their efforts and by the time the channel was reopened, dawn's crimson wings were spreading across the sky.

Hazar waited aboard El-Kifer's gunship, pacing the deck like a caged panther.

"Why are they still raking debris?" he demanded. "There's sufficient clearance right now. Let's be underway, before the tide ebbs."

"Since your miscalculation has already prompted one delay, your instincts must defer to proven experience," El-Kifer observed calmly.

Stung by his curt rejoinder, Hazar brooded in silence until the lion-maned chieftain eased his craft past the reefs and swung the prow west.

"It's Tingis she's bound for, not the bloody Canaries," the renegade blurted impatiently. "Head it northwest, before we lose them completely."

"You seem quite confident of their destination."

Hazar failed to note his probing air, being too preoccupied with setting their course.

"I know how the bitch thinks," he declared, scowling at the sun-laced horizon. "She headed straight back to Bouvier."

"How do you presume to know my daughter so well?"

This time Hazar caught the chieftain's barbed tone. "Forgive my vulgarity," he murmured, meeting El-Kifer's icy gaze. "But my poor manners have no bearing on my reason. If you want to save your daughter, heed my advice. There's no time to bicker. As soon as she rounds Safi, she'll be beyond anyone's help."

The chieftain arched his pale brows. "Beyond help, you say? This Count Bouvier of yours must be formidable, indeed."

Hazar veiled his annoyance with a wry smile. "Surely you don't think to attack Tingis? A force three times this strength would be cut to pieces. It's not only Bouvier you challenge. Every slaver, pimp, footpad, and pirate in Tingis will join against us. They'll blast us out of the sea before we can run up a white flag."

"I can't decide whether you're a traitor—or a coward," the chieftain replied casually.

Hazar's eyes glinted like ebony crescents above the grim curve of his smile. "It appears I'm dull as well as vulgar. I didn't consider your suspicions in this matter."

"Let's call it a lack of confidence," El-Kifer replied softly.

"Of course I might be forgiven my oversight in light of the circumstances," Hazar continued in a flat, steady, tone. "Truly one would be hard put to believe I came here to deceive you. What could I gain?"

"Vengeance is its own reward," the chieftain reminded.

"True enough," Hazar agreed. "Still I fear you overestimate my humble powers."

"You're too modest, sir."

"Merely realistic, milord. Indeed it would tax Merlin's skills to predict you'd spare my life, if defeated."

El-Kifer shrugged. "You forget your ace-in-the-hole."

"Kindly refresh my memory."

The chieftain stared at him coldly. "You knew I wouldn't kill you so long as my wife was hostage."

"Quite so," Hazar mused, folding his arms. "Put that way, it has a certain logic. All I had to do was pop back and forth to New Orleans within seven days' time. While the clipper you graciously donated to my cause is a remarkable craft, it still requires at least two weeks to make the trip. And *that*, I may add, is six days better than the world record."

"A hired accomplice could give you all the time you needed."

Hazar shook his head. "Your logic is foolproof," he admitted ruefully. "Therefore I must appeal to your emotions. For the sake of your wife and daughter, I beg you to trust in my judgment."

The chieftain's ice-tipped gaze flicked past him, and he nodded.

As Hazar glimpsed the shadowy figures moving stealthily toward him, he unfolded his arms.

The warriors stopped, eyes fixed on the derringer that protruded from his fist like a stubby black finger. Although only one bullet rested in the chamber, it pointed directly at El-Kifer's temple.

That small chunk of lead proved sufficient for Hazar's purpose. Calling Hashib to the bridge, he disarmed the guards, and bound El-Kifer to the mast.

"Now turn the prow north and keep it there," Hazar told the helmsman. "I don't wish to inconvenience your chieftain any longer than necessary."

Neither Hazar nor Hashib dared fall asleep during the brief voyage, aware that El-Kifer's warriors would take advantage of the slightest lapse in concentration. And their ability to fend off an attack was severely limited.

At best, Hazar could hope to kill his hostage before being cut down himself. *The margin separating us from death is mere seconds,* Hazar reflected grimly.

El-Kifer seemed to sense his misgivings.

"We're still forty-eight hours from port," he said, with a sympathetic smile. "Too long without sleep."

"You'd do better to concern yourself with Lady Trent's welfare," the renegade advised. "My own problems will soon be remedied."

In a few hours, El-Kifer understood what he meant. Hazar ordered the helmsman to swing east when they neared Essouira. As they sailed into the peaceful, tree-sheltered cove, the great white sails of *The Mercury* bobbed into view, making everything clear.

"I see this is where we part company," El-Kifer said, nodding toward the waiting clipper. "I'd almost forgotten your hidden resources." Hazar loosed his bonds and stepped back. "You also forget our unfinished business."

"Kill me and there's nothing to hold my men from attack," the chieftain reminded him, as the renegade extended the derringer.

Hazar regarded him with a bemused smile. "Why would I kill a favored guest?"

"Guest, you say?" the chieftain said, confused by the question.

"Of course. You will join me aboard my—that is to

say—*our* clipper, for the remainder of our voyage to Tingis."

"You have me and my son," El-Kifer said huskily. "There's no need to hold my wife and daughter. I offer my life in exchange for their freedom."

The renegade shrugged. "Most likely that's what it will cost."

"Then you agree?"

"What you ask is beyond my power." Hazar sighed, moving closer. "As I explained earlier, I had no part in your wife's abduction. But since you refuse my word—perhaps you'll accept this token as sign of good faith."

El-Kifer stared at the derringer the renegade pressed in his hand. He hefted the small gun as if to make sure it was real, then slowly lifted his gaze.

"It seems I owe you an apology."

"We've no time for niceties," Hazar murmured, clenching his sword. "By dawn tomorrow, your daughter will have forfeited all hope of redemption— save for death."

CHAPTER TWENTY-NINE

Count Bouvier was beginning to believe he'd have to kill Lady Trevor after all.

That he'd be denied the letter was no longer important. Nothing mattered except his determination to break her spirit.

With each passing day, he became more obsessed with the goal, devising new ways to torment his defiant hostage.

His visits to her cell became more frequent, until he found himself spending most of his waking hours in the dungeon, attending to Lady Trevor's education.

She resisted pain admirably, and endured privation with stoic stubbornness. Even when confronted by his pets, she refused to bend to his will.

For that alone she has to die, Bouvier mused, as he descended the steep stairway.

Lady Trevor was curled inside the cage that dominated the center of the floor. The adjoining cell was occupied by a swarm of large rats.

Naked except for a torn shift that exposed her ivory-ribbed torso and hollow hips, Lady Trevor's pale, gaunt body attested to her ordeal.

A few feet away, in the corner of her cell, was a crumpled carcass the size of a cat.

The previous evening he'd put her in the cell, then allowed a single rodent to enter. At the same time he tossed a chunk of meat into the cell—knowing the rat would be diverted from his prisoner long enough for her to yield, before being bitten. A slight wound could cause a variety of infections, not the least of which were rabies and the black plague.

But instead of recoiling, Lady Trevor attacked the animal. She grasped its furry neck when it nibbled on the meat and squeezed, gazing at Bouvier intently, as she strangled the rat. Then she hurled the dead creature at him, eyes glinting like broken glass.

For a moment, neither of them spoke.

"You have until tomorrow morning to decide," Bouvier said regretfully. "If by then you still refuse to comply, I'll have no choice. Do you understand, milady?"

She turned away, keeping her back to him as he departed.

She resolutely kept her face averted when he returned.

Her stubbornness far transcends her will to survive, Bouvier reflected with a trace of bitterness. *After all the harsh years in exile I've starved for this moment of revenge, it lacks the true bouquet of victory.*

"I take it you refuse my wish," Bouvier observed. "Therefore you must suffer the ultimate penalty. Is that clear?"

Receiving no answer he moved to the large steel panel that separated the two cells.

"Have you anything to say before my little executioners pay a last visit?"

Lady Trevor whirled. "Only that I curse the name Flaubert with my last breath."

"We'll see what prayers your last breath brings forth."

The man who now called himself Bouvier muttered, gripping the lever that controlled the panel. As he pulled back, the small door between cages slowly lifted. Tiny, glittering eyes filled the opening as the creatures peered at their prey.

"You've less than a second to reconsider," he reminded, as the opening enlarged.

"André!"

Bouvier paused, both annoyed and relieved by the interruption.

"André, come here!"

Evita's call provided Lady Trevor with a brief reprieve. Leaving the panel open to give her something to think about during his absence, Bouvier hurried to the narrow stone stairs.

He found his wife waiting in the main hall.

Clad in a scarlet chiffon frock that set off her snow-white hair, Evita's eyes were shining like emerald crescents above her icy smile.

"I've got a present for you, dearest," she murmured, taking his arm. "Come, I'll show you."

"This isn't the time for domestic games," Bouvier said gruffly. "I've decided to exterminate our hostage. I'm sure one of Lady Trevor's fingers would carry as much urgency as a letter to her dear husband."

Evita shrugged. "My intervention prevented you from making a serious error. I thought you agreed to take no action without my consent."

Bouvier scowled. "Is this a reprimand?"

"Call it a rebirth."

Evita's triumphant drawl ignited his anticipation as he followed her to the library.

Upon entering, he understood her triumph. Indeed, he reveled in it.

Seated on the couch like two ducklings in a pond were Lady Trent and her young protector.

"Why, Lady Kiferson, your presence is fully as welcome, as your leaving was mourned."

"I've come to ask for your sanctuary from Hazar. In repayment I'll lead you to his stronghold."

"What stronghold?" he asked sharply.

"A hidden port about three days sail along the coast."

Bouvier glanced at his wife. "El-Kifer's fortress, no doubt."

"Do we have a bargain, sir?" Trent said impatiently. "Otherwise I'm off to Gibraltar for help."

"Why of course, I'll help," Bouvier assured. "You must be starved after your harrowing journey. After I ring for refreshments you must tell me everything."

In a few minutes a tall, barrel-chested Turk named Vasy entered the study, bearing a large tray of food. As Trent wolfed down the sumptuous repast, she recounted how she managed to escape.

"Were it not for the good fortune of encountering Mister Gaines when I boarded the Kiferson ship, I might still be a Barbar slave."

"What of your sister?" Evita purred.

"My stepsister," Trent corrected. "It's possible that she's in league with Hazar. Perhaps she arranged my mother's abduction," she added, glancing at Malcolm.

Evita gave the boy a languid smile. "Do you think Lord Kiferson's stepdaughter could have been responsible?"

Malcolm cleared his throat. "Shan seemed to be concealing something," he admitted. "She insisted I remain aboard *The Indigo,* with a handful of men."

"That reminds me," Malcolm said, turning to Count Bouvier. "My crewmen are still under guard in port. I request that they receive fresh food and freedom of the harbor."

"I'll make sure they're taken care of properly."

At his nod the servant left the room.

"You must launch an attack as soon as possible," Trent demanded. "We're all safe enough, but my mother's life is still at stake."

Bouvier beamed at her with paternal sympathy. "No need to fret, my child. Lady Trevor is right here, under my personal care."

It took long seconds for his statement to penetrate her numbed brain.

"She's here?" Trent gasped, eyes wide with confusion. "But how . . . ?"

"Doubtless she'll be able to explain much better than I," the Count said mildly. "When you've recovered your strength, I'll take you to her."

Trent stood up, her thoughts stumbling through her surging emotions. "I'm ready now," she declared. "Where is my mother?"

She followed Bouvier into the hall, dimly aware of Malcolm hovering beside her. She also sensed Evita's trailing presence as they descended the stairs. A vague apprehension nipped at her perceptions and she glanced back.

Malcolm gave her an encouraging wink and patted the pistol butt protruding from his belt.

Reassured by the weapon, Trent continued following their guide. Her memory stirred as they neared the bottom of the stairs, and she recognized the bleak gray dungeon where Melba had been slaughtered.

Trent jerked to a halt, eyes rolling in panic.

Then her fears exploded into frenzied horror.

Her mother was crouched inside a cage like some red-maned wildcat, snarling at the dark horde of rats massed at the half-open passage between cells.

She turned when Trent screamed, her face dissolving like wax as she glimpsed her daughter. Trent's senses seemed to melt as well, fused by the realization of her monstrous blunder.

"Hold or I'll shoot!"

The cry smothered her searing remorse. Trent looked up and saw Malcolm jabbing at Bouvier with his pistol.

"Stand fast, Countess," Malcolm warned, as Evita took a tentative step toward him.

He extended the pistol and waved her closer to Bouvier. "Both of you get against the wall, if you please. And I'll have the keys to Lady Trevor's cell from you, Bouvier."

"Certainly," the count muttered, fumbling through the pockets of his brocade waistcoat.

There was a wet, smacking sound and something clattered to the ground. Trent's stunned gaze focused on the pistol on the floor.

Malcolm's fingers were still clutching the grip, thumb cocked on the hammer.

Then she saw his face.

He was staring at his severed wrist with fish-eyed astonishment, as if expecting his hand to reappear from the shiny red stump.

A moment later his skull exploded with violent force, spraying gobs of brain matter and chipped bone everywhere. Bits of hair-matted flesh stuck to Trent's skin as Malcolm toppled to the floor, a crimson ooze bubbling from the crack in his forehead.

Not until then did Trent see his assassin. The

brawny servant stepped from the alcove, wiping his gore-greased scimitar on his pantaloons.

Disbelief and despair collided in Trent's awareness and she collapsed, paralyzed by shock.

While only vaguely conscious of the rough hands pawing her breasts and her mother's anguished cries, one thought speared through the nightmare with sickening clarity.

Hazar had spoken the truth. And she was tainted by her father's cursed Barbar blood.

CHAPTER THIRTY

"Stop it! I'll do whatever you want!" Lady Trevor shouted hoarsely. "But get that butcher away from my daughter. Do you hear? I'll do whatever you say!"

Bouvier arched his brows in surprise. "It appears we've found your weak link," he observed with a small smile. "How delightful. I'd quite given up hope."

"Get him away from her!" she pleaded.

Slowly, deliberately, Bouvier turned and muttered something to his servant.

Vasy's flat features folded into a sullen scowl. Reluctantly, he released the half-naked wench and hovered over her like some giant bulldog straddling a freshly killed deer.

"We don't need the letter now," Evita reminded.

Bouvier gazed fondly at his caged hostage.

"Oh, but we do, my dear. We must make sure Lady Trevor carries out *all* of our demands."

Lust glazed Evita's features as his meaning dawned. "You know best in this case," she purred, green eyes flickering with excitement.

Bouvier had pen and paper in readiness, and for a few seconds nothing stirred the silence save for the scratching of Lady Trevor's quill and the restless scuttle of the rats.

Maddened by the scent of blood they clawed feverishly at the mesh walling their cage.

Before Trevor had completed the letter, Vasy stiffened, and moved to the doorway, curved blade cocked in front of his massive torso.

The serving girl who entered shrank back from the menacing figure, jabbering in panic. After blurting her message she beat a hasty retreat.

"So Hazar has returned with his tail between his legs," Bouvier crowed. "Having lost his gamble he comes sniffing at my door like a whipped cur, seeking my forgiveness."

He gave Evita a penetrating glance. "Instead he'll be grist for Vasy's blade."

"Wait, André," she exclaimed as he gestured to the brawny guard. "Don't kill him yet."

"You're still infatuated with this Barbar footpad," Bouvier snorted.

Evita met his contemptuous gaze without wavering. "You misunderstand," she said calmly. "I don't ask you to spare him—merely to let *me* dispose of the matter. It's really only fair, my darling. Just as you have certain debts to settle with Lady Trevor, so have I with Shareef Hazar. He belongs to me, not some Turkish mule. You owe me that much."

Bouvier bowed. "That I do, *ma petite*. It's a pleasure to dispatch my obligations. Hazar is yours."

It relieved Hazar to see Evita enter the study. Her presence insured his survival for the moment.

He wondered if he could rekindle her interest. *Passion would afford more leverage than penance,* he noted hopefully.

Her greeting shattered his hopes for a reconciliation. "So you're back."

"Obviously, milady."

The retort left her unamused.

"I should have you killed."

"*I* should have taken your advice," he conceded with a rueful grin.

"Your error was considerably graver than mere disobedience," she reminded crisply. "Being aggravated by assault, hijacking, and murder."

"That could become aggravating," he agreed. "Yet, it remains simple. I took a chance and I lost. Now you hold all the cards."

"And what do you propose I do?"

His eyes glinted like black diamonds. "You've only two choices, milady—either kill me or cut me in. Seems to me there's enough action to spare now that El-Kifer is cornered."

"He's yet to be defeated," Evita pointed out. "As usual you're impetuous, my king."

The familiar term of endearment salved Hazar's optimism, not to mention his vanity. "Certainly it was impetuous to come here. But I wanted to see you again."

"Curiosity?"

Her husky murmur suggested he'd breached her defenses.

"My motive was more akin to corruption than curiosity," he confided.

"We have a common vice, my king," Evita whispered, breath hot against his ear. "I can resist anything but corruption."

"What of Bouvier?"

"My husband is occupied with his new playthings. He won't leave the dungeon for hours."

"Dungeon?"

"Lady Trevor and her charming daughter," she explained, easing her fingers inside his black silk shirt. "I'll take you to see them in a little while."

It didn't take long for Hazar to discover how he'd been humiliated.

The moment they slipped out of Evita's boudoir, he felt cold steel biting his throat. After giving up his sword, dagger, derringer, and weighted belt to the surly Turk in Bouvier's employ, he entered the dungeon as an inmate rather than as an observer.

Evita led the way with Vasy's scimitar taking up the rear. She halted the short procession with a triumphant flourish, and waited for Bouvier to acknowledge their presence. Being preoccupied with the two women huddled inside the cage, the count ignored his new guests for a few minutes. Enough time to see escape was impossible.

The only exit was through the narrow alcove and up the steep stairs. That route was amply blocked by the barrel-chested Turk who carried a dagger to augment his scimitar.

Already armed with sword and pistol, Bouvier had added Hazar's derringer to his arsenal before he finally granted his visitors an audience.

"So, my young rival has worn out his welcome," the count said, beaming at his wife.

"Well worn indeed," Evita conceded. She moved to a padded bench near the wall and beckoned for Hazar to join her.

"Hold fast!"

At Bouvier's command Hazar paused in mid-step and raised his hands. Evita stood up, brimming with indignation.

"I thought we agreed."

"So we did, and so I'll abide," Bouvier said patiently. "I just wouldn't want your playmate to turn the tables on you. Have him bring the seat nearer to Vasy, so he won't be tempted to take you hostage."

She shrugged and stepped closer to the bodyguard. "I bow to your astute judgment."

"Perhaps it would be wiser to chain his limbs."

"Perhaps."

Evita's tone betrayed her reluctance. "It's worth discussing," she said, moving to her husband's side.

"I take it you have a personal reason for leaving him unfettered."

"I have only this day to destroy him," she said huskily. "Before he dies I want him to understand he's completely helpless—and totally under my domination. To chain him would lessen his manly responsibility as he watches you execute Lady Trevor. Unchained, his frustration will leave him no choice but to attack. And each time he tries, he'll be beaten back."

Bouvier smiled. "To prove my admiration for your exquisite sensibilities he'll remain *unchained, ma petite.*

"And to prove my wisdom," he added, ringing for the servants, "I'll have some men posted on the stairway."

Sensing Bouvier's anticipation, Hazar refrained from whipping the wooden bench against the Turk's shins and bided his time for a better moment.

The delay cost him dearly.

As he sat down a servant entered the chamber.

With a sinking heart, Hazar heard Bouvier order extra guards.

He had a slight chance against two men. But one

more made the odds astronomical, in favor of the house.

Time is on their side, as well, Hazar brooded. He'd arrived at mid-morning but had lost track of the hours while servicing Evita's lusts. *It couldn't be more than five or six* P.M., he speculated glumly. *Which leaves me two hours short.*

As planned, Hashib and El-Kifer would launch their attack at nightfall. But that now seemed far too belated.

If not posthumous, Hazar noted as Bouvier strolled back and forth, inspecting his hostages. The count's intense fascination was accelerated by impatience, like a child in a candy shop.

No doubt he'll be goaded by Evita's sweet tooth, the renegade calculated, trying to control his panic-spurred instincts.

Without even looking, Hazar knew the guard was waiting for a sudden move, so he could show off his prowess with the machetelike blade.

Indeed, when Evita sat beside him, the burly Turk edged closer to the bench.

Hazar ignored them both, distracted by Lady Trevor's shouts.

"You promised her release if I wrote the letter," she ranted, clawing at the wire mesh lining the steel bars of her cage.

"I agreed to keep my bodyguard away from your daughter," Bouvier corrected. "I said nothing of the rats."

"Kill me instead," Lady Trevor pleaded.

"You've consumed your bargaining power, milady. Unless..."

She clutched at his unspoken thought. "I'll do anything."

"Very well. Since you seem so enthusiastic, I'll consider a reprieve. You'll both avoid my furry executioners for as long as your daughter entertains my guard. Poor Vasy was so disappointed the last time. I'd like to make it up to him."

"You promised he wouldn't touch her," Lady Trent hissed.

"And he shan't—unless *you* consent, milady. However, it would seem that pleasing a hearty male specimen like Vasy is much more palatable than assuaging a rodent's appetite. Don't you agree?"

Bouvier's question lashed through her sobs.

"You've ten seconds to make your choice," he prodded, mouth pressed in a tight smile.

"I agree." The crack in Lady Trevor's voice betrayed her exhaustion. *They've finally broken her spirit,* Hazar reflected, his own hopes sagging. *It won't be long until they tire of tormenting her. And when they do, the rats will have a grand feast.*

"Come here, Vasy," Bouvier droned. "Bring your prisoner with you. What do you think, *ma petite?* Hazar might feel offended by Lady Trent's reconciliation with our Turkish friend."

"I'm sure he'll be amused by the sporting gesture," Evita said, turning to her hostage.

"Isn't that true, my king?"

Without answering, Hazar moved to the cage, closely trailed by the Turk's blade.

Bouvier unlocked the cell door and beckoned to Trent.

"Your mother has spared you from a most unsavory demise," he declared briskly. "Now you must show Vasy how grateful you are. Or would you prefer the rats? Truly, it would be sinful to let such sublime beauty be shredded by vermin teeth."

He stepped back to allow Trent passage through the narrow door.

"She seems eager to comply," Evita purred, glancing at Hazar.

The Barbar chieftain watched impassively as Vasy sheathed his sword and shuffled toward the ivory-skinned girl being offered for his pleasure.

"Kneel before your master," Bouvier rasped, voice thick with anticipation.

Trent seemed barely conscious as she obeyed his command. Her wide, unblinking eyes were clouded and her features void of expression. They didn't flicker when the brawny Turk tore away the remnants of her shift and roughly pawed her breasts.

But within seconds, Hazar's control snapped. Roaring with rage he threw himself at Vasy and rammed his head into the guard's kidneys.

The force of the blow drove the burly Turk to the ground, where he lay gasping like a beached whale.

"Touch it and she dies."

Hazar froze, fingers a scant inch from the guard's fallen sword.

"I need only pull this lever and Lady Trevor will be devoured by my pets," Bouvier reminded sharply.

As he spoke, the guard lurched to his feet.

"Our last guest was also impetuous," the count continued, nodding at Vasy. "Show him how we deal with our enemies."

Though Hazar knew what was coming, he was unable to defend himself against the guard's fury.

The first blow caught him in the belly and as he doubled over, Vasy spun him around and heaved him against the cage.

A dark mass of squealing rats rose up in frenzy when Hazar's body crashed against the steel bars.

They shrank back, squirming like some furry octopus with a thousand red eyes.

As they retreated, Hazar saw a pile of rags and rotted wood near the bars.

His stunned brain slowly realized it was a human skeleton. The heap of dirty, flesh-patched bones expanded as the rats scuttled back, flooding his senses with horror—and for the first time Hazar felt an icy current of fear caress his soul.

Even as the Turk's fist crushed his thoughts, the rats' hellish squeals echoed through the shattered darkness.

CHAPTER THIRTY-ONE

The men crammed into the dark, airless cargo hold were becoming restless.

Kevin listened to their shuffling and muted coughs with growing trepidation, knowing that if discovered, they'd be trapped. There were too many warriors jammed beneath *The Mercury*'s deck to launch an effective counteraction.

It doesn't take a veteran to understand we'd be butchered like a herd of buffalo, the youth noted, unable to restrain his own itching impatience. *Even death in battle is preferable to being suffocated in this foul hole.*

Kevin's dour reflections were cut off by the footsteps crossing the deck just above his head. The profound silence inside the hold amplified the sounds.

It seemed to Kevin that at least three men had boarded the ship. *Certainly not less,* he speculated as he crouched beneath the crude tarpaulin tents concealing them from casual observation. He gripped his sword as the sounds of gruff voices drifted down the stairs.

Then he heard the hatch-bolt rattle. He peered through a crack in the canvas and saw his father.

Poised beneath the stairway with a dagger between his jaws, Lord Kiferson resembled some golden effigy of a saber-toothed tiger as he waited in the shadows, without moving or blinking an eye.

A shaft of light burst across the darkness when the hatch door lifted.

Kevin unshouldered the padded bundle he carried, and carefully set it down.

A man descended the stairs, swinging his lamp back and forth as if looking for something. He paused at the bottom step, then continued further along the passage between the canvas-covered crates glutting the hold.

Abruptly the lamp dropped to the floor as a pair of hands covered the man's face and dragged him into the shadows.

Someone darted out to smother the fire and silence veiled the darkness.

"Medwi! What are you doing down there?" someone bellowed.

He thrust a lamp through the hatch and descended a few steps.

"Medwi? Where are you?"

Then he spied the broken lamp and slowly moved to investigate, pistol at ready.

He stopped and lifted the lamp above his head, then suddenly stiffened. El-Kifer stood behind him, one hand clamped firmly over the man's mouth, while the other pressed a dagger against his throat.

"One false word and you're dead—understand?"

The man nodded frantically, lamp still raised.

Kevin saw Hashib emerge from his hiding place and claim the man's pistol.

"How many aboard?" he grunted as he took the lamp.

The man rolled his eyes, unable to speak.

"Careful, now," El-Kifer said, slowly releasing the man's jaw. "Keep it low."

"How many aboard?" Hashib repeated.

"Fi . . . five of us," the man said hoarsely.

"How many ashore?"

The man turned his face from the lamp.

"Ten. Maybe a few more. They're waiting for our report. If we're not back . . ."

El-Kifer's hand cut him off. As he dragged the man to the stairway, Hashib followed with the lamp. Kevin heard his father murmur something but couldn't make out the words.

A moment later the man raised his lamp toward the open hatch and called out.

"Omar! Omar, come down here."

There was a hasty shuffle of footsteps and a third man poked his head through the hatch.

Since his companion held the lamp high, Omar was half-blinded by the brightness. "What is it?" he demanded, averting his face from the light.

"I've found something down here. Send the others away."

"Found what?" His scowl dissolved as Medwi lifted his hand. Even from afar Kevin could see the gold coins gleaming in the lamplight.

Omar uttered a long, low whistle as he squinted at the gold. "How much is there?"

"Send the others away, and I'll show you."

Still wary, Omar plucked a coin from his outstretched palm and bit down on it hard. Satisfied it was genuine, he grunted assent and hurried to comply.

Kevin heard voices on deck, and the clatter of footsteps descending the gangplank. As the sounds faded, Omar reappeared.

"I gave them a half hour for supper," he confided breathlessly when he reached the bottom of the stairs.

Hashib clubbed him with the pistol butt and dragged his unconscious body out of sight. Then El-Kifer went on deck.

Long, anxious minutes passed before he returned. "It's clear!" he hissed. "Move out!"

The warriors emerged from their hiding places and began filing up the stairs. Directed by El-Kifer, they slipped off the ship at ten-second intervals, to avoid drawing undue attention.

Though *The Mercury* was deserted, it was wedged between the many slave ships crowding the harbor. The sun hadn't quite submerged beneath the gold-studded horizon and Kevin could see men standing at the rail of the adjoining vessel no more than fifteen feet away.

However, the warriors trickling off *The Mercury* aroused no special interest. Most went ashore in pairs, and while Kevin and Gediz were among the first on deck, they remained aboard ship—having a special mission to carry out.

The evacuation went smoothly enough, but over a hundred warriors were still below decks when the inspection party returned.

Before they could reboard *The Mercury,* El-Kifer gave the signal. A few moments later a deafening explosion rocked the sleepy port.

The guerillas had chosen their target well.

Their first charge blasted the doors of a large slave pen facing the docks and scores of freed captives spilled onto the streets.

The next explosion unleashed a shouting melee as men began running in every direction. At the same time El-Kifer's remaining troops poured out of the hold.

The warriors rushed ashore unnoticed in the wild confusion. Not until the Barbar guerillas started cutting people down with sword and shot, did their enemies realize they were under attack. By then El-Kifer's advance force had penetrated the city walls.

Kevin's mission was also well underway, having been launched with the first blast. With the aid of grappling hooks he and Gediz boarded the vessel adjoining *The Mercury*. They unpacked the padded bundles strapped to their backs and quickly went to work.

The surprise attack drew attention away from the docked ships, enabling the pair to set their explosive charges virtually undetected. After lighting the fuse Kevin and Gediz moved to the rail. The next vessel in line was barely six feet away making it a simple matter to leap to its deck.

They hurriedly set the charges they carried in their padded sacks, then carefully inserted the fuse.

"What are ye doin' back there?"

Both youths whirled at the same time but Gediz drew first blood.

He felled the intruder with a single pistol shot, then returned to his task. As Kevin attached a fuse to the metal container packed with gunpowder, Gediz glanced back and saw two men drawing near. One had a pistol and the other a musket.

"Get up slow, little brother," he muttered under his breath.

"Hold or we'll shoot!"

Kevin and Gediz lifted their hands and turned.

The man with the musket gestured at the body sprawled nearby. "They killed Ben."

The other man pointed his pistol at Gediz.

"Here's the bastard what did it. Let's even the score right now."

A fiery blast from the adjoining ship shook the decks.

This time it was Kevin who struck first, flinging his dagger the moment the charge exploded.

The man dropped his pistol and clutched the knife protruding from his chest. As he fell, his companion jerked the musket toward Kevin and fired.

His aim was skewed by Gediz's sword. The Barbar youth thrust his blade between the man's ribs and the shot went wild, blowing a deep crater in the mast, mere inches from Kevin's head.

"You're still one up on me," the blond youth observed, retrieving his dagger.

Stepping back to the mast, he primed the charge and struck a match.

Then he rejoined Gediz and they strolled to the gangplank, as if the burning fuse was nothing more than a memorial candle for the three dead crewmen behind them.

When they reached shore, however, the raging battle swept over them with hurricane force and Kevin lost sight of Gediz amid the blurred figures whirling around him.

Suddenly his father burst into view astride a dark stallion, his sword flashing like a beacon. But as Kevin raced across the body-strewn pier he saw two men leap in front of the stallion and fire their weapons at point-blank range, hitting both rider and steed.

Mortally wounded, the horse collapsed, hurling El-Kifer to the ground, where his blood merged with that of his fallen mount.

CHAPTER THIRTY-TWO

Lady Trevor's relentless pounding had torn a section of the wire mesh lining her cage.

The ragged metal ripped her skin as she pushed her fist through the opening and clawed at Bouvier, who stood just out of reach, ignoring her curses in favor of more ephemeral pursuits.

Both the count and his wife watched avidly while Vasy pressed his sweat-greased belly against Lady Trent's naked skin.

The foul odor steaming from his giant body fogged Hazar's battered senses as he struggled back to consciousness. From where he lay he could make out Vasy's hulking form and the blank despair veiling Trent's face as the Turk violated her unresisting flesh.

Bouvier seemed pleased to see Hazar stir his bruised limbs.

"Most men don't recover so quickly from Vasy's beatings," he congratulated. "Now that you're back with us, we can proceed."

Hazar gleaned two facts from the mocking salutation: that he'd only been unconscious for a short time, and that Bouvier wanted him to witness Trent's execution. For that reason he feigned a relapse and rummaged through his throbbing brain for some un-tapped resource.

Reluctantly, he grasped that his only hope of staving off her death was to endure another beating.

He pushed himself to his feet and charged.

"Watch out!"

Being otherwise engaged, Vasy didn't hear the warning in time.

Hazar rammed his head into the rutting Goliath's back, aiming for the area he'd bruised earlier. His second blow was more effective.

The Turk bellowed in pain and tumbled forward, tripping over Trent's body. Surprise and pain kept Vasy on the floor for precious seconds.

But as Hazar spun toward Bouvier he saw it was too late. The count was standing beside the cage with his hand on the lever.

"Hold or I kill this one now!"

"Don't worry about me!" Lady Trevor pleaded. "Stop him!"

Seeing Hazar crouch as if to attack, Bouvier jerked the lever, opening the panel between Lady Trevor's cell and the caged rats. At the same time, the Turk lurched to his feet.

Having nothing to lose, Hazar leaped at Bouvier and shoved him to the floor. Then he pushed the lever, sealing the panel off from the rats jammed around the small opening.

In their rabid frenzy to get at Lady Trevor, the beasts clogged the passage, thus only four or five of them got through before Hazar shut the panel. As he pounced on Bouvier, he saw Lady Trevor kicking at the white-fanged creatures nipping at her ankles. Her shrieks were battlecries rather than screams of fear, ringing clear above the animal growls outside the cage.

As Hazar struggled with Bouvier for possession of the pistol, the huge Turk unsheathed his scimitar and shuffled forward. Unable to get loose, the count swung Hazar around, exposing his back to Vasy's blade.

Just as the Turk poised to chop Hazar in half, Lady Trevor thrust her arm through the torn wire and tossed a squirming rat at the Turk.

Vasy screeched and twisted, swiping wildly at the fear-crazed beast that was digging its sharp claws into his back. Hazar managed to wrest the pistol from Bouvier as the flailing guard stumbled back.

Clubbing the count to the ground he crouched to retrieve his dagger, and saw the howling giant charge at him, sword sweeping down like a scythe.

Without hesitation Hazar fired.

As if colliding with a stone wall, the huge Turk stopped short, then toppled backward, blood spurting from his mouth.

Evita's sharp cry silenced the roaring confusion.

Looking up, Hazar saw her bending over Trent, both hands pressing a knife into the girl's naked breast.

"Drop the gun and the dagger," she ordered calmly.

Bouvier hurried to pick up the discarded weapons.

"Are you hurt, *ma chérie?*"

"No harm done," Bouvier reported.

Evita nodded at Hazar. "We've wasted enough time with this Barbar puppet. Cut his strings and be done with him."

"With pleasure, *ma petite,*" Bouvier murmured.

The count took careful aim, one eye squinting between the barrels like an ice-blue sun in the valley of death.

He pulled the trigger and the falling hammer eclipsed his eye.

Bouvier looked up, expression shadowed by annoyance.

"The damned thing misfired."

Hurling the pistol aside he drew his sword and advanced warily toward Hazar.

The chieftain edged away until the metal bars at his back told him there was no place to run. He dodged as Bouvier's blade flashed into view but a jolting shock squeezed the breath from his lungs.

Then the thundering blackness crushed his awareness like an avalanche.

Gediz and Hashib reached the estate first, closely followed by Kevin, who transported El-Kifer in a buckboard he'd commandeered after his father was shot. Kevin glanced back anxiously as he whipped the team along the steep curves.

"Can you make it?" he shouted at the blond-maned figure huddled against the side.

El-Kifer nodded and continued wrapping his useless arm with bandages torn from his shirt.

"The bastard didn't get my swordarm."

Some fifty yards behind them was a large wagon carrying a platoon of warriors, and Kevin could see the deep orange glow of the flaming ships flickering across the bay far below.

He whipped the horses up the steep grade, then reined hard when he rounded the corner and saw Hashib and Gediz standing beside their horses.

Gediz signaled for the trailing wagon to halt a few yards below the turn, out of sight of any roaming patrol guarding the walled estate that loomed above them.

Being most familiar with the terrain, Hashib led the way up the rock-strewn hill. On reaching a plateau concealed by a group of boulders, the attackers split into two groups. Kevin and Gediz took a squad to the rear of the house, while Hashib and El-Kifer approached the entrance from two sides.

The main force waited for Gediz and Kevin to set off their explosives then stormed the fortress. Using grappling hooks, the Barbar warriors scaled the walls as easily as climbing stairs. They scattered immediately, and swarmed toward the house before anyone realized they'd penetrated the grounds. The guards had been drawn to the rear by the series of blasts that shattered a section of the mansion, giving the marauders a chance to establish position. One squad entrenched themselves behind the verdant pines that shaded the veranda, while the rest rushed the house in alternating waves—three men from the right side of the tree-lined entrance, followed by three from the left.

Six warriors managed to make it to the front before the guards opened fire, cutting down the next wave. El-Kifer was among the first to reach the door. Raising his pistol, he blew the lock with one shot, then blasted a guard with his second. He discarded the empty weapon and unsheathed his sword, as Hashib fired at another defender.

As they entered, armed guards rushed from every direction into the large hall. The attackers greeted Bouvier's men with a salvo of bullets that sent them scrambling for cover.

A score of dead warriors littered the marble floor and the domed ceilings rang with the shouts of the living, as Bouvier's guards mounted a counter-offensive. Their sword-lanced charge drove the marauders back and cut them off from the doorway. The swift, efficient maneuver bore testimony to their deadly skill. By massing at the entrance they kept reinforcements from entering the fray, and blocked the marauder's retreat.

Since Bouvier's men outnumbered the half-dozen intruders by a wide margin, their advantage escalated with every blood-scored moment. All of the attackers were wounded and each one who dropped diminished the chances of the rest.

El-Kifer snatched up a pistol lying beside a dead guard and fired both barrels into the crowd. The shots set off a violent chain of events. As one of the guards toppled, two or three others were struck by a sudden salvo from outside. Almost at the same time, a powerful explosion rattled the house, clogging the hall with a thick black cloud.

In the chaos that followed, El-Kifer and Hashib broke through the defender's line and sprinted down the smoke-filled corridor. Hashib led the way to a stairway behind the kitchen, but the stout door was bolted shut.

El-Kifer ransacked the pantry and found a heavy meat mallet, studded with steel nails. Gripping the tool tightly, he began to hammer at the knob.

His relentless strokes cracked the wood and he finished the job with a powerful kick that left the door listing on one hinge. As soon as it crashed open, a musket shot lashed through the blackness like a fiery tongue.

The blast scorched El-Kifer's eyebrows and he staggered back, momentarily blinded. Hearing Hashib's cry, he lifted his sword and dodged as a blurred figure

roared out of the haze. He somehow parried the
guard's blow, but was still off balance. Dimly he saw
the figure thrust his arm forward and for a frozen moment he watched the blade slicing through the smoke
with tantalizing slowness.

He stumbled, trying to twist away from its lazy tra-
jectory, but gravity yanked him directly into its path.

Abruptly, the sword paused in midair, then plummeted like a steel-beaked hawk. A moment later the
guard dove to the ground.

Blinking to clear his spotted vision, he saw Hashib
crouch down to retrieve his bone-handled dagger
from the fallen guard's back.

"Thanks," he grunted, moving toward the stairway.

"Wait!"

El-Kifer stopped and saw Hashib reloading the
musket with some powder and shot from the dead
guard's pouch. When the weapon was primed and
cocked, he crept to the edge of the door, then suddenly darted inside and fired point-blank down the
stairs.

The two guards stationed below were chopped to
pieces by the burning lead pellets that flooded the
narrow passage. They resembled nothing more than
mangled slabs of raw meat when El-Kifer leaped
down the stairs.

He paused to wrest a pistol from a severed hand,
then continued after Hashib. Just before they reached
bottom, two men emerged on the landing.

El-Kifer blasted the leader, but his companion
speared Hashib's leg, who tumbled headlong into the
guard's arms. Both men fell, struggling wildly. In the
heaving confusion, El-Kifer glimpsed an opening and
struck. His blade sliced past Hashib's gullet with

barely an inch to spare, on its way to the guard's heart.

"We're even," the renegade muttered, but El-Kifer was occupied with another foe.

Despite his useless arm, the blond-maned Barbar bobbed from side to side with catlike quickness, eluding the guard's sword as well as his wild pistol shot. The flash illuminated his wide yellow eyes and clenched grin as he sank his blade in the gunman's chest.

Without hesitation he kicked the skewered body off his sword and leaped down to the landing. But when Hashib jumped after him, his wounded leg gave way. As he tried to pull himself erect, a violent explosion threw him to the ground and an avalanche of broken rocks crashed down the stairs, clogging the narrow passage with thick, choking fumes. Unable to breathe, he tried to crawl into the alcove and found he couldn't move. His leg was buried under a mound of rubble, leaving him pinned like a prize butterfly for the next trophy hunter who descended the stairs.

Hashib pressed against the ground, struggling for air, then jerked his head up toward the footsteps that suddenly filled the passage. He listened helplessly as the sounds loomed closer, roaring through the dust-clouded gloom like death's invisible cavaliers.

The explosion flung El-Kifer to the floor, a few meager inches beneath the bullet from Bouvier's derringer. His marksmanship was commendable, considering the circumstances. The blast sent everyone sprawling, including the rats who swarmed over the walls of their cage in a squealing frenzy. When the chieftain saw his wife imprisoned in the adjoining cell, and his daughter's bruised flesh, he was seized by a soul-shaking fury that flung him across the room.

While hurried, Flaubert's next shot plucked El-Kifer's sword, but even as it flew from his grasp he was yanking the dagger from his boot. Bouvier hurled the empty gun and dove to the floor, both actions combining to sway El-Kifer's knife from its mark. As it was, the dagger struck high, embedding itself in Bouvier's shoulder as he rolled aside.

"I'll kill her!"

Frozen by the cry, El-Kifer looked up and saw a snow-haired female cradling his daughter, her stiletto pressed against Trent's neck like a long, silver fingernail.

Hazar was crouched about ten feet away, poised for any opportunity. There was none at all.

"Drop your knife," the woman hissed.

El-Kifer did as she ordered.

"Take off your belt, as well."

As he loosened his metal-tipped belt, Flaubert jerked the dagger from his arm and collected the fallen weapons, including the derringer, which he began reloading immediately.

Scanning the room, El-Kifer noted a heavy scimitar half-concealed beneath a hulking corpse that lay near the cage.

"Don't try it!" the woman warned, puncturing Trent's skin with her sharp blade.

Blood oozed from her ivory throat, glistening like a large, tear-shaped ruby.

"Put the belt down slowly."

Relaxing his bunched muscles, El-Kifer placed the weapon on the floor, gold-flecked eyes nailed to her wounded hostage.

Shock and disbelief hammered at his brain as the man kicked the belt aside and cocked the derringer.

"Surprised?"

The familiar voice dissolved all doubt. El-Kifer's scowl seemed etched in iron but his thoughts were whirling like leaves in a hurricane as he stared at his old enemy.

"Less surprised than disappointed," he said softly. "For all these years, my spirit has drawn comfort from the memory of Count Flaubert's demise."

"You've been living in a fool's Eden," Flaubert agreed, his smile twisted by triumph. "When Flaubert died, Count André Bouvier was born—rising like a phoenix to claim his vengeance. And today, your loved ones will discharge that debt to Flaubert's dishonored memory with their lives."

"We'll start with Lady Trevor," he added briskly, as if inviting them to take tea.

"Shoot him now," Evita insisted.

"Not just yet, *chérie*," Flaubert said in a coaxing voice. "I want him to see the rats crawling over his wife. He'll beg me to kill her . . ."

He glanced back, leaving Hazar momentarily out of view. That instant's lapse allowed the renegade to pounce on El-Kifer's discarded belt. In a single blurred motion he snatched up the weapon and lunged, flicking the weighted thong toward Evita.

The steel knobs lashed her neck like a braided noose, dragging her forward. As Bouvier whirled and fired, El-Kifer sprang.

His powerful frame uncoiled like a golden cobra driving a fist into Flaubert's face with stunning force.

The sharp crunch of broken bone lanced his arm, as the impact crushed Flaubert's nose. Part of his cheek collapsed as well, and one eye popped from its shattered socket like a pulpy red plum when his skull smacked the steel cage.

His shrieks became a frothing babble as blood bubbled from the soggy red mass that had once been a face.

By chance, his wildly flailing arm hooked the lever that controlled the locks, and both doors slid open, loosing the hoard of rats.

Evita screamed as the creatures covered the floor like a squirming carpet, swarming in every direction. Her cries were snuffed by a violent blast that cracked the archway and an instant later the ceiling caved in, flooding the room with hurtling stone. A massive rock smashed Evita against the wall, snapping her spine like a dry twig.

Unable to move, she rolled her eyes upward and saw Hazar straining to lift a heavy chunk of rubble from El-Kifer's chest.

A loud cry drew her gaze as a golden-maned figure appeared in the ruined archway. Eyes bulging with stunned disbelief, she watched El-Kifer's ghostlike figure float through swirling dust-choked chaos.

Gediz had five containers of explosive in his shoulder pack when they reached the walled estate. After creating a diversion by blowing up the north wing, he and Kevin ran to the rear of the house and crawled underneath the veranda.

They quickly wedged a second charge into a small crevice separating the stone walls, then scrambled outside, unrolling a long fuse as they hurried toward a pine-sheltered grove.

The well-placed explosive decimated the rear wall, digging a ragged hole large enough for a wagon to pass through.

The blast's rumbling echo hadn't yet faded when Kevin and Gediz emerged from cover and dashed into the steaming breach. Once inside the house they raced down the marble corridor to rejoin the warriors storming the entrance.

When they saw the massed defenders cordoning off the passage they slid to an abrupt halt and doubled back the way they came.

That route was also blocked. A squad of armed men were rushing into the jagged hole at the far end of the corridor, while two other guards leaped out of a door beneath the rear stairs, pistols blazing.

Both shots went wild, but Kevin's bullet found its mark, killing the first man who emerged. As he toppled, the other guard tripped over him, allowing Gediz an unchallenged thrust.

A shot careened off the wall, spraying them with chipped marble.

At the same time Gediz hurled a can of explosive across the smooth floor, bright sparks fanning from its stubby fuse. Moments before it ignited, they slipped inside the doorway and pulled the bolt shut. They barricaded themselves in a small armory stocked with a variety of weapons from pistols to broadswords, and abundant stores of powder and shot. Each took two pistols and Gediz seized the opportunity to fortify his remaining charges, pouring an extra measure of powder into the steel containers and tamping it down with the priming cap. His task completed, he primed the powder barrel, and concealed a long fuse beneath some gun crates. He paused to make sure it was burning smoothly before unlocking the bolt.

Kevin kicked the door open and rushed into the hall with both guns roaring. The squad of defenders fell back in panic as Gediz followed with another volley. Leaving four dead men in their wake, the youths sprinted along the corridor, closely followed by the survivors. Then he glimpsed his father at the end of the passage, and called out.

But El-Kifer was already gone, having ducked into an alcove.

Trapped between two groups of defenders, the youths took the same route to safety and found themselves in a cramped stairwell strewn with corpses. Kevin peered down the steep passage, ignoring the pounding footsteps of their pursuers.

Having wisely tucked an extra pistol in his belt when they left the armory, Gediz kept the guards at bay while Kyle reloaded his weapon, then primed another charge with an inch-long fuse.

Since the door to the alcove was smashed, Kevin had to rely on accuracy and speed to prevent being hurt by the blast. As Gediz fired a covering shot, he darted out of the alcove, heaved the sputtering container into the hall, and retreated back down the steep stairs.

The narrow passage amplified the explosion, shoving them against the stone wall with its force. A hail of pebbles showered over them as they stumbled down the stairs.

"Extra powder make strong bomb," Gediz grunted proudly.

Before Kevin could speak a fierce eruption shook the house like a raging fist. A series of rumbling aftershocks pounded deep crevices in the stone walls and a long crack undulated down the center of the stairway.

Realizing the charge they'd set in the armory had detonated too soon, they crouched against the shuddering wall until a large section collapsed, rammed by a thundering jolt that sent them tumbling amid an avalanche of crashing stone.

Miraculously, the stairway remained intact and

when Kevin and Gediz lifted themselves from the rubbled floor, they suffered from nothing more than minor cuts and bruises. A low moan drew them to Hashib, who was lying behind the stairs.

Leaving Gediz to bind his wound, Kevin warily entered the adjoining room, pistol ready.

He lowered his weapon when he stepped inside and saw his father.

El-Kifer was sprawled underneath a heavy slab of rock, eyes closed and limbs perfectly still.

Hazar was crouched beside him, straining vainly to budge the huge stone with his one good arm. Calling for Gediz, Kevin rushed to help him and with his companion's assistance, managed to ease the crushing burden from his father's chest.

The chieftain's eyelids fluttered open.

"Take care of Trevor," he mumbled weakly.

Kevin complied at once, searching through the tangled heaps of steel and rock until he found his mother and sister. Both women were unable to walk, which left only Kevin and Gediz to haul the four survivors up the steep stairway.

As Kevin dragged his sister across the floor he wondered if they'd be able to escape after all. The only exit from the dungeon was through the ruined passage and when they reached the main hall there'd surely be more guards to deal with. Even without any handicap it was a high-risk operation.

The greasy black smoke rolling down the stairway smothered his doubts.

"The house is on fire," Kevin declared, removing the last container from his shoulder pack.

"We'll have to blast our way out."

They deliberated for long moments before placing the charge, acutely aware that the thick walls had withstood a severe pounding. Then they sheltered their companions behind the stairway and ignited the fuse.

As the roar faded, Kevin reentered the dungeon and saw silvery moonbeams slicing through a gaping crater in the far corner. Afraid the remaining section might collapse, he and Gediz hurriedly assisted their wounded charges to the pine-scented grove behind the house, their flight illuminated by the orange flames spurting from the mansion's upper windows.

They remained hidden in the grove until the echoing gunfire faded to sporadic flurries. Then Kevin took a quick tour of the battleground and found it almost deserted except for the dead guards. There were no Barbar casualties in evidence, nor had he expected to see any. According to code Barbar warriors took their dead and wounded with them when they retreated.

However, seven unfriendly miles separated them from their rendezvous with the rescue ships and Kevin knew they'd never make it without horses to transport the wounded. A glittering stream of sparks danced across the sky as the mansion slowly disintegrated, folding at the center, like a cake melting in the heat. When it crumbled, the bright yellow flames leaped high, and Kevin saw a wagonload of armed men careening toward him. Having reloaded his pistols, he stood his ground and took careful aim at the lead horses.

Someone in the wagon fired at him, the bullet snapping past his ear, as the galloping steeds surged into range.

Kevin fared no better than his foe. One shot misfired, and the other went astray, leaving him nothing but a sword against the horde of warriors hurtling toward him.

"Hold, you bloody bastards—it's El-Kifer!"

Despite the misnomer, they were the sweetest words Kevin had ever heard.

Half-buried in rubble and paralyzed from the waist down, Evita was the last person left alive in the flaming mansion. While certain she'd be consumed in the fiery holocaust when the structure collapsed, she lived longer than she expected. Long enough for her stoic resignation to degenerate into soul-gutting terror.

Shortly before dawn, the rats returned, by the score, scuttling across the smoldering ruins in search of food. Drooling with fear Evita watched the squealing beasts swarm over the Turk's bloated corpse, their sharp fangs tearing away his skin. Within minutes they'd gouged a ragged crater in his belly and were burrowing inside his rib cage like a mass of furry maggots. Evita tried to scream as one of the rodents brushed her hair, but the only sound that emerged was a hoarse wheeze.

Having retained control of her left arm, she doggedly kept the slime-covered creatures at bay by tossing small rocks whenever they came near.

She prayed the Turk's abundant flesh would assuage their hunger but their ranks expanded rapidly.

The thin stream of blood trickling from Bouvier's ravaged face bore horrifying evidence that he was still alive when the rats covered his unconscious form like a dark, squirming cloak.

When the rippling horde finally eased away from Bouvier's body, nothing remained but some crimson strips of raw meat patching a splintered web of bones.

Evita shuddered convulsively as the creatures edged

closer, darting between the rocks on every side.

They ignored the rocks bouncing harmlessly off their backs, and crawled nearer, beady eyes glinting like razors behind their frothing, gore-matted jaws.

Suddenly they scattered and began scrambling for cover, their piercing squeals shredding the thick silence.

Warm tears of relief spilled down Evita's cheeks as she lay back, gasping for breath. Suddenly an icy dizziness sucked the air from her lungs when she glimpsed the ominous brown cloud hovering over the ruins like a tattered umbrella, partially obscuring the dawn sky.

Mesmerized by shock, she stared at the vultures circling lazily above her, following their descent with the unblinking fascination of a condemned prisoner inspecting the gallows. Indeed, Evita had no delusions about her fate. Her death warrant was posted overhead and she clearly perceived every inexorable agony of her impending execution. As the predatory birds swung closer, Bouvier's voice tolled through her memory like a church bell.

If ever you're wounded in the field be sure to roll on your belly. The buzzards always peck out the eyes first, to render their victims helpless . . .

Barely able to raise her arm, Evita could do nothing as one after another of the vultures plummeted from the hazy, pink sky—talons extended like barbed hooks and beaks twisted by a hellish grin.

That malevolent smile was the last thing she saw before the yewning talons speared her brain and a host of screeching demons burst through the soul-searing blackness, their inhuman cries mocking her mute, convulsive agony, as their merciless claws gutted her pain-crazed flesh.

CHAPTER THIRTY-THREE

"I could lie on this spot forever," Trent purred, gazing at the emerald sea.

"In two weeks you'd be pining for a fancy dress ball."

She lifted her head. "Have you noted any such symptoms during the past seven weeks?"

"Can't say that I have," he admitted reluctantly.

"Then you withdraw the remark?"

The flaring indignation in her crystal eyes withered his resistance.

"Consider it withdrawn, milady," he murmured, sealing the apology with a kiss.

In truth Trent had adapted to Barbar custom with astonishing ease, becoming a favorite among the women and children who vied for her company. The tribesmen were more reserved, aware of Hazar's interest in the flame-haired princess.

They'd also noted Trent's attraction to the renegade king. Her crisp self-assurance seemed to soften in his presence, and a trace of shyness shaded her voice when they spoke, which was often.

They also often found cause to disagree since Lady Trent was quite outspoken, even for a Barbar female, and Hazar displayed a goodly measure of temperament as befitting his royal station. When they clashed they erupted like twin volcanos, steaming the air with their fiery arguments.

Usually, their differences flared without prior warning, but after a few weeks it became apparent that there was a serious rift in their stormy courtship.

Trent began spending more time with the tribeswomen, ignoring the handsome young chieftain in favor of her handiwork, while Hazar busied himself aboard his ship.

One evening, however, Hazar rowed to shore and invited the princess for a stroll. They climbed the winding path in silence but when they reached the tree-sheltered cliff, the renegade drew her close.

"I'm growing impatient for your answer," he murmured.

Trent averted his gaze. "You'll just have to exercise more control," she said coolly. "There are many things I've not yet decided."

"And I suppose I'm to twiddle my thumbs like a good little boy while you plan my life."

"If it pleases you to think that way, you may do so," she snapped, easing out of his embrace.

"Take care, wench, you're not dealing with some Bourbon Street fop."

She whirled, crystal eyes blazing with fury. "It seems I'm dealing with a stubborn savage who doesn't know how to behave among civilized ladies and gentlemen."

"Enough of this, missy," he warned, making an effort to suppress his anger. "This game of yours has gone far enough. Now I'm calling your bluff—will you marry me, or no?"

Trent folded her arms. "I'm not sure. I need a little more time."

"You've had two weeks," he reminded. "Seems to

me your indecision is merely a case of buck fever—or perhaps *bridal flush* would be more soothing to your sensitive ears."

His wit failed to salve her indignation.

"It's not easy to decide to spend the rest of one's life with an unreasonable, selfish, foul-tempered ruffian," she explained coolly.

Hazar arched his brows. "Have you considered the possibility that *you* might also be selfish? After all there're two of us getting married. There're also a few tribal formalities to be considered."

Trent bristled at the thought. "It's customary for the intended bride to accept before formalities are considered—even my tribal sisters enjoy the luxury of choosing their own mate."

Hazar regarded her thoughtfully. "Then you believe your refusal to discuss the matter is justified?"

"Certainly I do."

"Clearly, there's no reason to expend energy on a useless cause."

Trent tossed her head scornfully. "You have my full agreement on that point, sir."

"Very good," Hazar said, as if coming to a decision. "Then my path is also clear."

Before Trent could reply, he grasped her wrists and swiftly bound them together with his braided leather belt. She tried to kick but he looped the thong around her ankle. After knotting her bonds tightly, he swung her over his shoulder, and strode briskly down the steep path, to his waiting ship.

El-Kifer was untroubled by his daughter's abduction, knowing the young chieftain was driven by passion rather than profit. He had no doubt Hazar would insure her safe return, and secretly endorsed his impetuous act, having learned long ago the futility of trying to reason with his daughter.

A trait she shares with her mother, he observed ruefully.

To be sure he was well pleased with Lady Trevor's recovery from her ordeal. In fact his entire family had benefited from the extended sojourn in the lush, cliff-sheltered village. Now that his children could share the fruits of their heritage a great burden had been lifted from his spirit.

However, Trevor was disturbed by some unexpected developments in her family situation, Trent's recent abduction being foremost on her list. Another sore point was Kevin's engagement to Shan.

"He's just a baby," Trevor objected. "It's just too soon to be thinking of getting married. He's barely out of grade school."

"He passed every test as a warrior with flying colors," he said gently. "He saved our lives. You can't deny him the manhood he's already earned."

"The battleground is hardly a fit training ground for a husband, *and father.*"

Her emphatic rejoinder left no room for discussion, so he tried another tack. "He couldn't have chosen a finer mate," he reminded. "Shan has been closer to us than our own Trent in some respects. I thought you felt the same."

"Of course I do," Trevor said quickly. "Don't misunderstand me on that point. I hold Shan as dear to me as our other two children. Her welfare is as great a concern to me as Kevin's. Which is exactly why I question his maturity. He is, after all, almost five years her junior."

"Shan herself seems to approve of his qualifications. Which is something she doesn't bestow lightly," he added, taking his wife's hand. "Now tell me true, missy, isn't it really the thought of losing your darling young son that agitates you? From what I've seen, no mother likes to give up the apple of her eye, whoever her rival."

Trevor shrugged and looked away. "Perhaps I have become a silly old woman. There's no denying Shan has more sense than any three ballroom belles in New Orleans. And I suppose Kevin proved his own good sense by his choice of a bride."

"Silly you may be," he murmured. "But never old. You're as beautiful now as the day I first saw you."

"Why, thank you, milord," she whispered, pale features tinted rosy pink. "You'll make a most attractive grandfather in your own right."

The blush deepened as he kissed her, and she remained silent for long moments. Then she rested her head on his chest and heaved a long sigh. "I share your high opinion of Hazar. But I still can't help being worried about her. She's so proud and so very stubborn."

He gently tilted her chin upward. "If *anyone* can tame her, it's Hazar. Or would you rather she wed Gavin Radcliffe after all?"

His lips suppressed Trevor's impolite reply.

The wedding feast lasted for three days.

On the third day Django announced his own continued wedding plans.

"Man *needs* a home port. And this place is the closest to paradise I ever been. So with your leave, Cap'n, I'd like to get hitched," he declared, grinning at the plump Barbar female beside him. "Tama will make a fine wife—soon as I teach her how to cook."

"You know you'll have to undergo certain rigid

tests before you can be initiated as a member of the tribe."

The muscular sailor gave El-Kifer an emphatic nod. "I'm ready, Cap'n."

El-Kifer plucked a white rose from the flower-strewn wedding table, and gave it to Django's beaming fiancée. "Both of you have my blessing. May your children know the bounty of peace."

"I'm so pleased you allow their union," Shan confided, as the happy pair departed. "You know it's good luck to have a new union announced at your wedding."

"It does solve the problem of entrusting this port's location with an outsider." El-Kifer smiled at his son, who sat on an ivory throne gazing over the sea.

"What do you think, Kevin? Or are you too love-struck to ponder affairs of state?"

"In my humble opinion," Kevin murmured, eyes still fixed on the horizon, "this problem is easier solved than the one just arriving."

Following his son's gaze, El-Kifer saw Hazar's ship cleaving through the sun-gilded waves.

When informed of Kevin's wedding the renegade sent an aide back to his ship, while Trent offered Shan her congratulations in private.

The aide returned with a carved teakwood chest inlaid with jade chips.

Inside was a crystal and gold decanter, corked by a large emerald, which Hazar presented to the young couple as a wedding gift.

"It's magnificent," Shan said in a hushed voice. "I'm truly grateful. But you really shouldn't have gone to this great expense."

"Not too great for a sister-in-law."

Startled by Hazar's statement, Shan looked at Trent. "Then you've decided to marry?"

Her sister examined her nails. "Not quite. You see, we're already wed."

"How wonderful," Shan exclaimed, embracing her. "That's truly the richest gift I could wish for."

"Though somewhat suddenly bestowed," Lady Trevor observed coolly.

Hazar turned to her and bowed. "I pray you'll forgive my insensitivity in failing to secure your blessing, milady. Please accept my apologies and my pledge to do everything in my power to insure your daughter's happiness."

Trent took Lady Trevor's hand. "Please forgive me, mother. It wasn't my intention to slight you."

"In fact, she didn't even know the ceremony was going to occur," Hazar interjected. "I'm afraid it's my fault entirely."

"Not entirely," Trent corrected, still staring at her mother. "Two of us were wed, not one. So two must share the blame, as well as the blessing. I hope someday I can make it up to you."

Lady Trevor smiled and kissed her daughter on both cheeks. "We've both suffered enough to learn to forgive. I give you my blessing, and my love."

"I'll always treasure your words. As I treasure your past sacrifices on my behalf. I promise you'll never have cause to regret your generosity."

"Well said," El-Kifer congratulated. "I wish you both all the joy we've found in our own union." Trent embraced him warmly. "Thank you, dear father. You've already given me great joy this day."

"Let me be first to welcome you to the family,"

Kevin offered. "I'm proud to be able to call you brother."

Hazar took his extended hand. "Our family seems to be expanding quite rapidly."

"Certainly we can use two experienced hands to expand our shipping lanes," El-Kifer reflected. "I've long needed some trusted partners."

"Partners?"

"Yes. As my wedding gift I'm giving both you and Kevin equal shares in the shipping company. As did my father-in-law."

Trent glanced at Hazar.

"Please don't think we're not grateful, but I think my new husband has other plans. As do I."

"What sort of plans?" Lady Trevor asked with a note of trepidation.

"Well you see, I—that is to say *we*—have decided to stay on here for a while. Having only just discovered my true roots I want to learn much more, so I can become a proper Barbar wife."

"I'd rather hoped to follow the same course," Kevin said hesitantly. "Except for the wife part."

"There's a simple solution," El-Kifer assured.

"Half the year one couple will reside here and perform the duties required of a Barbar chieftain; the other six months can be passed in New Orleans pursuing business affairs. That should give you both the best of both worlds."

"And what will *you* do?" Lady Trevor inquired.

"Something I've been planning for a long time," he confided, taking her in his arms. "I'm going to abduct my own bride and chart a second honeymoon. Think you can stand my company for a few years while we cruise around the world?"

Bright tears filled her crystal eyes like sparkling wine. "It will be the most wonderful bounty I've ever received," Lady Trevor said softly. "Except for my wedding day."